Praise for
All Kinds of Tied Down

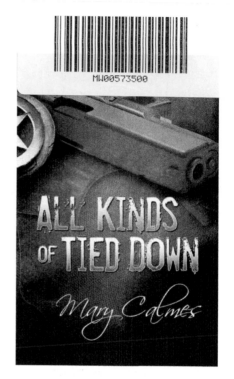

"Oh, how I loved these boys! ... I adored the two of them together so much, I didn't want the book to end!"

—The Blogger Girls

"Overall, this book is delightful and I already want to reread it. I can say with certainty that this book will be one of my top reads of 2015. I just loved everything about it."

—Series-ously Addicted

"*All Kinds of Tied Down* is angsty, exciting, sweet, romantic, funny… heck, it's all the feels rolled into one gigantic ball of freaking awesome."

—Joyfully Jay

"I seriously love, love, LOVED this book."

—Smitten With Reading

"For a little over half of *All Kinds of Tied Down* you the reader will be all kinds of tied up over the sexual tension. ... Once Ian and Miro get on the same page... holy hell! This book gets hot quick."

—The Jeep Diva

"You can't go wrong with this book!"

—Top 2 Bottom Reviews

By MARY CALMES

Acrobat
Again
Any Closer
With Cardeno C.: Control
With Poppy Dennison: Creature
Feature
Fit to Be Tied
Floodgates
Frog
The Guardian
Heart of the Race
Ice Around the Edges
Judgment
Just Desserts
Mine
Romanus
The Servant
Steamroller
Still
Timing • After the Sunset
What Can Be
Where You Lead

CHANGE OF HEART
Change of Heart • Trusted Bond
Honored Vow • Crucible of Fate
Forging the Future

L'ANGE
Old Loyalty, New Love
Fighting Instinct

MANGROVE STORIES
Blue Days • Quiet Nights
Sultry Sunset

MARSHALS
All Kinds of Tied Down • Fit to Be Tied

A MATTER OF TIME
A Matter of Time: Vol. 1
A Matter of Time: Vol. 2
Bulletproof • But For You • Parting Shot
Piece of Cake

THE WARDER SERIES
His Hearth • Tooth & Nail
Heart in Hand • Sinnerman
Nexus • Cherish Your Name
Warders Vol. 1 & 2

ANTHOLOGIES
Grand Adventures
Tales of the Curious Cookbook
Three Fates
Wishing on a Blue Star

Published by DREAMSPINNER PRESS
http://www.dreamspinnerpress.com

FIT TO BE TIED

Mary Calmes

REAMSPINNER
PRESS

Published by
DREAMSPINNER PRESS

5032 Capital Circle SW, Suite 2, PMB# 279, Tallahassee, FL 32305-7886 USA
http://www.dreamspinnerpress.com/

This is a work of fiction. Names, characters, places, and incidents either are the product of author imagination or are used fictitiously, and any resemblance to actual persons, living or dead, business establishments, events, or locales is entirely coincidental.

Fit to Be Tied
© 2015 Mary Calmes.

Cover Art
© 2015 Reese Dante.
http://www.reesedante.com
Cover content is for illustrative purposes only and any person depicted on the cover is a model.

All rights reserved. This book is licensed to the original purchaser only. Duplication or distribution via any means is illegal and a violation of international copyright law, subject to criminal prosecution and upon conviction, fines, and/or imprisonment. Any eBook format cannot be legally loaned or given to others. No part of this book may be reproduced or transmitted in any form or by any means, electronic or mechanical, including photocopying, recording, or by any information storage and retrieval system, without the written permission of the Publisher, except where permitted by law. To request permission and all other inquiries, contact Dreamspinner Press, 5032 Capital Circle SW, Suite 2, PMB# 279, Tallahassee, FL 32305-7886, USA, or http://www.dreamspinnerpress.com/.

ISBN: 978-1-63476-487-2
Digital ISBN: 978-1-63476-488-9
Library of Congress Control Number: 2015945759
First Edition September 2015

Printed in the United States of America
∞
This paper meets the requirements of
ANSI/NISO Z39.48-1992 (Permanence of Paper).

Once more for Lynn.
Thank you.

CHAPTER 1

I COULDN'T control the whimper of delight. Since we were out in Elmwood, where we never were, I'd begged and pleaded with Ian to stop at Johnnie's Beef and buy me a sandwich before we got to the house we were sitting on. I hated stakeouts; they were so boring, and I tended to use them as an excuse to eat *good* instead of the alternative. It could be argued that an Italian beef sandwich with sweet peppers was not, in fact, a gourmet meal, but anyone who said that had obviously never had one. Just opening it up, with the smell that came wafting out... I was salivating.

"This better be worth the long drive outta the way," Ian groused.

No amount of grumbling was going to get in the way of my happiness. And besides, he owed me. The day before, on our way to the same stakeout, I'd stopped and gotten him hot dogs at Budacki's—Polish with the works, just how he liked it. I'd even broken up a fight over ketchup between a native and an out-of-towner while I was there and still managed to deliver the goods. So swinging by the beef place was the least he could do.

"You wanna screw the sandwich?" he asked snidely as he started on his pepper and egg one.

I lifted my gaze to his, slowly and purposely seductive, and I got the catch of breath I was hoping for. "No. Not the sandwich."

He had opened his mouth to say something when we heard the shots.

"Maybe it was a car backfiring," I offered hopefully, having peeled back the wrapper, ready to take a bite. On this quiet tree-lined suburban street, the kind with white picket fences and people walking their dogs and little A-frame houses with picture windows, it could definitely be something other than a gunshot.

His grimace said no.

Seconds later, a man came flying across the street and down the sidewalk past our car that was sitting quietly on the storybook street at a little after one on a Tuesday afternoon.

"Motherfucker," I groaned, placing the sandwich gingerly on the dash of the Ford Taurus, out the passenger-side door seconds later.

The guy was fast—I was faster, and I was gaining on him until he pointed a gun over his shoulder and fired.

It would have been a miracle if he'd hit me—he was moving, I was moving—but still, I had to make him stop. Stray bullets were *bad*, as we'd learned in our last tactical seminar, and more importantly, we were in a small, quaint residential neighborhood where at this time of day, women could be jogging with strollers, followed by beagles or labradoodles. I would make sure reckless discharge of a firearm was tacked on to the charges as soon as I had the guy in custody.

He shot at me a second time, missed me by a mile again, but it was enough of a threat to make me alter my course, cross into a heavily foliaged yard, and cut through two others—one with a swing set, the other with wildflowers—to catch him at the corner. Arm out, using the classic clotheslining move I knew from my days of fighting in foster homes, I had him off his feet and on the pavement in seconds.

"Oh shit, what happened?" Ian asked as he came bounding up beside me. He put his boot down on the guy's wrist, pinning it painfully to the sidewalk as he bent to retrieve the .38 Special. I'd been the one stepped on before, so I knew the pressure hurt like a sonofabitch. "Look at this. I haven't seen one of these in years."

I nodded, admiring my FIORENTINI + BAKER suede boots on him, not even caring if he messed them up, loving more that what was mine, he considered his.

"This is a nice gun that you tried to shoot my partner with," he said menacingly, his voice icy.

"I'm fine," I reminded him. "Look at me."

But he didn't; instead he lifted the gun and bumped it against the stranger's cheek.

"Fuck," the man swore, his eyes wild as they rabbited over to me, pleading.

"How 'bout I make you eat this," Ian snarled, much more pissed than I'd realized as he hauled the runner up off the sidewalk and yanked him close. "What if you'd hit him?"

The man was either smarter than he appeared or his survival instinct was exceptionally well honed. He correctly surmised that talking back to Ian at that moment, getting lippy, was a bad choice. He kept his mouth shut.

"Everything's fine," I soothed Ian as police cars surrounded us.

"Freeze!" the first officer out of the car yelled.

Instead of complying, I unzipped Ian's olive green field jacket, which I was wearing, and showed them my badge on the chain. "US Marshals, Jones and Doyle."

Instantly they lowered their weapons before surging around us. Ian handed off both the prisoner and the gun, and told the officers to add reckless discharge of a firearm to whatever else they were charging the guy with.

I was surprised when he grabbed hold of my arm and yanked me after him a few feet down the street before jerking me around to face him.

"I'm fine," I assured him, chuckling. "You don't have to manhandle me."

But he was checking, looking me over, still scared.

"He missed me clean."

He nodded, hearing but not listening, not taking my words in. I was about to tease him, wanting to nudge him out of his worry, when I realized he was shaking.

"Come here," I prodded, tugging on his sweater, getting him closer, unable to hug him—not with so many people around—but able to whisper in his ear. "I'm okay, baby. I swear."

He muttered something under his breath, his shoulders dropped, and his fists unclenched. After a second, he seemed better. "I bet your sandwich is cold," he whispered.

"Fuckballs," I muttered, turning to trudge back to our car.

"So what'd you learn?" he teased, normalcy having been restored with my swearing.

"Not to run after other people's suspects when we're supposed to be eating."

Ian's snicker made me smile in spite of myself.

A LITTLE more than eight months ago we were Deputy US Marshal Miro Jones and his partner, Ian Doyle, but it hadn't meant what it did now. Then, it was us living apart, him dating women, me wishing he was gay so there would be hope that I could have him instead of comparing every man I met to my very straight, very unavailable partner. Everything changed when I finally saw what having his full and undivided attention actually meant, and when he got up the guts to tell me what he wanted and needed from me, I dove in quickly, drowning in him as fast as I could so he wouldn't have time to think that maybe, since he'd only recently discovered he was bi, he might want to try the dating scene before settling down. The thing was, though, Ian was one of those rare guys who wanted the one person in the world who fit him like a glove, and that person, it turned out, was me.

So, yes, Ian was still technically bi, but was exclusively now Miro-sexual and wasn't interested in trying the buffet. All Ian wanted was to stay home with me. I couldn't have been any happier. Everything was mostly working in my life. Professionally I was in a great place, and personally I was ready to put a ring on Ian's finger. Like really ready. Like maybe even too ready for Ian, but all in all, my life was perfect except for the grunt work we were currently doing.

After our interrupted lunch, we had to drive all the way back downtown to file a police report to be in compliance with Chicago PD— since we'd been the ones to make the collar—and then turn around to head back out to Elmwood.

"This will teach you to help," Ian grumbled, and even though I knew he was kidding, it was still a huge pain in the ass.

We were supposed to sit on the house of one William McClain, who was wanted for drug trafficking, but I got a call from Wes Ching, another marshal on our team, asking us to help serve a warrant out in Bloomingdale instead. He and his partner, Chris Becker, were already in Elmwood on another errand, so they would take my and Ian's crappy stakeout chore and we would take their more—in theory—interesting warrant duty.

I was not a fan of the suburbs, any of them, with or without artery-clogging food, or the hours it took to get to them from each other or the city itself. Traffic in Chicago, all day every day, was a beast, and added to that was the fact the radio in the new car didn't get Ian's favorite channel—97.9 The Loop—and the crappy shocks that let us feel every bump and dip in the road. Because we drove whatever had been seized in a criminal investigation, sometimes the cars were amazing—like the 1971 Chevrolet Chevelle SS we had for two weeks—and other times, I worried if maybe I'd died and gone to hell without anyone letting me know. The Ford Taurus we were in currently was seriously not working for me.

"It's fuel-efficient," Ian prompted me, reaching over to put a hand on my thigh.

Instantly I shifted in my seat, sliding down so I could get his touch on my cock instead.

"What're you doing?" he asked slyly even as he pressed his palm against my already thickening shaft.

"I need to get laid," I said for the third time that day.

It was all his fault.

Instead of getting right out of bed that morning like he normally did, he'd rolled over on top of me, pinned me to the mattress under him, and kissed me until I forgot what day it was. He never did that; he was so by the book in the morning, so on task and barky with the orders. But for whatever reason, I got Ian in languorous vacation mode, all hard and hungry, hands all over me, putting hickeys on my neck, instead of the drill sergeant I normally had to deal with until he got the first cup of coffee in him. He was ravenous and insistent, but then our boss called and Ian was up, out of bed, doing the "yessir, right away, sir" thing and telling me to hurry up and get in the shower fast.

"What?" I roared, sitting up in bed, incredulous when I heard the water running. "Get your ass in here and finish what you started!"

He actually cackled as he got into the shower and was still chuckling as I sat there in bed, fuming, before I fell back to take care of myself.

"Don't you dare touch that!" he yelled from under the water.

I groaned and climbed out of bed and plodded downstairs to get coffee. Chickie Baby was happy to see me, mostly because I fed him. Stupid dog.

"There was no happy ending for me this morning," I complained to Ian, back in the present. "You didn't take care of me."

"What?" He chuckled, moving his hand back to the wheel. "I woke you... up nice... and... crap."

I wanted Ian, needed Ian, but he was distracted as he slowed the car, and when I dragged my gaze from his profile to the sight in front of me, I made the same noise of disgust he had. Immediately I called Ching.

"You fuck," I said instead of hello when he answered.

Snort of laughter. "What?" he said, but it was muffled like he was chewing. "Me and Becker are doing stakeout for you in Elmwood and then following up on a lead from the Eastern District warrant squad."

"Where the fuck are you?" I snarled as I put him on speaker.

He said something in reply, but it couldn't really be categorized as a word.

I was instantly suspicious. "Are you at Johnnie's Beef?"

"What makes you think that?"

"Asshole!" I yelled.

"Oh, come on, Jones, have a heart. We're doing you a favor, right?"

"I'm sorry, what'd you just say to me?"

All I heard was laughing.

"You know we'd rather follow up a bullshit lead than serve a warrant with a task force, you dick," Ian growled from beside me. "This is fucked up, Wes, and you know it."

"I have no idea what you're talking about," Ching finished with a cackle. "You two get to work with the DEA and the Chicago PD for the second time today. That's awesome."

I should have known when he offered; it was my own fault.

Ian reiterated my thoughts almost perfectly, which made things that much worse. "You have no one to blame but yourself."

After Ian parked the car, we walked around to the trunk and got out our TAC vests, put the badges on our belts, and Ian put on his thigh holster that carried a second gun. Walking over to the group, Ian asked who was in charge. It turned out to be exactly what Ian and I expected; it was a clusterfuck better known as a task force. We saw both district and regional groups, this being the latter because I could see local law enforcement as well as guys from the DEA who all looked like either grunged-out meth addicts or *GQ* models. There was no in-between with them. I had, as of yet, never met a DEA agent I liked. They all thought they had not only the toughest job, but also the most dangerous. They were a bunch of prima donnas I had no use for.

It was amazing how many people thought that marshals did the same things other law enforcement agencies did. They assumed we investigated crime, collected evidence, and sat in front of whiteboards to try to figure out who the bad guy was from a list of viable suspects. But that was simply not the case. Much like it was in the Old West; we tracked people down and brought them in for trial. As a result, a tremendous amount of time—when we weren't out on loan to a joint task force, for instance—was spent running down leads, watching houses, and basically doing surveillance. It could be a little mind-numbing, and so, occasionally, when the usual was broken up by things like traveling to pick up a witness or taking part in an undercover operation, it was viewed as a welcome diversion. But neither Ian nor I ever thought working with the DEA was a good thing.

Today the task force was looking to pick up three men with ties to the Madero crime family who'd slipped federal custody in New York and were apparently hiding out with one of the guys' distant cousins in the burbs of Chicago. That was what serving a warrant meant. It was fancy phrasing for taking someone into custody.

The plan was for us to go into the five-story apartment building like thunder with battering rams, the whole deal. The raids were my least favorite, but I understood why we were there. Normally a Fugitive Investigative Strike Team consisting of Feds, local police, and other state agencies extracted a witness, and FISTs fell under the purview of the marshals service. It wasn't a task force without us, so our office had been tacked on.

Chicago PD went in first, the DEA douchebags following. Ian and I stayed put on the first floor until we heard shots fired in the stairwell. We went straight up while people yelled that there were men escaping onto the roof.

I yelled first to let anyone else around know what was going on, then for backup, but they'd all scattered to the lower floors, so that left Ian and me to charge up to try and head off whoever was up there.

"Do not go out that door!" I yelled after Ian, who, as usual, was in front of me. The only reason he'd been second earlier in the day was because I'd been in the passenger seat when the guy ran by the car. Nine times out of ten, I followed Ian into whatever the situation was.

He burst through the heavy metal door leading to the roof and, of course, drew immediate answering gunfire.

I ran out after him in time to see Ian level his gun and fire. Only in the movies did people yell "don't shoot" when people were *actually* shooting at them.

The guy went down, and I watched another turn and run. He didn't have a weapon that I could see, so I holstered my gun and took off after him as Ian rolled the guy he'd shot onto his back and roared at the men who had followed us up to take him.

I raced across the rooftop hard on the fugitive's heels, churning my legs and arms to catch him before he reached the edge. He sped toward the building's ledge, then launched himself into the air. I had no idea if there was another building there, but since there had been no scream, I pushed myself harder and followed after him into the sky.

The rooftop of the four-story building across the narrow alley was a welcome sight, and I landed easily, somersaulting over onto one knee, then pushing up into a dead sprint again. I guessed we were out of real estate when the man abruptly stopped, whirling to face me. Pulling a butterfly knife from his back pocket, he flipped it open and advanced on me.

I pulled my Glock 20 and leveled it at him. "Drop the weapon, get on your knees, and lace your fingers on top of your head."

He was deciding—I could tell.

"Now," I ordered, my voice dipping an octave into a cold, dark place.

He muttered under his breath but released the knife and went to his knees. I moved fast, reaching his side before he complied with the entirety of my request, kicked the knife away, and pulled a set of Plasticuffs from my TAC vest. Shoving him facedown, I waited for backup.

My phone rang and I winced upon seeing the caller ID. "Hey."

"What the fuck was that?"

"That was the Ian Doyle special," I teased, trying to lighten the mood.

"Oh, no, fuck you! I don't jump off shit, Miro, only you do that!"

I did have a bit more of a history with that than he did. "Yeah, okay."

"Are you hurt?"

"No, I'm good," I replied, smiling into the phone. "Promise. I'll meet you downstairs as soon as I get some fucking help up here."

His inelegant snort made me smile.

Moments later I was swarmed by police officers ready to take the fugitive off my hands. As I was following the men down four flights, I asked the sergeant in front of me if we were transporting the criminals to their station, whichever one that was, or if they were going in our holding cell downtown.

"I think the DEA is taking custody of all three."

That meant all three men would be questioned and the one with the best information would be given a deal. The others would be turned over to the police. It was a waste of time for Ian and me to have even been there.

"Did you hear this bullshit?" I groused at Ian as he came hurdling up to me. "We don't even get—"

"Shut up," he growled, grabbing the armhole of my vest and yanking me forward. His gaze ran over me and I heard how rough his breathing was.

"Oh, baby, I'm sorry," I whispered, leaning close so he could hear me but not touching, the motion making it seem like I was relating privileged information and nothing more.

"I have faith in you, don't get me wrong," he said quickly. "But you know as well as I do that you leaped without knowing what was there, and that's plain stupid."

He was right.

"Don't fuckin' do it again."

"No," I agreed, leaning back to search his face. "So am I forgiven?"

He nodded, and I finally got a trace of a smile.

We were going to head back to file a report when we saw the people who were flushed from the apartment, three guys in all, now sitting outside on the sidewalk.

"What's goin' on there?" I asked the closest officer, gesturing at the men.

"We're about to let 'em all go."

"Why?" Ian asked, clipping the word, clearly irritated.

"Hey, man," the cop responded tiredly, "we ran those guys through NCIC for outstanding warrants already, and they all came up clean. There's no use keeping 'em."

"Mind if we check?" I replied, trying to make my tone soothing.

"Only if you take custody," he replied petulantly. "I don't have time to stand around here with my thumb up my ass waiting on you."

"Sure," Ian agreed, his tone silky and dangerous. "Transfer custody to us."

It was done in moments, and the freed officer jogged over to let his sergeant know. His superior gave us a head tilt, clearly thinking we were DEA since he couldn't see the back of the vests. Had he known, he wouldn't have given the go-ahead. No one ever turned people over to the marshals because with our warrant information network we could always find something extra, just that bit more and being shown up pissed them off like nobody's business. No one ever hated asking for our help to pick someone up after the fact or on a lead that'd gone cold, but having the marshals show them up at the scene of a bust made everyone bitchy.

Ian pulled out his phone as I squatted down in front of the first guy.

"So who the fuck are you?" our first suspect asked.

"Marshal," I answered. "We're going to run you all for warrants again."

No one seemed concerned.

Mike Ryan and his partner, Jack Dorsey, were on desk duty that morning, which meant they got to look up the records of the men sitting on the curb. We released the suspects one by one—Ryan and Dorsey making a note of it over the phone—removed their cuffs, and wished them a good day. "Go to hell" was the most popular response to Ian's cheerfulness while "fuck off" ran a close second.

It turned out a warrant for attempted murder and aggravated battery came back for the last guy.

"Winner winner chicken dinner," I announced, smirking at him.

"Fuckin' marshals," Dario Batista griped. "I thought this was a DEA bust."

Ian cackled as we hauled him to his feet.

"Come on, man," he protested. "I have information I can give you. Let's work out a deal."

"We're marshals," Ian said as the three of us began walking back to the Taurus. "We don't make deals."

I called in as we stuffed him into the backseat.

"What the hell kind of clown car is this?" Batista complained.

"It's fuel-efficient," I rationalized as I set the childproof lock on the back door before getting in.

"God, I hate this car," Ian growled irritably.

I promised we'd check on a new one when we got back to the office.

IT TURNED out Batista was the one moving money for the Madero crime family that had ties to the Solo cartel out of Durango, Mexico. The DEA could maybe, possibly, get him to roll on the family if they could get witnesses to make the money laundering and racketeering charges stick, but it was a long shot. They would have loved to try, but San Francisco PD had him solid on attempted murder and aggravated battery charges. So since San Fran had put out the warrant for him, and since that was why we'd picked him up, we processed him, notified them of his capture, and they had people scrambled and on a plane within the hour. All of that activity happened faster than it took the DEA to figure out precisely what had happened to their potential informant.

After the DEA agents pulled their heads out of their asses and ran down the information from Chicago PD that the marshals office had, in fact, taken custody of Batista, they finally showed up about six that evening.

The guy in charge was Corbin Stafford, and he barged into our office with four of his men and demanded to speak to the marshals who were on-site in Bloomingdale that afternoon.

That was a mistake.

Maybe if they'd come in tactfully, respectfully, something different might have occurred. As it was, my boss, newly promoted Chief Deputy US Marshal Sam Kage came out of his office and waited while Stafford yelled at him and told him in no uncertain terms why he needed to turn Batista over to the DEA immediately.

Kage waited until they were quiet.

"Well?" Stafford barked.

"No," Kage replied flatly.

It took a moment for the word to sink in. "No?"

Kage waited.

"What the hell do you mean, no?"

Kage let out the sigh we all normally ran from. "US Marshals are the enforcement arm of most federal agencies, including yours, and as such, we reserve the right to make arrests as we see fit."

Everyone opened their mouths to say something, maybe even to yell, but my boss lifted his hand to shut them up.

"As the main enforcement agency, this gives us more power than you were obviously aware of in your limited understanding of our office."

"I—"

"Therefore, in this instance, we see fit *not* to honor your request."

"We'll see what your boss thinks about—"

"My boss, Tom Kenwood, was confirmed by the senate only a week ago and is the new US Marshal in charge of the Northern District of Illinois," Kage explained, and I could see the glimmer of evil in his smile. "I'm sure he would love to have one of his first orders of business be you questioning a decision of his chief deputy."

The room fell very still.

"But do have *your* boss give *my* boss my regards," he finished cheerfully.

As Kage returned to his office, Stafford's gaze swept the room.

I waved.

Ian did too.

The "fuck you" was implied.

CHAPTER 2

THAT NIGHT at home, without me even seeing it coming, Ian and I got into it again. It was good that we kept it out of work—both of us were being really careful about not talking about our personal life—but the second we crossed the threshold, the underlying issue exploded.

It was all my fault.

I wanted more than he had ever even considered, and because I'd given voice to my desire, I'd fucked everything up. What was sad was that I always did that, always wanted it all instead of being happy with what I had. My friends had different theories about why I pushed when the person I cared about—and in this case: desperately, madly, loved—wasn't ready. The idea everyone liked the best was that because I was a foster kid who was passed around from pillar to post until I was legal, when I saw my happily ever after, I went after it like a charging bull. In Ian's case, and only his, I could concede their point. In the past, it had been a test, me pushing to see how serious the other person was, see if they'd stay if I got serious too fast. But with Ian, it was all about me having him right there for the rest of my life. I couldn't imagine it any other way.

In my defense, I thought Ian wanted me not simply as his partner on and off the job, but for *more*. It felt like it, it looked like it, so I assumed. There was a reason that was bad, and my mistake was in not checking.

"It's not that I don't want the same shit you want." Ian sighed from where he was sitting at the table, peeling the label off an empty bottle of the Gumballhead I kept for him. "I just don't get why it has to be *that*."

"You don't get why I want forever and ever, 'til death do us part?"

"No, that I get. I just don't get the need for the ring and the piece of paper."

Maybe it was stupid, but I couldn't help how I felt any more than he could help how he didn't. It was *that* part that was killing me.

The issue, he said, was not that he didn't want to get married; the issue was that he didn't understand why I wanted to so badly.

"Forget I asked," I snapped, clearing the table after dinner.

"How can I forget it?" he replied irritably, following me to the kitchen. "You want something, you asked, I said no, and now everything's all fucked up."

"So it's all on me," I retorted, rounding on him.

"Well, yeah, you know it is."

"You're saying it's stupid to ask for what I want?"

"No, but it didn't go like you planned, and now you're saying just forget it, but how does that work? You can't just erase it and pretend nothing happened. You want something and you put it out there, and now we have to deal with it."

I crossed my arms. "Why don't you want to be married to me?"

Heavy sigh. "You know why."

"Tell me again."

"Because it limits you and it makes my life hard."

"In what way?"

"You'll never be promoted," he said, his voice charged with annoyance.

"I disagree."

"You're an idiot."

"Fine, I'm an idiot. I don't care."

"Well, I do! The guys on my team might be okay with me, but no one else will be. You're basically asking me to end my military career just so you can have a goddamn piece of paper!"

"It's not just a piece of paper," I argued, my voice brittle. "It's a lot more than that."

"Not to me," he replied coldly. "It won't change how I feel, I won't love you any more or any less. It's nothing, and it takes away who I am, what I do, and how far I can go."

His words hollowed me out, and it physically hurt for a moment, like a punch in the gut, because it was the exact opposite for me. I wanted it all, always had. Husband, house, dog, and maybe even kids—I wasn't sure about the fatherhood, not certain about the kind of dad I would make, but I sure as hell wanted the choice.

Ian was good with how things were, with the status quo, with us living together and being partners on the job, lovers at home. He was done moving forward; he was dug in where he was.

"Why can't I be enough for you?" he asked hoarsely, clearly hurt.

"That's bullshit," I fired back. "It has nothing to do with enough and everything to do with wanting everyone to know that you're with me."

"But why does that matter?"

"Because I want the Army to have to call me if, heaven forbid, something happened to you. I want to be the person a doctor has to ask to treat you. I want you to wear a ring. I want to be your husband."

"And it doesn't matter what I want?"

"Of course it matters. I just need you to make me understand why you don't want that."

"I told you already, it doesn't work for me."

"Because of why?"

"Because of my job," he yelled.

We'd been going round and round for weeks. He was sick to death of talking about this. The difference was, I kept hoping he'd wake up one morning with a completely changed opinion on the subject. I was waiting for a miracle.

"Ian—"

"You're going to impact what I do and who I am because you wanna play house!"

"I'm sorry, what did you just say to me?" I asked icily.

Instantly his hands went up. "Okay. That was shitty, but c'mon."

"Come on what?" I demanded.

"Why do I have to explain myself to you? Why are you pushing alluva sudden?"

"I—"

"Why's it so important that we get married?"

"Because I love you."

He moved fast, into my space, hands on my face, staring into my eyes. As always, love and desire and heat all swirled together and nearly stopped my heart. I wanted him desperately.

"I love you too, M, but being married is not in the cards for me."

"But it would be if I were a woman."

He dropped his hands and stalked across the kitchen, pivoting around before leaving completely. "Why do you say shit like that?"

"It's true, though. If I were a woman, you'd marry me. There'd be no problem then."

"But you're not."

"No."

"So the question is stupid."

I was quiet for a long moment, and so was he, before I said, "We need to just forget this. I'm tired of fighting about it, I'm sorry I ever fuckin' brought it up."

He shrugged. "But you can't change how you feel and neither can I."

"So then what?" I began, holding my breath like I'd been doing around him lately. My stomach was tightening and twisting into knots with incredible regularity because of Ian Doyle. But it was better to finally ask and hear his answer so we both knew where we stood. Wondering, imagining the worst-case scenario, none of that was productive. It was cowardly, and tiptoeing around the elephant in the room was no good for anyone. My body went cold, hands fisted at my sides as I croaked out the question. "You're just gonna leave?"

"Leave?"

Quick inhale. "Walk out, bail, ask to be deployed for like— ever. I dunno."

"Why would I do that?"

"To get away from me."

"And why would I wanna do that?"

He seemed genuinely confused and I took that as a good sign.

"To give us both time to sort things out."

"Fuck that," he growled. "I don't run away and I'm not leaving you, so you can figure out a way to live without me. That's—"

"I don't ever wanna live without you, that's the whole fuckin' point!"

"Well, I'm not going anywhere, so I guess you're just gonna be miserable for the rest of your life."

"I'm not miserable," I muttered under my breath.

"Could've fooled me."

"Listen. I'm not leaving, either, that's not what partners do."

"How would you know?" he volleyed. "All you've been thinking about is yourself and what you want. What you have to have to be happy."

"Ian—"

He shook his head. "You can't want a change and not think about the consequences. I know what I can do, what I can give and still be me. I thought you'd ask before you went ahead and threw out ultimatums."

"I never threatened you," I insisted.

"Oh no?"

"Fuck no! I said what I wanted, but that was all."

"That wasn't all. How could that be all?" He crossed his arms, in his battle stance, ready to fight. "You asked me to marry you; you had a ring and everything."

"And you said no," I husked, feeling the pain all over again.

I had made his favorite meal, the beef stroganoff he loved, and then in the kitchen, right about where I was standing now, I had gone down to one knee, and with the plain thick platinum band, asked him to spend the rest of his life with me. His face, in that moment, had turned my blood to ice. I saw fear there, pain, not a trace of happiness, not a drop of joy.

"Because I want to spend the rest of my life with you. But why do I have to wear a ring to do it? Why is that bullshit important?"

"If I was a woman, would it still be bullshit?"

No answer.

"See," I sighed. "Marriage is what straight people do, right?"

Still silence.

"Do I not deserve to be married?"

"I just don't understand why you want to be."

"Because I love you."

"Love me, M, not a piece of paper that says you have to."

"Fine," I sighed, giving up, so tired of it being a thing. "I'm sorry I ever brought it up."

"Yeah, but you did."

"So what," I muttered, turning to the sink to rinse the dishes. "Like I said before, let's just forget it."

"I already told you we can't. You can't let it go and neither can I. We're both screwed."

"But we wouldn't be if you just married me."

"Sure," he replied stoically. "And we wouldn't be if what we have now was enough for you."

"You—"

"We need to go to bed. We gotta work tomorrow and it's already midnight."

"You're going to bed *now*?" I was incredulous. "In the middle of a fight?"

"We've been fighting about this for three weeks, what's another night?"

"How can you sleep?"

"Training," he said flatly.

"Clearly this is not that important to you."

"You're wrong," he replied. "But I think we both need some time to think about what we want and what we can do."

"What we want? What're you talking about?"

"You want a husband, right?"

"Ian—"

"If that's not gonna be me, then what?"

"Then fine, I'll deal with it."

"Why should you have to? Why shouldn't you find someone who wants the same things you want and will give in?"

"I don't want someone to give in. This isn't about winning."

"Isn't it?"

"No, idiot, it's about me wanting to spend the rest of my life with you."

"Which is all I want, but without the fuckin' ring and the bullshit piece of paper!"

"Why do you always gotta call the marriage license a piece of paper? It's more important than that."

"To you," he reiterated.

"To a lot of people!"

"This isn't about *a lot of people*; it's about you and me, period."

"Fine."

"What's fine?"

I sighed. "You figure out what you want, and when you do, you'll let me know."

"I already know. I want things just like how they are."

"Okay," I sighed, too tired to fight with him anymore.

He murmured something I didn't catch and pounded up the stairs. In his absence I cleaned the kitchen, got the dishwasher running, and was preparing to take our dog, our werewolf, Chickie, out for a run.

"What're you doing?" he yelled down to me.

Normally I walked out into the living room so I could see him when I yelled up into the loft. "I gotta take Chickie out."

"Just let him go in the backyard. I'll clean it tomorrow when we get home."

"No," I called up to him. "We could both use the air."

"Whatever you want," he grumbled. "I'm taking a shower."

I didn't wait to hear the water running. Instead I went to the front door, took a breath of the crisp fall air, and stepped out into the night. It was already getting chilly, but not cold enough for me to put on a heavy jacket. The hoodie I had on would be enough.

Closing the door behind me, I went quickly down the stairs and was almost to the end of our street in Lincoln Park when I heard my name yelled out.

I turned in time to have Ian run into my arms. He hit me hard, grabbing me tight, crushing me, wedging his head down in my shoulder.

"Don't," he whispered.

I realized I hadn't even been breathing moments before. Only Ian could do that to me, freeze me in absolute limbo—physically, mentally, emotionally—and turn me into the guy who waited.

Inhaling deeply, I clutched at him, my lips on the warm skin of his neck, savoring the feel of him in my arms, not wanting to let go, terrified that what we had was slipping away and we were both trying so desperately to hold on.

"We'll figure this out," he said shakily. "Don't do anything like take my name off the deed to the house or anything."

"I can't do that," I said around the lump in my throat. "And I wouldn't even if I could."

He nodded into my shoulder.

"There's a middle ground," I sighed, tightening my hold. "We'll figure it out. I swear."

"I thought I was gonna throw up when you walked out of the house."

"We just have to figure this out. It's not terminal."

"No," he agreed quickly.

"It'll be all right," I said, easing back so I could see his face.

Fucking Ian. Only he could turn the tables and get me to reassure him that everything would be okay even when I wasn't sure I was telling the truth. For fuck's sake, I was the one who was the most upset; I was the one with the hurt feelings and wounded pride, like I had skewers in my heart because he didn't want to marry me. I should have punched him in the face, but he was covered in worry. I could see it in the pinch of his eyebrows, the darkness in his eyes, the tight press of his lips, and the clench of his jaw. He was spooked good, and because I was the one who always took care of that, fixed that, I couldn't stop now just because it affected me.

"Okay."

"We're supposed to be together," I said as much for my benefit as his.

"I know."

I took a step back and still saw the haunted look in his eyes, like I'd been gone and it had scared the crap out of him. It turned out, from how shaky my knees were, that I felt the same.

We walked Chickie together, and when we got home his phone was ringing. I was anxious for a second that he was being deployed. Ian was Special Forces so whenever they called him up, since he served at the pleasure of the president, he had to get on a plane. But since he didn't stand at attention as he listened, only swore a little, I knew we were being called back to work.

"What happened?" I asked when he got off the phone.

"Your boss just loaned you, me, White, and Sharpe to the FBI for the night."

"How come he's my boss whenever he does something shitty to us?"

"Lemme think," Ian said, grinning evilly at me.

It was nice to have even a small amount of normalcy restored. We needed a ceasefire between us even if neither of us was sure how long it would hold.

CHAPTER 3

"WHAT WERE you even shooting at?" Chandler White asked from where he sat across the table from me the following night.

"At the guy trying to run you over with his car," I explained again, since he'd missed it. I should have been on the receiving end of some serious gratitude, but instead all I was getting was grief.

"Yeah, but you missed," Ethan Sharpe, White's partner, reminded me.

"I didn't miss," I argued. "*You* missed."

He scoffed. "In your dreams, Jones. I'm the one who shot the car. I made him swerve and run into the side of his own house!"

"Again with this?" Ian sounded bored as he sat down beside me at the table, having returned from the bathroom. "Just wait for the damn ballistics report to come back. Why're you even wasting your time arguing?"

After work on Wednesday night, White and Sharpe had invited us to have dinner at Haymarket Pub & Brewery down on Randolph. Since it wasn't far from work, right there in the West Loop, and since we were both on our second wind—not having slept in a full twenty-four-hour period—we went along. Normally, White went straight home to his wife, but apparently she was out having drinks with her friends, so he had decided to hang with his partner and colleagues. I was wishing Ian and I had begged off, though, if White was going to keep believing his partner instead of me. I got that, the loyalty, but not in the face of overwhelming empirical proof otherwise.

"I shot the car," I reiterated to Ian, growing more indignant by the second.

"Okay."

"No, not okay, you have to believe me."

He shrugged, taking a sip of his beer, the Angry Birds Belgian Rye IPA he liked. He preferred the Mathias Imperial IPA, but that wasn't always on tap. I was not the beer drinker he was, but I did like The Defender American Stout I was drinking at the moment—on my second glass, feeling better than I had when I came in.

Because we'd all been involved in a shooting that day, our primary weapons were collected for processing, and we were all carrying our backups at the moment. A deputy US marshal had to be strapped at all times. That didn't mean it had to be the standard issue Glock 20, as long as the gun was approved to carry. It also didn't need to be in plain sight, which, when we went out, it normally wasn't. I'd been caught without a weapon on a few occasions, once even by my boss, who'd been good enough not to write me up for it, but since then, I'd never once been in breach of protocol.

"Not from where I was."

"What?" I was lost, thinking about our guns.

He snickered, pointing at my glass. "How many of those have you had?"

"Two," I said defensively.

"Try four," he said with a chuckle, draping his arm around the back of my chair.

"Who cares, not the point," I flared. "I was in the driveway. How could you even see what I did or didn't hit when you were in the front yard?"

"Because I ran up behind you."

"Not before I fired."

"Yes, I did," Ian said patronizingly. "It was way before you fired."

"Obviously not, since you didn't see me shoot the car."

"I shot the car from the street," Sharpe chimed in.

I turned from Ian to him. "How? You were behind me."

"You don't think I can shoot from behind you and not hit you?"

"That's not what I said," I muttered. "I know you don't have to hit me, but I also know you didn't hit shit."

"No, you're right, I didn't hit shit—I hit the car, asshole."

"No, you didn't," Ian groaned before eating another of the smoked chicken wings we'd ordered for an appetizer. He really liked the buffalo ones while I preferred the barbecue.

The thing was, Sharpe thought he got the car, but I knew it had been me. It wasn't like Tony Bayer, the driver of the car, could tell us who put the bullet in the radiator of his Ford Focus, thus making him swerve and hit the side of the split-level ranch, because he'd have to come down from his PCP high, first. He'd violated his parole in Austin, Texas, and then skipped town. But we'd gotten a tip from the Dallas field office that he was out in Northbrook, laying low at his sister's, and it had turned out he was.

He'd come running out of the house—naked—with a gun, car keys, and his brother-in-law's wallet. Once he was in the vehicle, he came barreling down the dirt and gravel driveway from the back of the house and tried to run over Deputy US Marshal Chandler White. It was then that I fired at, and hit, the subcompact getaway car. The best part of the whole thing was that his brother-in-law, Bobby Tanner, came out of the house after we had Tony cuffed and facedown on the front lawn and brought us some of Tony's clothes. He hadn't wanted to see the guy naked any more than we had.

Sharpe interrupted my thoughts as he pointed at Ian. "Wait. You think Miro shot the car too?"

"No," Ian grunted. "I shot the car."

White's laughter drew all our attention. "Are you kidding? You too? All you fuckers hit the car? Are you fuckin' kidding me?"

"When," Ian began sanctimoniously, indicating us all with an imperial wave of his hand, "we get the ballistics report back, you two are gonna be really fuckin' embarrassed."

"I hit the car," I repeated as our waitress brought burgers for me, Ian, and Sharpe and a grilled chicken breast for White. "What the hell is that?" I asked, horrified, pointing at his food.

"That's why I will outlive all of you by a great many years," White assured me.

"Maybe," Sharpe said in disgust. "But we're gonna have way more fun."

"I'll say nice things about you at each of your funerals."

We all threw fries at him.

AFTER DINNER White got a call from his wife and she wanted him to meet her at the club she was at in Lakeview. He of course didn't want to go alone, and Sharpe had no choice, as a partner never did. Ian and I begged off, but White was insistent and very whiny, so we all piled into a cab and took the twenty-minute ride, in traffic—because there was always traffic—to join her and her friends.

"Maybe the ballistics report will come in tonight," I said from the backseat where I was sandwiched between Ian and Sharpe. White was in the front seat with the driver.

"Oh, will you let it go," White groused, turning in his seat to gesture at Ian. "He's supposed to be the competitive one."

Normally Ian was, and for whatever reason, that filled me with affection for him and I let my head fall sideways onto his shoulder.

I realized what I'd done as soon as it registered how comfortable I was, and felt my stomach drop. We had agreed that work was work and home was home and never would we mix the two. With how things were going lately, it was especially important. And even though we weren't on the clock at the moment, we were still with Sharpe and White, and they fell more into one category than the other. Plus, we didn't want to make anyone uncomfortable. It was great that no one on our team cared that we were together, but none of them wanted to sit through us making out, either. At least none that I knew of.

I lifted my head a bit, but Ian reached up and pressed gentle fingers into my hair, keeping me there, wanting me there. I loved it when he was affectionate, whenever he let me see his desire, and it took more concentration than usual, as tired as I was, not to simply burrow against him. I really wanted to go home and get in bed with him.

White was texting his wife and Sharpe was asking him about her friends—who was single, if any of them were hot, and which, if any, were married. That last part caught my attention.

"Why does that matter?" I asked, sitting up and turning my head so I could look at him.

"What?"

"The married?"

He shrugged. "If they're married, they just wanna screw around. There's no bullshit."

"Ohmygod," I said, thoroughly revolted.

"You're a pig." Ian passed judgment on him.

"What?"

"You cannot sleep with a married woman," the cabbie informed Sharpe. "You will go to hell. Consider your immortal soul."

"And the fact that the husband who finds out might be packing," White added.

"And if he *is* packin', I might not be there to shoot him for you," I threw in.

"I shot the car," Ian insisted.

"Jesus, where is the fuckin' ballistics report?"

What was interesting, even to my inebriated, exhausted brain, was that no one in the car, even the driver, gave a crap that Ian and I were very obviously together.

THE CLUB was noisy and packed in the front but not in the back, where it was more lounge than bar. White's wife, Pam, had a table with her girlfriends and three male admirers who were buying the five women drinks. I noticed the round of cosmopolitans on the table that looked untouched.

"Ladies," Sharpe announced as he got close, and Pam was up quickly and in his arms, hugging him tight before turning to the others and introducing her husband's partner.

"This is Deputy United States Marshal Ethan Sharpe, everyone, who's very newly single."

The marshal part did the trick, and the guys, apparently looking to score, disappeared and a waitress came by to collect the drinks no one wanted.

"I liked your partner better when he had a girlfriend," I told White.

"My wife is trying her damnedest to fix that," he snickered.

Sharpe ordered a round of Kamikaze shots for the women, and Ian turned and stepped into my space before I could order a beer.

"You wanna drink or go home with me?"

What was I, nuts? "I want to go home with you," I replied adamantly.

His laughter was warm. "You're so wasted, but it's nice that even though you are, you pick me."

"Always," I burped. "But I've been much more wasted than"—*Eric Lozano*—"than now and—wait."

"Why am I waiting?" he pried, leaning in like it was noisy, so that's why his mouth was so close to my ear, but in reality his breath was there, on my skin, and—

"Shit," I gasped, jolting away from him, reaching out and grabbing his bicep. "Ian, I think Eric Lozano walked into the bathroom."

"What?" he asked harshly, clearly annoyed. "I'm trying to—"

"I swear to God."

And that fast, because he was not only my lover but my partner as well, he brushed off seductive mode and stepped back into the marshal. "Let's go."

There was no thought given to alerting Sharpe and White. We simply bolted.

Ian went first, as usual, and we waited until we were outside the bathroom to draw our guns. But as soon as we stepped into the bathroom, we first, quickly and quietly, made sure it was clear, and then walked to the last stall, where it sounded like Lozano was getting lucky.

I myself had had many encounters in restrooms over the course of my sex life, but never with women. So I was impressed, really, by the balance displayed by Lozano's lady friend, who had her legs wrapped around his waist, her back arched like a rainbow, and her hands on the rim of the toilet. It was important to note that she had wads of toilet paper between her palms and the seat.

"Why didn't you simply bend her over?" I asked from where I stood, up on the toilet in the next stall over.

"It's a good question," Ian apprised from where he was standing on the toilet in the stall on the other side of them. We had them bookended.

Lozano's head snapped up and his eyes bugged out, glancing from me smiling at him to Ian, who was scowling over the top of the dividing wall on his other side, and back to me.

"It would've been faster."

"And easier," the girl said, because, really, what the hell—why wouldn't she weigh in?

"I'll fuckin' kill you guys," he threatened, which really showed a lot of balls, because for one, his pants were around his ankles, and for two, there was no way he was getting out of the stall without getting her legs off him.

"We're federal marshals," I informed him, holstering my gun under my sweater even as Ian lifted his over the side of the divider so Lozano could see the P228 clearly. "You wanna maybe rethink that?"

He sighed deeply. "I thought I gave all you guys the slip when I left Des Plains."

Ian lowered his gun, knowing as well as I did that Lozano wasn't going to give us any trouble. We were already talking like regular people, and we'd been marshals long enough to know what that meant. Lozano, like most of the people we busted—when they knew we had them—was going to come along easy.

"You were in Iowa?" I grimaced. "Aww, man, I'm sorry."

"Hey."

The new voice made me look up, and I saw three men behind us, all in trench coats, all in suits, and I wondered, as I often did, why these guys didn't simply put on nametags that said "Hi, I'm a mob enforcer."

"Hey," I greeted them loudly, putting on. "Come watch my buddy take a shit, man. We're putting it on YouTube!"

"He's gotta stand over the bowl," Ian announced, even louder than I was, before he pretended to fall off the toilet in his stall. "Oh fuck!"

I howled with fake laughter. "Awww, man, you didn't get shit on you did you?"

The one in front pressed his closed fist to his mouth, one of the guys behind him turned and darted, and the third guy almost retched.

Shooting people in the head was one thing. Getting some other guy's fecal matter on you was a whole other ballgame.

The guy in front was breathing quickly in and out through his nose in an effort, I assumed, not to hurl. "You assholes see anybody else come in or outta here?"

"No," I cackled, lifting my phone. "Dude, you gotta see this… it's epic!"

That was it—he pivoted, shoved his friend who was also trying to not throw up toward the door. They were gone seconds later.

Ian came out of the stall and knocked on the one Lozano and his girl were in. "Kick your gun out under the door, and then you and—"

"Donatella," she chimed in.

"You and Donatella come out of there."

His Heckler & Koch P30 slid out under the door and Ian stopped it with his foot.

"Do you want mine too?" Donatella asked.

"Yes, please," I answered as Ian did a quick brass check on the gun.

Donatella's micro Uzi was a surprise.

"I have a big purse," she said defensively as the door opened and she and Lozano stepped out. And she was right; her Juicy Couture bag was enormous.

I held up the automatic weapon for her. "Why do you need this?"

She gave me a look like I was stupid, made all the more obvious as her eyes were so heavily frosted and her lashes so very fake.

"Okay, fine. Tell me why you're meeting Lozano here to fuck in a bathroom stall. You seem classier than this."

"Oh, do I?" she baited.

I took a step forward and stared her down. "Yeah, Donatella, ya do. I think the Four Seasons or something. I think this is slumming, for you."

And with that, the dam broke and she launched herself at me, wrapped her arms around my neck as she sobbed and chanted over and over that she loved him, hand to God.

"For crissakes, Lozano," Ian said, waving the gun he'd picked up. "Why didn't you tell the marshals that took you in that Donatella had to come with you?"

His brows lifted almost to his hairline. "I can do that?"

Ian groaned and Donatella lifted her head to peer up at me with her now swollen raccoon eyes. "I can go to Iowa too?"

"Well, it won't be Iowa anymore," I assured her as I pulled my iPhone from the breast pocket of my slim-fitting motorcycle jacket and called the office. We needed backup.

"Yeah? Could it be Brooklyn? I got family there."

I rolled my eyes as she sighed and cuddled against me, fiddling with the hem of my gray cashmere sweater.

"You gotta girl at home, marshal?" she asked seductively.

"What?" Ryan barked from the other end of the phone.

"That is not a greeting, asshole," I assured him.

"What the hell do you want?"

"I need Ching and Becker and an extraction team to meet me and Ian at Kid Lobo over on Clark Street. We've got Eric Lozano and his friend Donatella—"

"Fenzi," she purred, tightening her arms and nestling even closer. "I hope you have a girl, marshal, 'cause all this here should not be going to waste."

"Fenzi," I repeated as Ian grabbed her arm, spun her around, and shoved her at Lozano.

"Are you fucking with me?" Ryan cracked, sounding incredulous. "You and Doyle caught Eric Lozano, accountant for the Tedesco crime family?"

I moved the phone from my mouth and watched Lozano smiling down at Donatella, who was wrapped around him even tighter than she'd been around me. It was easy to see the difference between the friendly, appreciative hugging I'd been getting and the seductive body press she was giving Lozano. Sadly, Ian didn't have any female friends, so he didn't know what the friendship kind of snuggling looked like.

"You're an accountant?" I asked Lozano.

He looked over at me. "Yeah."

"I thought you killed people."

"No, man—I do taxes, I launder money, move it around, shit like that."

"Do you even know how to fire a gun?"

He made a face like maybe and then nodded.

"What the fuck, Jones," Ryan grumbled over the phone.

"Extraction team," I insisted.

"Coming now."

"We're in the bathroom."

"Of course you are," he said as though he were in pain, clearly appalled. "Where are White and Sharpe?"

"Doing shots."

"You know what, don't tell me anything else. I'm hanging up now. Just stay there. Ching and Becker will be on site in twenty."

"Way-way-way—is the ballistics report back on the shooting?" I asked eagerly.

"What shooting?"

"The car!" I rasped, dying.

"The car?" He was indignant.

"Come on," I whined. "Are the guns back yet?"

"You look like a grown-up, but you're actually only ten," he groused.

"Please," I begged with a little whining thrown in for good measure.

"Doyle shot the car," he informed me. "You hit one of the tires and Sharpe hit a tree. Happy now?"

"What? That can't be right."

"You were running; so was Sharpe. Do you have any idea how hard it is to hit something when you're moving?"

"Shit."

"You will never hear the end of this."

He had no idea.

"Ching and Becker are eighteen minutes out. Do not move from that bathroom."

"Did you just tell me to stay in the bathroom?"

Apparently I was too annoying for words, as evidenced by him hanging up on me. I was going to explain to Lozano and Donatella that these were their tax dollars at work, but as they probably didn't pay taxes, the observation would be lost on them. Also, they wouldn't have heard me anyway because they were much too busy making out. I would have made them stop, just to be a dick, but I felt lips on the back of my neck.

"Get off me," I complained, not meaning it.

"I told you I shot the car," he murmured in my ear.

Yes, he had.

"We should go to the shooting range, and I can give you some pointers."

I stalked away from him and went to the bathroom door, making sure no one could come in.

"You want me to come over there and protect you since I can shoot straight?" he teased.

"I have the Uzi," I volleyed.

"Yeah, but what can you hit with that?"

"Fuck you, Ian!"

He lost it.

IT TOOK the whole night and into the early morning before we were done processing Lozano and Donatella, and when we finally got home, I was not only hungry and sober, but tired and prickly, having been rubbed raw by the ribbing from every single person on my team, including my partner.

I was surprised when I was seized from behind and shoved down on the couch. Ian followed fast, curling over me, grabbing hold of my legs and wrapping them around his hips.

"What're you—"

"Kiss me," he demanded huskily, rubbing his groin against mine before bending to capture my mouth.

I evaded his lips. "That teasing was brutal, Ian."

"No, it wasn't."

"You were an ass."

"Yeah, but you love me when I'm like that, so who cares?"

He was right, I did. I loved him like crazy.

"So," he said, his voice cracking as he gripped my thighs, making sure I stayed there, "could you get over being annoyed and kiss me already?"

"You know, that was pretty great what you did earlier."

"What was that?" he asked as he shifted over me.

"Just the way you followed me, no questions asked."

"Always," he said, smiling at me. "So… about that kiss?"

"Yeah," I sighed, taking hold of his tie and easing him down to me. "I think I can manage that."

CHAPTER 4

OCTOBER IN Chicago was already cold, so as we sat outside in the car on the moderately busy city street, I turned the heater on. The problem was, though, that once Ian got warmed up, he was out like a light. Because of his military training, if Ian wanted to sleep, he could do it on command. It took maybe a minute for him to be dead to the world, and it was annoying as hell, because I had to power down my brain to reach that same REM sleep he could achieve so easily. Even sex wasn't a certainty for knocking me out, and I was frankly more than a little resentful.

"Will you wake up?" I growled, jabbing him with my elbow to roust him.

"What?" he complained, sitting up, scowling at me. "Don't be jealous."

I went back to checking the street with the binoculars as he got situated again, leaning his head against the driver's-side door. We were a street over from the house we were monitoring, our fellow marshals, Eli Kohn and Jer Kowalski, were across the street, and Chicago PD was there with cars on the other three corners of the block. It wasn't for our case, or even a fugitive the marshals were looking for, but instead another task force op.

"Hey."

My gaze flicked over to him.

"Why don't you just tell me already?"

I had no idea what we were talking about. "You lost me," I said, again glancing around the perimeter to make sure I hadn't missed anything.

"We both know that ever since Altman was here you've been even weirder than usual."

This wasn't the marriage thing. This was something else, and I really didn't want to get into it. "I don't know what you're—"

"Stop," he ordered. "Spill."

His Army buddy, Sean Altman, was one of the guys in the twelve-man team Ian was a member of, and whenever Ian was away on a mission, Altman was with him. He was in charge of communications, while Ian was a weapons specialist. Altman had expounded, because I'd asked, what kinds of tasks Operational Detachment Alpha did. He talked about training, and that each member of the team had an insertion specialty—which of course made me snicker, because no matter how old I was on the outside I was still a little boy in my head—but didn't give me more details about the group. And while I understood, I felt like he shouldn't have asked what I wanted to know if he really couldn't say.

I had excused myself to give the two men time alone, but I got annoyed that Ian didn't stop me, didn't want me there. Upstairs in bed, I realized how possessive and idiotic I was acting, made peace with the fact that I was being an asshole, and let it go. They stayed up into the early morning hours talking, and I finally fell asleep around two. When I woke up to make coffee, I was surprised that Altman wasn't passed out on the couch where he'd been the day before.

"Where's your buddy?" I asked Ian as he walked up behind me and planted a kiss on my bare shoulder.

"He had to go," was all he said.

But there had been more to it than that, because another week later, Ian had to report to training because Altman had been replaced with a new guy in their group. When I prodded him, he told me he wasn't sure why Altman had transferred but he was certain the man had his reasons.

"Everyone has reasons, Ian. Don't you care what they are?"

"It's none of my business?"

"He's your friend."

"He is."

I was confused. "So I could go ahead and request a new partner, and you wouldn't want to know why?"

"That's different and you know it," he husked, leaning in, hand on my cheek to keep me still as he kissed me. He put his coffee cup down and used his free hand to divest me of my sleep shorts. When he dropped to his knees, I forgot why I cared that Altman hadn't stayed in my house.

As the weeks wore on, my mind kept returning to Altman, and now, in the car on a stakeout, I had no way to tiptoe around the subject.

"Miro?"

I was good and caught. "What?"

"Don't do the what, just ask your fuckin' question."

I coughed softly. "I want to know why Altman left that night and then later left your group."

Ian let his head roll sideways so he could see me. "He wanted to fuck me."

I accidentally inhaled the water I was drinking and nearly drowned right there. "Jesus Christ, Ian!" My roar was loud in the car. "Are you tryin' to fuckin' kill me?"

"Nope," he sighed, "only answering the question."

"Ian!"

"Stop yelling," he said with a yawn.

"Then explain."

Quick shrug. "He told me he was gay."

"Why? Why would he do that just outta the blue?"

"It wasn't like that. He trusted me 'cause I came clean with my team the last time I saw them."

"You did?"

"Sure I did," he explained. "I couldn't have them find out by themselves down the road. It wouldn't be fair. So I told my CO first and then the rest of the team."

I was overwhelmed. "I can't believe you did that."

"You have to be honest with the men you serve with—they have your back."

"And do they still have yours?"

"Of course," he said irritably, like how dare I doubt them. "They know me. They've been in combat with me. What would have changed?"

"People are stupid sometimes, and the gay part freaks them out."

"Yeah, okay, but not—you know, my guys. They're soldiers first. The only thing that matters is do you carry your weight."

I understood that too.

"But so I told them, and that night Altman was here, he propositioned me."

I tried hard not to sound defensive. "And what'd you say?"

"What the fuck do you think I said?"

It was the niggling fear in the back of my head... what Ian could have or could do with someone other than me. I wasn't the only man able to tie him down; he knew others.

I stared at him. He stared back.

I relented. "You trust those guys too."

"Meaning what?"

I shrugged.

"I'm that easy to give up?"

"You know that's not how it is."

"Oh yeah?" he taunted. "How is it, then?"

I leaned into him, close, my mouth hovering over his so we were sharing breath. "I want to know what you told your friend."

"And I wanna know what's going on in your head."

I went to ease back, but he slipped his hand around the side of my neck and held tight, making sure I stayed where I was.

"I'm not the only one who could be in bed with you." It was true. "We both know it."

"There are other guys," he agreed. "There's no doubt."

My mouth went dry because this was another fear that rode me, along with him thinking that marriage was not for him.

When we'd started, I'd thought it was only me who could give Ian what he needed physically, but if the men he entrusted his life to were also vying to fuck him... it would be hard for me to compete.

He asked the question I didn't have the balls to. "So why you, then?"

I pulled away, hating the conversation, mad that I'd brought anything up and wanting it to all just go away. Why I always had to push, I had no idea. I didn't need to know this badly what had happened with his friend.

"M."

The streetlights had all my attention.

"Look at me."

I did as he asked, slowly, reluctantly.

"You're such an idiot."

"That's helpful," I muttered, letting my head thump sideways against the window.

"Kohn," Ian said softly, and I realized he was now on his phone. "Miro and I are out for twenty. We gotta eat."

"Where the fuck are you eating out here? This is Englewood."

"Meaning what?"

"Meaning just stay in the fuckin' car. It ain't safe."

"It's not that bad."

"The hell it's not," he scoffed, and I could hear Kowalski chuckling in the background. "Is your vest on?"

"Could you shut up already and cover our position."

"10-4," he said snidely.

I needed air, so I shifted to get out of the car, trying to remember what was close, but Ian grabbed the front of the wool hunting jacket I'd changed into at the office and held tight. "What're you doing?" I muttered.

He yanked me forward, framed my face with his hands, and kissed me hard, rough. I opened for him as he shoved his tongue inside, seeking mine. It was a hot, brutal onslaught, and I whimpered in the back of my throat as he reached around me to lower the seat so that once he leaned over the console, I was under him, taking what he was giving.

He loosened the long, gray cashmere scarf I had on and made me jolt under him when he suckled the side of my neck.

"Ian—"

He kissed me again, biting my bottom lip to shut me up before his lips settled hungrily, possessively, on mine.

Not much of a talker, my boy, but I heard him anyway, loud and clear.

"I trust you," he panted in a broken whisper before he went back to mauling my mouth. "Only you."

Only me. There was only me.

So yes, he could have other lovers, but he only trusted *me*, and because he did, that translated to a singular desire.

I needed air, so I shoved him back enough to gulp some.

"If I fuck someone else," he rasped, "I'll lose you, and I can't have that." He looked good all excited and hot for me, with his blown pupils and swollen lips and flushed face. "When Altman said what he did, all I could think was—if I fuck him, Miro'll leave me, and then he'll be lookin' for a new guy to take home and put in his bed, and I wanna be the only guy who ever gets to be there."

He was the only one I wanted. I didn't even *see* anyone else but him.

"And besides, you're way prettier than Altman."

I snorted out a laugh. Having Ian—the man who was physical perfection himself with his sculpted body and gorgeous eyes; the smoky, seductive sound of his voice and his wicked grin—think I was beautiful was overwhelming. Him wanting me did fantastic things for my ego.

"Miro," he rumbled, bending to kiss me again, "I'm yours."

And I knew that, I did.

"Don't second-guess me. Don't think stupid shit anymore, all right? I don't stay 'cause you're the only guy who *could* hold me down or tie me up or whatever. I stay 'cause it's us and we're real and I'm safe, so"—he growled—"stop."

He was safe because I made him feel that way. There was nothing else he needed and nothing else I wanted. I had an opening there, because in that moment he was vulnerable and I could've pushed. It would be easy to bring up the marriage thing again, say that if he felt the way he so obviously did, then there was, in fact, a logical next step. But it was nice between us now, and I didn't want to screw it up by returning to an already sore subject.

"Okay," I agreed, sighing as I accepted another kiss, "okay."

"I wanna go home," he said raggedly, and when I reached down between us and rubbed over his rock-hard cock straining against his zipper, his moan was sweet.

"You want me bad," I teased, tilting his head and licking the base of his throat.

"Don't gloat," he cautioned, twisting around to flop down into his seat and then gripping the steering wheel tight. Moments later he called Kohn and told him we were back.

"Hold on, I'ma put you on speaker 'cause Jer wants to—"

"That was fast. What'd you eat?" Kowalski wanted to know.

"Nothing," Ian said, his voice brittle with annoyance. He wanted to leave.

"Ohhh-kay, so—oh, wait. We have movement on the north side of the house. Everyone hold position."

We were out front, so we couldn't see anything.

"Shit!" Kohn yelled. "Go-go-go—suspect is fleeing on foot down 77th Street east toward Racine."

Ian exploded from the car and took off running. I had no choice but to climb into the driver's seat and whip the car out from between the two parked ones and into the street. I hated driving when Ian was running, and it was only worse at night when I had a harder time following him.

My phone rang seconds later. "Do you have a visual on Doyle?" I yelled at Kohn. "I can't see him anywhere!"

"In pursuit down an alley—he's on Bishop now, headed toward 79th!"

Shit.

I made a U-turn in the middle of the street, much to the annoyance of other drivers if the blaring horns, screeching tires, and yelling was any indication.

"Shit, wait," Kohn gasped, "it's Loomis, not Bishop."

It was good he told me since I had been poised to make a hard left and instead drove by, flying down the street to the next one and turning in, barreling down it probably much faster than I should have. Alleys were dicey; you never knew who could pop out of one of the buildings.

A man was in a dead sprint toward me, and my partner was in quick pursuit. I came to a lurching stop, and as the guy went to veer around me, I threw open the driver's-side door. He hit it hard, slamming it shut, but it stopped him.

Ian was there a second later, hauling the dazed man roughly to his feet so I could get out. He cuffed him, then spun him around and shoved him against the car.

"This is police brutality," he gasped.

"We're not the police," Ian stated, not even winded from his run, pulling his badge from the inside of his coat so the guy could see the star. "We're marshals."

"Shit," he groaned. "I don't wanna go back to the joint."

"Too late," I replied cheerfully as Kohn and Kowalski came whipping down the alley—we all drove too fast—followed by three police cars, blue lights pulsing, sirens screaming.

We were surrounded in seconds, but Kowalski had more important things on his mind than the apprehended fugitive.

"Did you guys really eat?" Jer wanted to know before anything else, big bear of a man that he was. He looked like one of those powerlifters in the Olympics, all barrel chested and huge. In contrast was his partner: sleek, metrosexual Eli Kohn, who apparently took a new woman home every single night. I always wondered where he got the energy.

"What?" Ian asked, clearly annoyed.

"What? Why you gotta say it like that? I was gonna treat for dinner, but not if you're gonna be a prick. I'll take your partner and leave your ass here."

Ian's scowl got darker, and I apologized for him and said we'd love to have dinner at any restaurant of Jer's choosing.

"There, ya see, douchebag—that's how not to be a dick."

"Where's Sergeant Joyner?" I asked everyone around me.

"Here," she called out, striding up to me as the men cleared a path.

I passed her the fugitive's wallet when she reached me. "I release into your custody one Derek LaSalle, formerly of Gresham, Oregon, wanted for assault and battery."

Sergeant Adele Joyner out of the Portland PD was more than happy to take him off our hands. "Thank you," she said, shaking my hand and then Ian's. "Without these task forces, I'd never pick up the criminals who aren't involved in our open cases."

It was true. Most cops were so busy not drowning in their day-to-day caseload that people who evaded capture, ran to other states, or crossed jurisdictional lines slipped through the cracks. Many PDs didn't have the resources or manpower to simply follow a fugitive across the country. But what they could do was bring their missing violent criminals to the marshals service, and we would form what basically amounted to a posse made up of federal, state, and local law enforcement personnel to hunt down whoever they were after. Joyner had approached the marshals in Portland, and they had in turn accessed case records in Chicago and found a lead on her fugitive. The rest was simply waiting and watching.

"I appreciate this so much, gentlemen."

"It's our job," Ian assured her.

"It is," I agreed.

"So tell me a good place to eat before we go back to the hotel."

I suggested Girl & The Goat downtown, but Ian wanted meat and beer so we decided on Trenchermen over on North Avenue. I'd taken him once before and the hanger steak there was his new favorite thing. Sadly, when I called to check, the dining room was closed, and since it was past 10:00 p.m., our options were dwindling. Ian's second idea was Mexican, El Charro over on Milwaukee Ave. He went on and on about the extralarge super burrito with scrambled eggs and chorizo until even Kowalski was salivating. Joyner and some others agreed to follow us there.

He was excited to see that the driver's-side door on the Taurus was caved in from the fugitive's impact, so we had to have it towed back to our garage. We technically weren't allowed to drive a vehicle in any condition where the structural integrity could be called into question.

"Gimme a break, it's fine," I told Ian. "It's still drivable. That's only a ding."

"It's a big fuckin' ding," Kowalski informed me.

I pointed at Ian. "He just doesn't wanna drive it anymore."

"Yeah, I can't blame him," Kohn admitted, looking revolted. "It doesn't scream armed and dangerous, more middle management."

Kowalski shivered. "I can't even fit in that."

I snorted in spite of myself, and Ian cracked a grin. "Fine," I relented. "We'll have it towed back so the dent can be banged out."

Ian's whoop of happiness made me smile.

"Call it in," I directed, shaking my head when he hit my abdomen in excitement.

HEADING TO the restaurant, riding in the back seat of the Mercedes Benz that was Kohn and Kowalski's vehicle, I complained about how slow he was driving.

"Miro's used to me taking the corners on two wheels." Ian snickered.

"I try and keep all tires on the road at all times," Kohn affirmed in his superserious voice.

I approved of that, just not the lack of speed. When I complained some more, he actually hit the gas, but not enough to make me happy.

"I could die of old age back here," I insisted, leaning forward between him and Kowalski. "Lemme drive."

"Not on your life," Kohn assured me as his partner put a massive hand on my face and shoved me back.

I turned to Ian. "You gonna let him treat me like that?"

Since he couldn't stop laughing, I figured my backup was not forthcoming.

After we'd eaten, we walked three doors down to a bar Ian knew, and he and the marshals from Oregon, along with me and Kohn—Kowalski bailed to drive Joyner and one of the other detectives back to their hotel—got down to some serious drinking.

When the stories started getting swapped, I was ready to go. It was well after midnight and we all had to work later today. But Ian got talked into darts and more drinks and finally, around one thirty, I had to take drastic measures.

I caught him coming out of the bathroom as I lay in wait.

"Hey."

He turned fast, saw me leaning against the exposed brick wall, and strolled over.

"What're you doin'?"

I shrugged. "I'm beat, so I'm gonna head out."

"Without me?" he asked, instantly concerned.

"I don't want to keep you from having a good time."

He took a breath.

"Unless you'd rather come home with me?" I asked softly, taking hold of his hips and pulling him into me, my eyes locked on his.

"I... yeah," he rasped, inhaling sharply as I opened my stance, allowing him to push in closer, my thigh sliding between his legs.

"I wanna kiss you," I promised softly, gently. "But I can't do that here."

"But you will at home."

"Oh yes," I said, smiling at him.

"Okay, let's go," he replied hoarsely.

"Good," I agreed, glad that we didn't have to go pick up Chickie from my friends Aruna and Liam, since they'd agreed to keep him overnight. I'd had no idea how long the op would run, so I'd made arrangements.

When we got back to the table, the others wanted to know what bar we were hitting next. I got it, I did, we worked a crazy scary job, and the unwinding was necessary and allowed people to bond. But I was beat and could barely make conversation, let alone sing "Kumbayah" with all of them.

"Actually we're both going," Ian apprised them. "Work and all that."

We were called lightweights, but Kohn called it a night, too, and we caught cabs, Kohn over to Roosevelt and State where he lived in some new high-end apartment building, and me and Ian down to the Loop where we caught a bus out to the Fullerton stop in Lincoln Park. It took longer than a cab would have, but that would have cost a mint. As it was, the walk from the stop to the Greystone was short.

I was about to start telling Ian all the hot sweaty, sticky things I had planned for him the second we got home when his phone rang. As soon as he looked at the caller ID, I saw his face fall.

"Oh no," I said without meaning to, because I'd had a few drinks. "No-no-no."

But it was obvious and unchangeable. He was leaving on a mission later this morning—I caught that much listening to his yes-and-no answers—and all we'd have would be a few hours, for God knew how long. His smile after he hung up tried hard to show me that everything was going to be all right.

Once inside, Ian locked the front door before we both took off our jackets and hung them up, and then he turned to say something to me, but I grabbed him instead.

"You're leaving me again," I whispered, shoving him against the door, my chest plastered to his back, holding him in place. I caught his left wrist with my right hand and pinned it above his head, using my other to reach up under his shirt and pinch his left nipple, hard.

"Fuck!" he yelled, writhing against me as I pulled him away from the door just enough to run my hand down his abdomen, savoring the feel of his muscles flexing beneath my fingers.

I let go of his wrist and worked open his belt and jeans and got under the elastic of his briefs to take hold of his gorgeous cock, already dribbling precum.

"Someone's ready for me," I husked into his ear before he tilted his head back and to the side and offered me his mouth.

I milked his length as I devoured his lips, breaking the kiss only after he was squirming against me.

"Let me—I need to get these down," he whispered before shoving his jeans to his knees. When he reached behind him and pressed a lube packet into my hand, I was surprised.

"Where the fuck did this come from?" I asked, my voice thick with need as I let go of him, only moving away far enough to shuck my pants and briefs down and slather my dick.

"I carry these for you," he said, splaying his hands on the door, arching his back, offering me his hard, beautiful body, "just in case."

"Very smart," I growled, taking hold of my slicked, seeping dick and pressing slowly into his body.

"Miro!" he gasped, shivering, jolting back against me, impaling himself on my length, pushing in deep, hard, wanting me, needing me to fill him fast, the gentle and slow saved for another time. "I wanna feel it when I'm gone."

"I would never hurt you," I whispered, thrusting quickly, holding on to his lean hips tight, dragging myself from him gradually on the retreat, only to piston back inside a moment later.

"Fuck, you feel good," he rasped brokenly, the yearning there. "Don't... stop."

He was slick and hot, and I wanted to be gentle, but he wouldn't let me.

"Miro, fuckin'—hurry!"

I could do nothing less. His demand, with the dark strain in his voice, the breathless catch, the way he trembled—I wanted all of him.

I drove into him over and over until we were both sticky with sweat and he was braced against the wall with one hand, jerking himself off with the other.

"I'm gonna... come," he ground out.

I ran my hand up the back of his head into his hair and fisted tight, yanking hard to claim his mouth. He opened for me and I sucked on his tongue, the kiss brutal and desperate. I wanted to absorb him into my skin, have him with me all the time, and it was heartbreaking and joyful all at the same time.

God, I loved him.

His muscles clamped around me as he broke the kiss to yell, spurting onto the door, shuddering against me as my own orgasm followed his and I pumped into him, filling him up, semen dripping hot and thick between us.

I leaned heavily, still buried in his ass, and kissed along his jaw as he let his head fall back on my shoulder. "I love you," I said, licking the sweat from his skin. "Be careful while you're away from me."

He moved his head, just barely acknowledging my request. "Kiss me more."

It was all I wanted to do.

CHAPTER 5

IT WAS standing room only on the opposite side of the vet's office downtown off Cicero. Even though my boyfriend, and therefore his dog, now both lived with me in Lincoln Park, we hadn't looked into finding a new vet for the werewolf yet. So Chickie and I made the trip out to frighten the locals even without meaning to.

No matter what I said, no one believed that the bear-sized dog sitting beside me wasn't going to eat anyone. He was simply too big. His paws were as large as my hands splayed out, his head dwarfed mine, and up on his back legs, he could drape his front legs over my shoulders—and I was five eleven in my bare feet. It wasn't his fault that he made two, or even three, of most dogs. He wasn't a creature out of a horror movie; he just looked like one.

"Hybrids are illegal in Chicago, you know," a woman scolded me from where she was cowering with her cat carrier against the far wall.

"Yes ma'am, I know," I said, letting my head thunk softly back against the wall, as Chickie Baby stretched and put his head in my lap, the movement causing a gasp from the entire left side of the room.

"Someone should report you to the authorities," another concerned pet owner chimed in.

"Mrs. Gunderson." Susannah, the perky vet tech, sighed as she walked into the lobby and toward Chickie and me. "If this dog was, in fact, a wolf hybrid, do you think we'd be taking care of him or reporting him to animal control?"

No answer to that.

She reached us and squatted down beside Chickie, who wagged his tail but otherwise didn't move. "What's the matter with Ian's baby?"

"I dunno, but he won't eat, and that's cause for concern. I mean, normally he eats his own weight in food a day."

She chuckled. "Well, let's go ahead and bring him on back."

Once the door closed behind me, I heard movement on the other side. "You realize that now everyone can fan out, right?"

She laughed softly. "He is a big dog, Miro."

"Yeah, but he doesn't actually eat people."

"No, but he certainly could."

I lifted the sweet face with the black muzzle. "Look at those eyes. Are those the eyes of a cold-blooded killer?"

When she looked at him, Chickie eased his nose out of my hand and licked my fingers.

"Awww," she crooned. "No. He's a sweet baby."

"Yes, he is," I agreed, following her down the hall to the exam room. After we weighed him—110 pounds of powerful muscle—I took a seat in the chair. Chickie rested his head in my lap, under my hand, and I petted him as Susannah said that he was down three pounds from a year ago.

"Which is a tiny amount of weight for a dog Chickie's size," she cautioned.

"All right," I said, getting worried anyway, scratching behind his ears.

"Is it possible he just misses Ian?" Susannah offered. "How long's he been gone?"

"He's only been gone three weeks, so I doubt that's it."

"Was he deployed?"

"He was," I answered, trying not to sound as dejected as I felt. The relationship part of us was still only about six months old, so when he was home I could barely keep my hands off him. Three weeks without him with no end in sight, and I was ready to climb the walls. I hated that since Ian was a reserve officer, the Army could call him up at a moment's notice. The worrying was taking its toll on me, and I missed having him in my bed.

"Miro?"

I coughed. "Sorry, I just don't buy Chickie starving himself 'cause Ian's not home."

"Oh no?"

"No. That dog doesn't miss a meal for any reason, and normally he eats *more* when Ian's gone."

"Why?"

"'Cause Ian's really careful with how often he feeds him, but me, not so much."

She nodded. "I see. Well, I'd take his temperature, but our large animal thermometer broke last week, and we're waiting on the new one to come in."

"That's okay. His nose is cold, so I think he's good."

She shook her head like I was ridiculous.

"What?"

"That's adorable. Been watching lots of Lassie reruns, have you?"

I smirked at her, and she cackled before promising to send the doctor right in as she closed the door behind her.

I sat there with Ian's dog and petted him more. "Whatever this is, Chick, we'll figure it out."

He yawned wide to show me he wasn't all that racked up about it, himself.

When the door opened, the vet came in—Dr. Alchureiqi, who was one of the nicest men I had ever met. Chickie liked him as well, as evidenced from his quick rise and trot over.

"Oh, Mr. Wolf, why aren't you eating?" he asked Chickie in his warm Egyptian accent. "Is it your stomach or—oh, what do we have here, wedged in our tooth?"

It was simple, but what the hell did I know? It wasn't like Chickie was going to let me floss his teeth or something. But seriously, what kind of dog got a piece of bark stuck between his incisors? What the hell was he doing, gnawing on a tree?

A hundred and fifteen dollars later, I had an appointment to get his teeth cleaned, dog treats that helped clean off plaque, and a stern reprimand about keeping an eye on him when he went outside. I did the patronizing nodding, and everyone in the office was surprised when teeny Susannah smacked me on the arm.

"You broke your hand, didn't you," I teased.

"No," she sulked, even as she shook out her fingers. My bicep was bigger than her thigh; there was no way it hadn't hurt. "You're built like a damn lumberjack or something."

I chuckled and she turned a charming shade of scarlet.

We walked out the front to scattered gasps, having scared everyone again. Watching them all clutch their pets, I rolled my eyes before we hit the front door. Outside, we startled a woman when we arrived on the sidewalk, and she grabbed her kid tight as she rushed by.

Chickie was going to get a complex. It was ridiculous. I wanted to yell out that he only ate men and women, no kids, but since that would in no way help the situation, I let it go.

We crossed the street to the small parking lot, and I put Chickie in the passenger seat of my Toyota Tacoma pickup, buckled him in, and then went around to the driver's-side door.

"Give me your wallet" came the demand at the same time I felt a gun muzzle shoved between my shoulder blades.

I froze as Chickie began barking inside the cab.

It was a side street right off normally bustling Cicero Avenue, but it was Saturday morning, not quite as much traffic, so I shouldn't have been as surprised as I was.

"Don't turn around and no one's gonna get hurt," the man promised. "Just pass the wallet over your shoulder."

Deliberately, I pulled my ID from the breast pocket of my Burberry wool-blend military greatcoat and did exactly as he asked, holding it over my right shoulder for him.

"Oh fuck." He groaned as Chickie wriggled free of the seatbelt and flung himself against the door, pawing the glass, his nails clicking on it, snarling and growling, trying to get to me. "You're a cop?"

"Marshal," I corrected as he pushed the muzzle of the gun harder into my back.

"Fuck," he swore again as Chickie lost his mind and howled.

Grabbing the door fast, I opened it a crack and Chickie exploded from the cab, the force of the door opening knocking me back into the man, slamming us onto the asphalt at our feet.

He dropped the gun and my ID when he landed, scrambled out from under me, and ran. I was winded for a moment, but he was operating on far more adrenaline than I was. I knew the dog wouldn't rip my face off; he was under no such impression.

"Chickie," I yelled, but he was gone, barreling after the fleeing man.

I stood unsteadily, retrieving the gun and my ID, and watched as Chickie caught the guy in a flying leap, grabbed him by the shoulder, jaws clamping down, and lifted him off his feet in a blur of motion before hurling him to the ground like he was a rag doll instead of a man.

I groaned.

"Oh!" a bystander yelled from the other side of the parking lot.

"Jesus Christ!" another shouted from the sidewalk.

A good Samaritan who'd come running to see if I was all right grimaced in sympathy with the criminal. "Oh shit, that had to hurt."

"Dayum," a woman standing beside her Volkswagen Beetle two cars away called out as well, all of us watching Chickie dance around his fallen quarry.

The takedown had looked painful and the man wasn't moving.

It was fortunate that Chickie wasn't a trained attack dog or he would have gone for the jugular and the guy would be dead. As it was, he growled and barked, circled his victim, wagged his tail, basically waiting for his fallen quarry to twitch or move in any way. Jogging over to them, I called Chickie to me and petted him as the man simply lay there and moaned.

"I called 911 for you, brother," good Samaritan, who had followed me, said.

"Thank you." I sighed, squatting down and holding Chickie as the guy on the ground turned over.

"I think he broke my back, marshal," the would-be-robber said hoarsely, still not in possession of all the air normally in his body.

"And what did we learn?" I asked snidely.

Applause caught my attention, and I turned to see all the people from the veterinarian's office standing outside the front door, clapping. It was nice that they all saw Chickie for the good boy he was. As I heard sirens in the distance, I petted him while he took a seat beside me.

"Next time just grab the perp's leg, okay?"

All I got for my trouble was a wet nose in the eye.

I HAD to go down to the police station, file a report, have the vet fax over Chickie's medical records so I could prove all his shots were up to date and he didn't have rabies, and then sit for hours before giving a statement about exactly what had occurred. And that was fast!—with them throwing some professional courtesy my way after they found out I was a marshal. The sheer volume of paperwork involved in law enforcement was simply staggering.

"Why didn't you use your gun?"

"'Cause I figured the dog would hurt more," I lied. It took a lot for me to pull my gun on someone, certainly a life-and-death struggle, and those were few and far between.

"Really?" the officer taking my statement asked, chuckling as he filled out the report on his computer, leaning forward in his squeaky office chair.

"No, not really," I groaned. "I usually yell first, right? You warn people before you shoot at them."

"So then what happened?"

"My dog got there before I could even say 'Stop or he'll eat you.'"

The cop grinned wide. "What an idiot."

"You get a badge when you mug someone, you drop it and run."

"Right?"

I shrugged.

"Man, what're they teaching these clowns in the joint nowadays," the officer muttered.

Unfortunately for my mugger, threatening a peace officer, marshal, any law enforcement personnel at all carried with it a greater penalty than simply trying to rob your average person on the street. He was in for a world of shit.

It was a tedious way to spend my Saturday.

I had my phone out to call my boss and tell him about the robbery attempt as I was on my way home to Lincoln Park, but Chickie got out of the seatbelt and tried to climb into my lap while I was driving. How monster dog thought he was a Chihuahua was beyond me.

"Miro."

Not my boss. Never in a million years, even if I was dying, would he use my first name. I had obviously misdialed, but I couldn't make out who it was.

"Shit, Chick, sit—stupid dog, you're lucky you saved my life today or I'd shoot—" I growled, "Fuck. Hello?"

"Who saved your life?"

"The dog," I answered, not absorbed in the task of figuring out who I was talking to, more concerned with not dying in traffic because I had dog ass in my face. "Chickie, sit!"

"How did he save your life?"

"Some felon thought I looked like an easy mark," I said, trying to sound serious as Chickie sat in my lap, completely obscuring my view of the road. "Over there!" I snarled, shoving him into the passenger seat, only to have him twist around and lick my neck.

"Are you all right?" The voice took on a frantic tone.

"Yeah, I'm—" It hit me like a fist in the face. "Ian?"

"What the hell are you doing?"

"Oh," I gasped, my heart stopping. I pulled over quickly right before I got on Lakeshore Drive so I didn't wreck. "Baby?"

He was instantly surly. "Are you asking or do you know?"

"I *know*."

"You didn't sound sure."

"For crissakes, E," I snapped, shortening his name to the first syllable, which I hardly ever did, because how dare he doubt me even for a second. "I couldn't fuckin' hear you 'cause I'm fighting with your goddamn dog!"

"What? Why? Where are you?" he asked irritably.

"I'm in the car with Chickie."

"Doing what?"

"I had to take him to the vet 'cause he quit eating."

"Did you check and see if he got something stuck in his teeth? His gums are really sensitive," he said logically.

Perfect timing as usual. "No, I didn't."

"Is that what it was?"

"Yeah, that's what it was." I sighed, because even though we were discussing his annoying dog, I was in heaven talking to him on the phone. "Why are you calling? Are you hurt?"

"What?"

My heart stopped. "Oh shit. Ian—"

"And *you* called *me*, asshole."

I had, but how in the world was he answering? "Ian... honey—"

"No, I'm not fuckin' hurt!" he yelled. "Why would I get hurt? I'm not the one who had a run in with some—what? Was someone trying to rob you?"

"Yeah, I—"

"Did he pull a gun on you?"

"Yes, but it's fine, I'm fine, not a scratch on me. Can you say the same? No holes in you? Why are you answering? Tell me why you're answering!"

"I wanna know what happened with this guy!"

I had to rest my forehead on the steering wheel to try and get my breathing to even out. Chickie whined beside me, worried.

"Miro?"

"Just gimme a... sec," I said shakily.

He coughed. "Don't get all freaked out."

"Hard not to."

"Yeah," he grumbled, his voice gravelly. "Me too. When I'm not there and something happens, I—my mind goes to the worst thing I can think of."

"I know." After a minute, I took a breath. "So I called you?"

"Yeah."

"How did I do that?"

"You pushed the button on your screen, I suspect."

"You're such a wiseass."

"Yeah, well," he conceded. "Can't be helped, born this way."

We were both quiet for a long moment.

"So," he began, and I could hear the hesitation in his voice. "You called by accident."

"Yes."

"You happy I picked up?"

Stupid man, stupid question. Only Ian asked when the truth was so very obvious. "Yes. Very."

"'Cause why?"

I swallowed first so I wouldn't make a desperate, urgent sound in the back of my throat. "I miss you."

"Oh yeah?"

"Yeah."

"Like bad?"

"You have *no* idea."

He was silent again, and it hit me how whiny I must have sounded. "Sorry. I don't mean to come off so needy. You'll be home as soon as you can, I know that."

"Miro!" he snarled.

What was I missing?

"I want you to miss me."

"Well, that's good, then." I chuckled.

"And you know when I'm coming home."

I did? "How?"

"When have you ever been able to fuckin' call me when I'm deployed?"

"Never."

"So what does that tell you?"

The answer occurred to me, and it wasn't good. "Awww, man, did you accidentally leave your phone on? Did I uncloak your dagger?"

"You're fuckin' hysterical."

"No, I mean, since when do black ops guys get phone calls?"

"We don't when we're out in the field."

"Which means what?"

"Put it together, Jones."

It hit me after a second. "You're somewhere you can talk?"

The noise he made confirmed my deduction.

"*Where?*" I asked before I thought about it, desperate to know his location.

He coughed.

"No, wait," I muttered. "I'm… sorry. I'm just bein' stupid. You're probably on an unsecured line and so—forget I said anything."

He sighed, sounding exasperated. "Where are you exactly?"

I swallowed down my heart. "I was about to get on Lakeshore."

"Okay," he said simply. "Come home, then. I'm here."

I froze, afraid to even breathe.

"Miro?"

"Ian—"

"For crying out loud, are you coming or not?"

"You're at home?"

"Isn't that what I said?"

"Don't be an ass."

"Then get yours home!" he snarled.

I was silent a moment. "Well, that was clever," I apprised him, smiling like an idiot. My man was home.

"Yeah, well," he began, his voice bottoming out. "I missed you too."

And since there had been actual pining on my part, I made a very unmanly noise I wasn't proud of.

"Hurry."

He had no idea how fast I could make my truck go.

CHAPTER 6

OPENING THE front door of the Greystone townhouse Ian and I had done some work on over the summer—we'd painted the doors and cornice a deep purple-red, trimmed the boxwood hedges, and put in window boxes—I was happy to see his duffel bag and boots lying on the floor in the middle of the living room. The dog beat me to him since I had to close and lock the door behind me. Chickie rushed across the space, whimpering and whining, and flung himself at his master, knocking him down onto the couch hard.

"Stupid dog," Ian said affectionately, laughing as he hugged his werewolf. If I didn't know what I was looking at, it would have been scary. The licking looked like mauling, and honestly, if Chickie wanted, Ian was dog food.

I hung up my jacket on one of the pegs we'd added to the entryway and put my keys and wallet on the ledge above it before toeing off my sneakers. Ian had made changes to try to get me moving faster in the morning. He timed my rituals, which included putting product in my hair and figuring out what I was going to wear, and had made improvements. One of his biggest changes had been to put things by the front door: keys on hooks, badges on chains as well, wallets on the shelf above, IDs, earpieces, and pens in the cup. The only items that didn't live there now were phones and guns, and I had to give it to him, not having to hunt all over the house had sped up our exodus each day.

"Hey."

When I turned, Ian was standing there barefoot in frayed jeans and a plain white T-shirt, holding out his arms for me. Chickie was eating, which was good, and noisily slurping water.

Moving fast, I lunged when I was close enough, catching him hard—but more gently than the dog had—hugging him tight, soaking up the contact and the heat I was wrapped in as Ian squeezed me back.

"Fuck, I'm so happy you're home," I choked out, shivering with the feel of him, the strength of his body and the smell of his skin.

He turned and kissed behind my ear, my cheek, under my jaw, my chin, and then thrust his tongue in my mouth as he took me in a frantic, devouring kiss.

My brain shorted out because it was still new and still a dream: Ian all over me, easing me down onto the couch, following close, never breaking contact, pinning me under him. The movement was seamless, fluid, and the kiss deepened, became wild, ravenous, making me clutch at his back, dig my hands into the powerful muscles to keep him there, close to me. His knee wedged between my thighs, parting them, and I opened them wider so he could rest there, all of him on me, my feet on the backs of his calves.

I reached down between us and found the hard line of his cock straining against only denim before sliding my fingers under the waistband of his jeans, realizing instantly there was no other barrier there.

Quickly, with deft fingers, I unbuttoned his fly and worked the zipper down quickly, his erection filling my hand as I squeezed tight. The noise he made was pure ruthless need as he jolted forward, wanting the friction, driving into my fist as he ground out my name.

"You missed me," I said, trying to keep the smugness out of my tone as I stroked his dripping shaft.

His lashes lifted languorously as though he was drugged, and I was drowning in deep, dark blue. "I missed you," he whispered in agreement.

"Get your ass in my bed," I demanded, then softened my command with, "please."

"No," he said, his breath catching, shoving his hand behind one of the couch cushions and pulling out a small bottle of lube. "Here."

He pushed it at me. The fact that he'd had the foresight to put it there because he wanted me to take him on the couch was crazy hot. His desire for me was a gift.

"Get off me," I said, my voice gravelly and low.

"When?" he asked. Beads of precum rolled over my fingers as I continued to fondle his rock-hard erection.

"Now, idiot." I snickered, letting him go and trying to wriggle out from under him at the same time.

"I want you to… I want—" he rasped as he stood up beside me. "Miro."

Twisting free, I got up behind him, shoved him forward, bent him over the couch cushions, and rucked his T-shirt up at the same time I shucked his jeans to his ankles. He lifted one foot free so he could widen his stance, and I flipped open the bottle of lube.

"Hurry," he pleaded, and I heard the hard edge to his voice, the frustration mixed with the desire riding him.

"We should go slow. You've been gone."

"Screw that, just show me," he begged.

I didn't need to ask—I knew. He wanted me to show him that I'd missed him.

Slicking my cock fast, I clicked the bottle closed before dropping it to the wood floor. There would be no prep, no slow loosening of his muscles; it wasn't what he wanted or needed.

"Miro," he choked out, gripping the front of the couch tight, letting his head fall forward and lifting his ass, wanting me there, ready.

Taking hold of my painfully hard dick, I guided the dark, flared head to his entrance and pressed slowly inside.

The garbled noise he made worried me.

"Are you okay?" I asked, curling over him, my lips on his back, licking, kissing, and finally sucking.

"Yes," he groaned sweetly. "Just—I missed you being inside."

And I'd missed being there. "Hold on, baby."

"You feel so good. I need you to move… faster."

His body would not get time to adjust to the intrusion, I couldn't wait even seconds more. I thrust into him hard and hot, burying myself to the balls in one snap of my hips, his clenching muscles unable to keep me from the breach. The inexorable slide, me filling him, all at once, had taken his breath.

"Fuck," he growled, muscles cording as he squeezed the frame of the couch, bracing there.

Slipping out a fraction, I shoved back inside, stuffing him full, my flesh slapping against his, the powerful motion making him call out my name.

"Miro, just fuckin' use me."

Taking hold of his hips, I began a slow, rhythmic deep pumping, driving to the hilt over and over, loving the feel of the slick heat rippling around me as well as knowing that it was Ian taking me in, wanting me.

"Miro, I can't—"

"You can," I ground out. "Don't you dare come."

"But I'm so close."

"Yes," I agreed, convulsing all at once, no warning, simply *there*, climaxing deep inside his body.

He shivered as he held on through my aftershocks and my withdrawal, the cum dripping from his ass to between his thighs.

"Miro," he whispered as I sank to my knees behind him.

"Turn around and feed it to me."

He moved with all the coiled power in him, pivoting as I parted my lips, and shoved his thick, heavy cock into my mouth. It was lucky I had no gag reflex to speak of, or he would have choked me without thought. As it was, I sucked and laved, swallowing around his length as he grabbed hold of my hair and held me in place.

"Take it all," he growled roughly as he smothered my face in his groin.

I made the suction strong and felt him tremble against me. As much as Ian enjoyed me buried in him, watching my lips stretch around his cock never failed to get him off. He liked it too much, exerting power over me while he watched.

"S'good," he groaned before exploding down the back of my throat.

I swallowed fast, not breathing, only drinking, realizing after long moments that I could hear my own heartbeat in my ears as air went from a low priority to the only priority. It was a fight to get loose. He had me and he wanted me there, sucking his dick. But I shoved him back and gulped oxygen, slumping to the floor, my arms spread across the seat cushions of the couch.

He followed, sliding into my lap, straddling my hips, his saliva and cum-slick cock trailing a wet line down my abdomen as his ass wedged over my groin.

"I know why you didn't let me come," he said raggedly, his voice hoarse as he took my face in his callused hands.

"Why's that?" I teased, licking my lips, semen in the corners.

"'Cause you didn't want me to make a mess on the fuckin' couch," he said with a snort.

I nodded, grinning at him.

He released a low growl before tilting my head back to kiss my throat, making me laugh.

"Fuckin' Miro," he griped, kissing me, tasting himself in my mouth, licking me clean, sucking on my tongue until there was no air in my lungs and I was left panting.

"You sound mad," I said, chuckling, my hands on his granite thighs. "But I'm being rewarded, so I'm getting conflicting messages."

With a firm hand buried in my hair, he held my head in place, pinned to the couch cushion, and continued his sensual onslaught. He kissed me slow and deep, each kiss longer than the last until I lost track of starting and stopping, knowing only Ian and his hot, wet, ravaging mouth on mine. There were things I wanted to say, to tell him, but I couldn't keep a thought in my head as every inch of skin he touched felt branded by the hard grip of his hands on my body.

I couldn't stop him, even for air, but my stomach growled loudly, breaking the spell. I groaned and leaned back, severing the suction of our lips, laughing at the same time.

"You want me to stop kissing and feed you?" he asked softly, biting my bottom lip, tugging gently before leaning back to meet my gaze.

"No," I insisted, sliding a hand around the side of his neck and easing him close until his bruised, swollen lips hovered over mine. "Kiss me some more."

His smile was deliciously evil as he bent and took my mouth again. I would have gotten another kiss after that one, but the doorbell rang and startled us both.

"Miro?" someone yelled through the door. "Are you home?"

"Who the fuck is that?" Ian growled.

My phone, on the ledge by the door where I normally didn't leave it, rang a second later, and moments after that, whoever it was started knocking. I'd left my gun there as well, more intent on getting to Ian than putting it away in my nightstand.

"Why is there some—"

"It's Drake," I said quickly.

"Drake? Why?"

I shrugged. "I dunno. He called me yesterday and asked if he could come by. Apparently there's a new thing."

"Oh, fuck, no," Ian growled, letting his head thunk down on my shoulder.

I couldn't stifle my laughter.

"What the fuck is wrong with them now?" he asked as his phone rang.

Only one way to find out.

"THIS IS stupid," my partner, lover, and best friend said for the sixth time.

"I heard you the other five times," I replied drolly as we walked down Wabash toward Exchequer, the restaurant where Cabot Jenner—now Cabot Kincaid—worked as a waiter. He'd gotten the job because it was close to where he went to school at the Art Institute and he had to work for the first time in his life after he'd gone into witness protection with his boyfriend, Drake, formerly Ford, now Palmer, who was walking a good twenty feet in front of us. He was in a hurry—he always was when he went to meet his boyfriend.

Drake and Cabot—both eighteen, going to school, and hailing from a small town in Virginia—had been thrust into the hustle and bustle of downtown Chicago. Cabot, who I'd thought would be the one having trouble, was doing great. Drake, on the other hand, was floundering.

Two months in, Drake was sure Cabot was cheating on him. It was not the case.

Three months in, he wasn't sure if he wanted to go to school. I told him that while he figured it out, he should stay in school. Since that made some semblance of sense, he stayed.

Four months in, he thought Cabot wanted to move out. What Cabot really wanted was to try out new things in the bedroom—like different kinds of toys. Ian had nearly killed them both.

"Deep breaths," I'd cautioned at the time as I left him on the street and went into the sex shop with Cabot.

Five months in, Cabot was promoted from his busboy position to a waiter and found his niche: talking to people. With his golden hair and skin, big blue eyes, fragile and delicate features, and sunny personality, women tipped him, men tipped him, and he made friends at the drop of a hat. Between school and work, Drake felt like Cabot was slipping away. That had not been strictly true. They were both changing quite a bit, but while Drake was growing only scholastically, Cabot was changing into a social butterfly. He'd always been sheltered by his parents in the past, with country clubs and dressage and security and an impenetrable wall of money. Now the real Cabot was on display, the one who wasn't only Drake's "boy" and who was more than ready to stand on his own two feet.

Now, at six months, Drake had called me and said, "I think Cabot wants his own space." So I had to go and check it out. I had agreed to go mediate before I knew Ian was coming home.

"It's not our place to talk to a witness to determine if he does or does not need fuckin' space from our other asshole witness."

"It is if the answer jeopardizes their protection status," I corrected, waving at Drake to go on and not turn around and come back to us. Ian was newly home; I wanted him all to myself for at least another minute.

He shook his head. "I don't think so."

"But you don't know for certain."

He stopped walking to look at me. "I want to go home. I want to go back to bed. I want a long shower with you like we took before I left."

Ian Doyle absolutely loved me on my knees with his dick shoved down my throat. He was addicted to seeing me submit to him. I would have thought the desire would translate to him wanting to top, but so far in our relationship, he enjoyed me holding him down.

"All that is yours the second this is done," I promised, lifting my hand to his cheek and running my thumb gently over the stubble-covered skin. "You look so tired. You should just go home and take a nap. I'll bring you back some dinner."

He shook his head, leaning away from my hand. "Not without you. All I've been thinkin' about for three weeks is lying on the couch, watching TV with my head in your lap and listening to Chickie snore."

"He farts too," I reminded him, throwing an arm around his shoulder and dragging him close to me.

"If you ate that much, you would too."

The way he said it, so matter-of-fact, made me laugh.

"What?" he asked, gifting me with a lazy grin that tightened things low in my body.

"You're funny."

"Only to you," he sighed.

"Maybe," I agreed as we closed in on our destination.

Exchequer looked lifeless from the outside, even with the jaunty canopy over the entrance, but once inside, the place was huge. And yes, there were names carved into some of the tables, but supposedly Al Capone himself had eaten there a million years ago, they served great pizza, and it was one of the places I could get deep dish and Ian thin crust so we didn't have to rock-paper-scissors for who would be disappointed.

We asked to be seated in Cabot's section, and when he saw us, he jogged over to the table and planted a big wet kiss on Drake before turning to us with a big smile. I was on the outside of the booth, so he toppled into me, head down on my shoulder, hugging me tight.

The pointed look I gave Drake made him grimace as Ian ordered us beers and Drake a giant Coke.

"I can't bring the beers, guys," Cabot said, straightening up, hand brushing the hair back out of Drake's eyes, "but I'll have Terry bring 'em right out."

He knew what pizza we'd order—it was always the same—and when he bolted away, Ian leaned forward and smacked Drake on the side of the head.

"Fuck, Ian, what was that for?"

"For this, you stupid sonofabitch!" he grouched. "He loves you. He's into you, and you need to pull your head out of your ass and stop worrying about what he's doing and focus on you."

Drake nodded, slowly looking up at us. "I just—the other day he introduced me to some of his friends from school, and when I told them I go to the University of Chicago, they were like 'Really? You go there? How did you get in?' I was freaking out. I had no idea getting in was like getting into Harvard or Yale or something. Everyone wants to know how I swung it."

"Tell them grades, test scores, and extracurriculars," Ian replied quickly.

"Why couldn't you guys have enrolled me at Loyola or UIC or DePaul or—"

"You need to slow your roll," I cautioned him. "Where is all this coming from?"

He shook his head.

"You feel like you don't belong there?"

His eyes met mine. "I feel like Cabot would have fit in better there."

"I went there," I told him. "And it's a big place, right?"

"Yeah."

"I mean, just crossing the Quad for the first time is like, where the fuck am I going."

He made a noise of agreement.

"But pretty soon you'll know Cobb Hall like the back of your hand, and everything else, going to The Reg is—"

"The what?"

"The Regenstein Library," I teased. I knew he'd been there because I met him in front of it the last time I picked him up to take him over to The Medici to eat. "You'll know all the ins and outs pretty soon, just give yourself some damn time."

"Yeah, okay."

"Good," I said, smiling at him as Cabot returned with Drake's pop and Terry, Cabot's coworker, put down two bottles of Sierra Nevada Pale Ale, one for me and one for Ian.

"If we were home, we could have the beer I like," Ian muttered.

I leaned sideways, bumping his shoulder with mine. "We'll be home soon, I swear."

His grunt was grouchy, but the hand on my thigh under the table, possessive and firm, told me what I needed to know. The promise of home meant the world to him.

As I took a sip of my beer, I noticed Cabot in the kitchen, caught up against a wall by the same guy who had delivered our beers. He had his hand on Terry's chest, and it looked uncomfortable. Cabot was clearly distressed, and the thought of that made my stomach roll even as I saw the older man walk away from him.

Excusing myself, I got up and walked straight to the back. Cabot smiled when he saw me.

"Miro, I put the pizzas in."

"Perfect," I said, passing him quickly and walking up on Terry, who was now punching orders into a POS.

He was taller than me, but I had muscle on him, lots of it, and so when I grabbed him by the throat and pinned him to the wall, he didn't move. Instead he immediately began pleading.

"Miro," Cabot gasped, frightened for his job, I was sure.

"Listen to me," I said, leaning in close beside Terry's ear so I could deliver my threat in a whisper. "If you ever put your hands on Cabot again, eye fuck him, or even smile in a way that's pervy, I will come back here and rip out your lungs. Are we clear?"

He nodded quickly.

"Are you sure?"

More nodding.

"Excellent," I huffed, letting him go, leaning back so he could map my frame and get an idea of the muscle I had that he didn't. Normally I didn't go in for intimidation tactics, but in this case, it was necessary.

His eyes flitted to look everywhere but at me. After a moment, I turned, took hold of Cabot's bicep, and walked him back out to the dining floor with me.

"Miro, I could have handled—"

"Drake's worried that you're thinking of moving out because you need space, but it's not that at all. You've been trying to figure out how to deal with Terry without having to tell Drake, and it's been weighing on you, huh, kid?"

He was holding his breath, but after a moment, he gave up. "Yeah," he confessed, staring at his shoes like they were important.

"Look at me."

His gaze flicked up to meet mine.

"You have a problem, any kind of problem—money, scary neighbors, older guys pawing you, a teacher who hits on you, or Drake freaking out—you tell me. That's what I'm here for, to remove obstacles."

"Okay," he agreed.

"Whatever it is," I insisted, "I'll take care of it. And yes, it's my job, but you and Drake are a special case for me and Ian. You know that."

He smiled sheepishly. "Yeah, okay."

"So talk to Drake and clear the air, all right?"

"I will."

"Good. Now get me some food before I pass out."

He chuckled and returned to the kitchen as I rejoined Ian and Drake.

"Something wrong?" Ian asked as I slid in beside him, his hand immediately sliding over my upper thigh. It was intimate and sexy, and when he leaned in to listen to whatever I had to say, his breath on my ear gave me goose bumps.

"No," I managed to get out. "Cabot's bringing out our food soon."

"That's good," Ian rumbled, his voice like a caress.

"Let's go home after this."

"Good idea," he agreed quickly, his fingers tracing over the inseam of my jeans.

Ian, who had never been sensual in the past, had become sex on two legs. Ever since we first started sleeping together, he thrummed with a new understanding of how his body responded to pleasure, and the new ease with which he carried himself was irresistible. Ian had always been gorgeous, but now he oozed confidence and the promise of wicked pleasure. I wanted him under me again as soon as possible.

"Excuse me."

We all looked up and there, hovering over us, was a man I didn't know and Terry, whom I had just assaulted in the kitchen.

"I need you to leave," the man directed. "I'm Brad Rigby, the assistant manager here, and you—"

"What's the problem?" Ian asked, pulling his ID from the breast pocket of his leather jacket and flipping it open.

Brad blanched when he realized Ian was a federal marshal.

"Did you want to check his out too?" Ian asked, scowling, tipping his head at me. "Or are we good here?"

It was hard for someone to back down after they'd been charged up, adrenaline pumping, for a fight. Brad was doing his job, defending his employee; he simply didn't know that his guy was the one in the wrong.

Six months ago, Ian would have climbed over me to get out of the booth, physically pushed Brad, and backed him into a corner. The Ian sitting beside me now let Brad collect himself and back down.

I knew it was because of me. Because I loved him, because he had a home, because he was no longer a stray, it wasn't necessary for him to win at everything anymore. He didn't have to be the scariest and toughest. He could be himself, not only strong and brave, but also kind and gentle. Ian was now grounded and secure. He wasn't angry all the time. He didn't need to prove himself to anyone because I was the only one who mattered. If only he'd realize getting married was the logical next step in that transformation.

"Well?" Ian pressed the manager, bringing my attention to the present.

Brad swallowed hard. "I thought your partner threatened my guy."

"Yeah, no," Ian said flatly. "That'd never happen."

"I understand."

"Good," Ian replied, nodding.

When both men turned, Cabot was there with our pizzas. His boss smiled at him, told him he was doing a good job, and walked away with Terry in tow.

"What was that about?" Drake asked his boyfriend.

Cabot put the pizzas, my deep dish and then Ian's thin crust, down on the trivets already on the table, and his gaze met Drake's. "The short version is: I messed up and didn't tell you that I was having trouble here."

Drake reached for Cabot, who immediately took the offered hand and allowed himself to be eased down next to him.

"Forgive me. I've just never been hit on before."

Drake nodded.

"I had no idea what to do," Cabot said, taking Drake's face in his hands. "I didn't want you coming down here all pissed off, and, I mean, I'm an adult, right? I should be able to handle my own crap."

"But you should always be able to tell me anything."

"Yes," Cabot agreed, his eyes doing the melting thing they always did around Drake. He was completely smitten, and Drake needed to start believing in that. Their entire relationship had begun with him in denial that a prince could ever really want him. Now, finally, he had to start believing he was a catch, too, before his insecurity drove Cabot away.

"From now on, no more secrets," Drake said, turning his head to kiss Cabot's palm. "Swear."

Cabot nodded, catching his breath, seemingly unable to speak. The hug they shared said it all.

"Can you guys break it up so I can eat?" Ian grumbled, unrolling his fork and knife not because he needed either but because the napkin was necessary. "And take your break, Cab, and sit the fuck down."

Some things didn't change.

CHAPTER 7

DRAKE DECIDED to hang around for the last hour of Cabot's shift, and Ian and I left him the rest of the pizza, much to my annoyance.

"I'll get you more." Ian laughed at me as we walked out of the restaurant. "You might not want that for dinner anyway." I grunted and he bumped me with his shoulder. "I could maybe take you out."

Turning to look at him, I found him staring back at me. "What?"

"Like on a date. I could take you out on a date."

My grin conveyed my disbelief.

"What?"

"You wanna take me out?"

When he smiled, slowly, the laugh lines in the corners of his eyes crinkled, and the pleasure he got from looking at me was obvious and made me momentarily breathless. "Yeah, I do."

"Okay," I replied hoarsely, clearing my throat. "Bring on date night."

He was chuckling when his phone rang as we walked back toward the 1973 Ford Capri with a sunroof we were currently getting around in. I had enjoyed driving the muscle car, but with Ian home now, my days of riding shotgun had returned. He had, in fact, already taken over.

He moved by me, stepping off the curb to walk in the street to get in on the driver's side, but then he instead turned and took hold of my forearm to keep me close.

"No," he said quickly, his pale gaze meeting mine. "I didn't realize it was today. I wasn't staying away on purpose."

There went date night.

"Miro and I will be by at some point."

His grip on me loosened but held, sliding to my wrist and then lower, until he was holding my hand. Since Ian was not in any way a PDA kind of guy, the motion was odd and very telling. He was taking some sort of comfort from touching me, but for what, I had no clue.

"I don't know that we'll make it for din—cake is at six, I got it."

When he hung up, I waited.

"My father's sixtieth is today," he said, searching my face.

Colin Doyle was Ian's estranged father. While I had at one time thought the relationship might be on the mend, I was wrong. They hadn't seen each other in months. "That's short notice, huh?"

"Apparently she sent me an invite that was returned to her. I moved without filling out one of those forms for the post office."

"Oh."

"I mean, mostly it was just bills anyway."

"Sure."

"And I got all those taken care of, and no one ever writes me, they e-mail me."

I nodded because he was rambling about mail and I cared that he was feeling awkward while explaining it to me, but I couldn't have cared less that an invitation for his father's birthday party had gotten lost.

The move had been seamless. We spent a Saturday moving Ian from the cinderblock wasteland that was his apartment and into my Greystone in Lincoln Park. He went from renting a hovel to co-owning my eight-hundred-thousand-dollar home that would maybe be paid off—since I'd increased the payments—a year or so before I died. It had been quick, yes, but I'd asked and Ian was crazy about the idea of taking on a mortgage with me. He'd been touched that I'd thought to include him, moved by my faith in him, and finally, over the moon about signing a piece of paper that made us more than work partners. It made us *life* partners. It was my big gesture, shackling him to me, and he took it as it was meant, as permanency. We had told everyone important that Ian lived with me, but apparently that had not included Colin.

"So," I said after a moment, "we'll stop at a liquor store and get him a really good bottle of Irish whiskey."

"Because he's Irish," Ian teased, brought out of his thoughts by my ridiculous stereotyping.

I shrugged and his smile was there, curling his lip in a way that made my stomach flip.

He placed his hands on my coat, tightening, pulling me close. He laid his head on my shoulder without loosening his grip. "Stay by me when we get over there, okay?"

"Of course," I replied, hands on his hips, breathing in his warm, citrusy scent.

He lifted my chin and planted a kiss on me that lasted only a moment but ran through my body like wildfire, heating every cell and nerve ending.

As we got in the car, I was again reminded why Ian driving was always cause for concern. My hand immediately braced on the dash.

"This is what hanging with a stunt-car driver is like," I groused.

The chuckle made me smile in spite of myself.

IAN THOUGHT we spent too much, but we were arriving late to the party, plus how many times did a guy turn sixty?

The drive out to Marynook took some time even though it was Saturday. Chicago always had traffic—morning, noon, and night. Once I had been going home from a club at 3:00 a.m. and got caught in a bumper-to-bumper snarl. It was best never to assume that we'd make it anywhere on time.

The normally quiet street was loaded with cars, and to find a spot, we had to park a full block away. Once we got close to the house, I saw the front gate open and balloons and streamers decorating the yard.

"We'll just go in, wish him a good one, and bail, all right?"

"Whatever you want," I agreed, watching him tense, making me uneasy.

We walked around the side of the house and into the backyard filled with people. They'd set up picnic tables, card tables, those plastic scoop chairs that buckle if you're not careful, and a wide assortment of other benches, lounges, and folding chairs. The enclosed back deck had space heaters, and guests were walking in and out of the house.

I checked the bottle of Redbreast Non-Chill-filtered 21-Year-Old Irish Whiskey we'd bought, made sure the red bow was on securely and that there wasn't a price tag on it anywhere before I passed it to Ian.

Looking around, I saw his father in a group of men dressed as he was, in a long sleeved T-shirt under a bowling shirt.

When we were close enough, he saw us, and I could tell from the flush of his cheeks and the enormous smile Ian got that he'd been drinking. Normally his father was much more reticent.

"Here's my boy!" he yelled, spreading his arms for Ian to fill.

Ian took a quick breath and moved fast. The hug was hard, tight, and if it looked as awkward as it felt, I had no idea why Colin held on so long. But he thumped Ian on the back and then shoved him out to arm's length.

"It's so good to see you," he sighed, patting Ian's cheek. "What's it been, six months?"

I'd thought, back when Colin told me he couldn't watch Chickie for a particular weekend, that it was no big deal. I'd asked my friend Aruna and her husband, Liam, to keep the werewolf, and they'd jumped at the chance. But what Ian took that as, was he'd asked his father to do one thing, and that was to be the backup for his dog. So what to me was a nonissue, to Ian was being let down. If Colin had wanted to be there for him, he would have made other plans and kept Ian's dog. As he had not, Ian made other arrangements. Permanently.

He asked my friends Aruna and Liam to keep Chickie on a daily basis while he and I were at work, and since they actually wanted him, it was a task they willingly took on. Even though Aruna was a new mother, having Chickie around helped. He was her reason to walk to the store and not drive, to feel safe during the day wherever she went, and she could say "fetch the baby" and Chickie would very gently nudge Sajani Duffy in the right direction. The little girl, all of four months, could do what Ian called a commando crawl, but not any serious moving quite yet. She could sort of undulate across a room, and if Aruna was tired, Chickie would bump the baby with his muzzle to get her going. She would, apparently, follow the dog that dwarfed her mother anywhere.

The new arrangement had worked out wonderfully for Chickie, but not as well for Ian and Colin. Without a reason to see his father, Ian didn't see him at all anymore.

"Yeah, around that," Ian agreed.

"So you've been busy, then?"

"I was deployed," Ian said, which wasn't the whole truth but was nicer than the truth. "Just got back today, actually."

"Oh?" Colin said, and I heard the dare in his voice, like he was baiting Ian. "And you came right over, did you?"

"Stopped to get you this first," Ian answered in his modulated, matter-of-fact law enforcement voice as he passed his father the bottle.

"Oh, well now," one of the other men said, slapping Colin across the back. "That's a nice gift there, Col." All the men agreed the very expensive bottle was one of the best of the day.

Colin introduced Ian and then me to his friends and made sure to thank me for showing up as well. Just when Ian was about to make an excuse for our exit, Linda Doyle, Ian's stepmother, popped out of the house to call everyone inside for cake.

Ian wanted to leave, I could tell, but his father made sure to throw an arm around his neck and lead him inside.

There was a screen set up in the living room, and Colin's son Lorcan and his daughter, Erica, stood at each side of the screen, inviting people to sit down. Linda—a beautiful woman with gorgeous thick gray hair caught up in a chignon that appeared effortless but that I knew, from living with four women, was not—had everyone take a seat and quiet down.

Colin's family was all dressed casually but elegantly: his wife in a black wrap dress, his daughter in a denim shirt tied at the waist with black lace skirt and platform pumps, and his son in dress pants and a long-sleeved button-down. Ian in his dark denim jeans, gray Henley and John Varvatos lace-up biker boots—they were mine—didn't measure up.

I had tried to stay beside him, but there wasn't room for me on the couch at the front where Colin led him with that arm around his shoulders. Ian was still wearing my black Dsquared2 leather jacket. The fact he was the only one wearing outerwear, besides me, while inside was strange. It was like they'd hustled him in and not even allowed him to get comfortable. I was torn between wanting to walk up there and rescue him and knowing that if he wanted to leave, he would. Ian was more than capable of simply getting up and walking out. I just had to wait and see what he was going to do.

"Hello, everyone, and thank you for coming to Dad's sixtieth," Lorcan announced to the room, his greeting drawing applause, cheering, and happy whistles. "Erica and I put together this little walk down memory lane of Colin Doyle's life, and we hope you all enjoy it."

There are times when you can absolutely and without a doubt see both sides of something. If I were Colin or Linda or any of their friends or extended family, I would have been touched and awed by the amount of work and time and energy that went into creating the movie. The sheer number of pictures that had been scanned, uploaded, and digitally manipulated was staggering. It also included some home movies, interviews, and letters; it was like watching a documentary on ESPN where they do those 30 for 30 films I was addicted to, except with a side of gushing love. The narration was crisp, funny, and kept everything moving with no lull. There was no way to not be overwhelmed by the production values. Linda was crying; Colin, the man of the hour, was holding her; and everyone else was riveted.

Ian sat frozen, and it was hard to tell if he was even breathing.

I knew why.

The entire presentation didn't include one single picture of him or his mother, and in fact, there was no mention of Colin being married at all before the current Mrs. Doyle. During the show, Ian got to see family vacations he'd never been on, Christmases he hadn't been invited to, and graduations he had not attended. It lasted an hour but felt like five. The second it was over and everyone called for a speech, Ian stood as Colin made his way up to Lorcan and Erica, and bolted toward me.

People were clapping and moving around us, gathering close to see and hear Colin. No one noticed me grab for Ian, yank him toward me, and duck into the hallway.

"Breathe," I ordered.

"I'm fine," he said, his voice feigning nonchalance his eyes couldn't quite muster. He was good and hurt.

"I know," I replied, pretending to buy the fact that he was in no way affected by him and his mother being forgotten.

He inhaled deep, tugging on my jacket, fisting it in his hands, trying to get me closer.

"You can't—this is your father's house."

His eyes narrowed.

"Don't do that. Don't make any part of this about me not wanting you, because you know that's bullshit," I warned him.

"Okay."

"I will be all over you if that's what you want."

"Yes," he croaked out. "That's what I fuckin' want."

I lunged at him, hugging him tight, crushing him against me as I pressed my lips to his ear. "I love you, Ian Doyle. Only you, and every time you go away it fuckin' kills me. I don't ever want to us to be apart."

He leaned into me, and I felt the power in his hard, muscular frame as he gave me his weight and his lips opened against the side of my throat.

"Someday, when I have a movie of my life, all that'll be there will be you," I promised huskily.

He kissed up to my jaw and then made his way to my mouth. When he tilted my head back and mauled me, I breathed him in, taking all he was offering. Walking him into the wall, I banged him up against it, rattling the pictures, wedging my thigh between his, pressing, pushing, wanting him naked under me, under my hands, desperately.

It was too much to ask to watch him be forgotten. He was the man I loved, and the slight, I realized quickly, urged me to get him home to show him how cherished he truly was.

"Miro." He breathed out my name.

It was all I could do to not drag him out of the house, wanting, needing to be closer, to be inside him.

I could feel it as I stood wedged chest to chest against my lover, soaking in the hard drum beating of his heart as I lowered my mouth to the throbbing pulse in his throat and bit down.

His cry was hoarse but whispered as he bucked in my arms, took my face in his hands, and kissed me.

It was drugging and violent, hot and hungry, and I forgot where I was—all that mattered was him and my desire to have him.

"Fuck," he gasped, turning his head, breaking the kiss, his hot breath puffing over my face. "I can't even... think. Just—lemme go."

Moving slow, like honey, I made sure to put my hands everywhere before finally curling my fingers through the belt loops of his jeans as I stood, panting, my forehead resting against his.

His hands were up under my light cashmere sweater, on my skin, sliding over my abdomen as he fought to get his body, unsteady after my onslaught, under control.

"Oh."

Turning, I found his stepsister, Erica, standing in the hall, smiling tentatively at us.

"There you are, Ian," she said softly. "We were all going to say something to Dad, a quick toast, and then we'll have cake. Mom's going now, and after her, Lor. You can go before me, though, if you like."

She was startled. It was all over her face as she stood there, staring, watching us both panting and breathless from kissing. To her credit, her hesitant smile never wavered. There was no judgment in her gaze, merely surprise.

He shook his head. "No, Miro and I gotta go, actually. Duty calls."

She squinted at us, clearly confused.

I pulled my ID and flipped it open as I'd been doing for the past three, almost four, years. "Deputy US Marshal."

Her mouth dropped open.

"That's why we were out here," I explained. "I got a call and pulled Ian out."

Her look turned skeptical.

"I mean—" I shrugged, because we had not drawn apart. I still had my hands clenched on his hips, his were on my sides under my sweater. We weren't fooling anyone. "I was obviously all over him, but there was a reason for us being out here to begin with."

It was a lie, but I hardly cared. They had not included Ian or his mother in the "walk down memory lane." I was too pissed to care. "So, you know, you don't have to wait on Ian for anything. You all can go on with it like you did the movie."

She put her hand over her heart. "You're very blunt."

"Yeah, he is," Ian said, and I was glad to hear the trace of laughter in his voice. I'd worried for a second that I'd overstepped. "But that's how I like him."

He eased free of me but took hold of the front of my sweater. "So we'll see you."

"Wait, I—" she began, rushing down the hall after us. "Are you sure you have to go? I'd love to hear more about being a marshal."

Ian snorted out a laugh, which I loved hearing. It made it impossible not to lean sideways and kiss him. He covered his cheek where my lips had been and beamed at his stepsister. "You don't give a crap."

But unlike probably every other interaction they'd had, he was grinning in that wicked way where you were sure you'd never seen anything prettier in your life.

"No, I do," she argued, clearly mesmerized by him. It was easy when Ian was being charming. He was irresistible. "I had no idea there were still marshals around. I thought they rode horses and got posses together."

"We don't saddle up, but there are still posses," he assured her. "But now it's called a task force."

"Really?"

He nodded.

She took a step closer to him.

"Let's go," I growled, hand on the small of his back. "She doesn't really give a crap."

"But I do," she snapped, and I understood why. She wanted him to stay, and I wasn't helping. "Please don't leave, Ian," she pleaded, stepping in front of him, barring his escape. "If Miro needs to go, he should, but this is your father's birthday."

"Wouldn't have known that from the video everyone just watched," I said harshly, my annoyance there in the sharpness of my tone.

"That's not fair," she said defensively. "Ian wasn't here for us to get input or pictures from. I mean, certainly we don't have any of him or his mother."

"No," I replied icily, "of course you don't."

She was silent, seething in front of me.

For my part, I was shaking a little, too, realizing slowly that my hands had balled into fists. Ian being forgotten had turned me inside out.

We all heard her name called from the other room.

"Ian, I'm going to call you up first," she told him, and I could hear the quaver in her voice along with the threat. "So you best be prepared and you better not go anywhere."

I grabbed his shoulder and pulled even before she turned to walk back in the living room.

"Ian!" she stage-whispered after us.

"You know," he said as I shoved him forward, toward the sliding glass door, then hurled it open with far more force than was actually necessary, "you never get mad."

Which was a lie. I was just as prone to rage as the next guy. The difference was that this wasn't about me. This was about the man I loved.

Unfortunately, the door took the brunt of my frustration, and I threw it closed behind us so hard, it bounced back and forth, creating a hazard for anyone following. Not that I cared. I was too furious to give a damn. Slipping around Ian, I pounded down the stairs and kicked a plastic chair out of my way when I reached the bottom. I realized I was growling at the same time, getting angrier by the second.

The more I thought about it, the worse it got. How dare they act as though Ian's mother had never existed, and therefore him as well? What the fuck?

"Okay," he said, pouncing on me as I charged around the side of the house, yanking me back against his body, one arm thrown across my chest, the other curled around my abdomen. He buried his face in the side of my neck, inhaling deeply as he hugged me.

I couldn't breathe around the anger boiling in the pit of my stomach and the pent-up aggression searched for another outlet, as the chair had proven to be a poor target. I was ready to punch a hole through a wall.

"Miro," he crooned into my ear, his voice a husky whisper. "You really love me."

There was no talking around the lump in my throat or the fury throbbing in my temples. How *dare* his stepmother guilt him into coming and then treat him like he was nothing!

"I mean, I knew it 'cause you told me, but watching you get mad over me... holy fuck, that's hot."

I growled at him. It was all I could manage.

"I matter to you."

Needing him off me, unable to calm down, I tried twisting free.

"Oh no you don't," he said, his voice thick and sexy in my ear as he exerted more pressure, wedging against me. "You're not going anywhere."

He had the leverage, but more importantly, my body was starting to respond to his groin pressed against my ass. His hands dug into my chest, his lips opened on the side of my neck as he kissed up the side, and the brute force of him making me submit to his will was turning fury into bone-melting desire.

When his hand moved to my cock, I jolted in his arms, wanting him to touch and stroke me, craving him on his knees.

"Miro," he breathed out. "You're crazy about me."

My voice, when I finally spoke, was rough and crackly. "You're all there is."

He held me tighter. "Let's go home. I want to lay with you on the couch. I want your hands and mouth all over me."

Oh dear God, yes.

But I couldn't move. The rush of heat tore through me, and I let my head fall back on his shoulders, the anger dissipating, everything refocusing on Ian. "I missed you."

"I missed you too," he husked, giving me a final squeeze before letting me go. "Come on. Follow me."

Whatever he wanted, whenever he wanted, I was ready.

We were at the gate when someone yelled.

"You're breaking his heart, you fuck!"

Turning toward the sound, I saw Lorcan walking out the front door with other guys his same age following him.

"Go back inside," Ian called over, opening the gate and passing through. "I'm leaving, so don't worry about it."

"I don't want you to leave, you selfish piece of shit," Lorcan continued, quickening his stride, the others matching him. "I want you to come inside and beg his forgiveness."

I closed the gate behind Ian, staying in the yard, and then pivoted to face Lorcan as he closed on me.

"Miro, let's go," Ian ordered.

"You didn't put one picture of him or his mother in that fucking presentation, but he's the selfish one?" I attacked, all my hostility resurfacing and targeting Ian's stepbrother.

"Get out of my way, you fuckin' faggot," Lorcan snarled when he reached me, placing his hand on my chest to shove me out of the way.

I lost it.

I saw red and I… lost it.

One second he was touching me, the next he was on his knees and I had his wrist in my hand, bent backward at an angle that allowed no movement whatsoever. It was self-defense they taught you at the police academy—how to immobilize people so they couldn't hurt you. It was reflexive for me, ingrained so long ago even before I was a marshal, back when I was green.

"Say you're sorry," I demanded, my voice menacing and low as I put pressure on his wrist that I knew from firsthand experience sent ripples of pain up his forearm and pulsing up through his bicep.

"Let him go!" some guy threatened as he gathered himself to charge.

Ian vaulted the gate and put himself between the rest of Lorcan's pals and me. "Back the fuck off. He can break his arm like that."

Everybody froze.

Lorcan made a choking, sniveling sound as I stood there looming over him, watching beads of sweat break out on his forehead.

"Miro," Ian said gently. "Let him go and we'll bail."

"After he apologizes."

"No," Ian insisted, moving up beside me and patting my chest. "It's not worth it."

But it was to me. "Apologize," I said to Lorcan.

"I apologize," he heaved out, starting to tremble.

"Okay," Ian said, eyes on me. "Come on, let's go home."

Releasing Lorcan, I turned to face Ian.

His grin was wicked. "I'm supposed to be the asshole, not you."

I was going to yell, but he reached for me, grabbing hold of my jacket and dragging me close. "Let's go get the car, Jones," he ordered, and his voice, how low it was, and the smirk that accompanied it, made my stomach flutter.

I smiled as he held the gate open for me.

"You think it's funny to treat people like that?"

I heard the comment, but I didn't count on the guy coming over the top of the gate at me. I *should* have—they were young and hotheaded like Lorcan, plus they thought I was laughing at him when all I was doing was responding to Ian. So I shouldn't have been surprised when he caught me in a flying tackle… or tried.

He flung himself forward, Ian shoved me back, and the poor drunk asshole sailed between us and crashed down onto the middle of the sidewalk.

"Oh!" I yelled, stepping over the fallen man, looking down at him. "Did you break the sidewalk with your face?"

Ian squatted down next to the guy. "What the hell were you trying to do?"

Seeing their friend epically fail took the fight out of the others, and when he rolled to his back, Ian asked if he needed an ambulance.

My phone rang before I could hear the answer.

"Jones."

"Yessir," I answered, my back stiffening involuntarily because my boss was on the other end of the call.

"Listen," he said curtly. "I need you and Doyle to report in right now. Advise me of your present location."

I shared that we were out in Marynook, and he said he'd give us forty minutes to reach him. If it was going to be longer, he wanted updates from the car.

"May I ask what you need us to do, sir? Should we change or—"

"Don't ask questions, simply come in. I want you and Doyle here immediately."

It wasn't like him to not tell us what was going on.

"Yessir."

He ended the call and took in the situation. Lorcan's friend was scraped up, bruised, all of which had nothing to do with Ian or me, except if we were responsible for the impetus.

"We gotta go," I said to Ian, patting his shoulder as I moved by him to start down the sidewalk. "Boss man wants us now."

Ian rose, shot a look at Lorcan, who appeared both shocked and confused, and then started down the street toward the car.

"Don't come back," Lorcan spat after us, having recovered from his momentary daze to yell. "Neither one of you is welcome."

"Not a problem," Ian called back over his shoulder, grabbing hold of my hand and squeezing tight before he leaned in and kissed my cheek. "I got everything I need right here."

CHAPTER 8

I WAS surprised when we reached the office to find everyone there. It wasn't just me and Ian and our team, but other teams that now reported to our boss. As soon as we walked in, Kage called us into the conference room, where four other people were already sitting.

"Have you watched the news?" Kage asked before we even had a chance to find seats.

I glanced around the table before answering him. "No, sir."

He indicated where he wanted Ian and me, and we dropped into the chairs at the end of the long table.

"This is Special Agent Oliver and his partner, Wojno, as well as Rohl and Thompson."

I knew everyone but Oliver, who seemed to be in charge, judging by the way he leaned forward and stared at me. It would have been better if Wojno wasn't there, because now I'd have to tell Ian that I'd slept with the man before my last boyfriend, Brent Ivers. It was always uncomfortable to reveal past hookups to your significant other.

I nodded, and Oliver clasped his hands in front of him as he studied me before turning to Ian. "We're allowing you to be in on this briefing, Marshal Doyle, but it's a courtesy, as you're Marshal Jones's partner and therefore would be asking questions. We expect total confidentiality and your compliance in this matter must be absolute."

"Yessir."

Oliver nodded and then returned his attention to me. "So, Jones, it was reported that Craig Hartley escaped from prison today, but it was actually three days ago."

I was really proud of myself for not letting anyone see the jolt of fear that lanced through me, and for not throwing up right there on the table. Only Ian heard my sharp intake of breath, and I was thankful for his warm hand on my thigh under the table because it was the only thing real and grounding. My body flushed with a chill, and the heat from his palm coupled with the possessive hold was so much more than comforting.

"We were able to keep a lid on the information, as we wanted to run down leads before alerting the media, but now that all trails have gone cold, we need all the help we can get," Oliver continued.

Three days the man who wanted to kill me had been running around free. The idea that he'd been on the loose and I'd had no idea was staggering. I could have opened the front door and there he would have been. It was absolutely terrifying.

"Keep in mind, Jones, that the moment we learned of his escape, you were under constant surveillance."

Which would do absolutely nothing if Dr. Craig Hartley wanted me dead.

No amount of any kind of protection would be enough. I could never be kept safe, it wasn't possible. He'd get to me if he wanted, simple as that. He obviously didn't, which was why I was still drawing breath. I had no doubt that if he changed his mind, I was bound for the morgue. "Okay."

Years ago when I was a police detective, the last investigation I worked with my partner Norris Cochran was the Prince Charming case. Some guy was killing women and turning them into pieces of art. For a while they called him The Master, after all the great artists he mimicked, but it didn't stick. When we really dug in and found out the guy was like a walking, talking wet dream come to life up to the point that he killed you in your sleep... his name became Prince Charming. That had stuck.

Lots of detectives worked the case, and there were many viable suspects, but Cochran and I had a hunch about Hartley and neither of us could let it go. He was too squeaky clean, too calm under pressure, too nice—he used to send us doughnuts and lunch on occasion—but more than anything, he liked to talk. He especially liked to talk to me. At the beginning of the investigation, I thought maybe he was gay. But it wasn't even that. He just liked being around me, near me, close in my personal space, and he liked it when we had tea late at night together and I told him about the case.

The night I discovered a ring belonging to one of the murder victims in his house, accidentally left behind by his sister—he'd given her the expensive bauble—he put a chef's knife in my abdomen. I still carried the scar. But I'd pleaded with my partner for Hartley's life and, in so doing, sealed us together until one of us died. He owed me his life, it was true, but I knew that if I ever found myself helpless in his hands, he'd do vile, unspeakable things to me and make me pray for death.

The FBI telling me that I was safe was ridiculous.

"We've had eyes on you since Hartley escaped."

Uh-huh.

"Even your run-in with a mugger earlier today was witnessed."

I was quiet. So nice of them to step in and make me feel safe. What were they going to do, watch as the madman put a bullet in my back? Chickie was better backup than the Feds.

"We followed his trail as far as Maine, but he crossed into Canada and his track went cold in Quebec. We have agents coordinating with the RCMP there, but as of right now, we don't know where he is."

I nodded.

"Jones."

Turning, I gave Rohl my attention.

"Do you remember me from our trip out to Elgin?"

"Yes."

She smiled faintly. "Well, it's no secret that Hartley still has quite a following and many people willing to hide him and house him and do whatever's necessary to aid him in his flight from justice."

"Of course," I replied woodenly, focusing on my breathing, in and out, trying to keep it regular so I didn't hyperventilate.

"But even with those resources, we don't think he's stupid enough to return to the country. We can say with quite a bit of certainty that he'll leave Canada and go abroad, probably to France, as he has many friends there and speaks the language fluently."

I would have laughed if I could have made the sound. Jesus, how stupid were they? The man was an egomaniac. There was no way in hell he'd ever leave Chicago. It was *his* city, he'd terrorized it, he'd been news, people still brought up his name in fear if a friend started dating a guy who seemed too good to be true.

"Maybe he's Prince Charming?"

People still whispered it and scared themselves and then checked Google to make sure Hartley was still incarcerated.

It was scary, I knew Hartley so well. He'd never leave his people, and he would never, ever leave without dealing with me.

"Marshal?"

My gaze met Agent Rohl's. "Yeah, he won't do that."

She frowned at me. "He won't do what?"

"Leave."

"You don't—"

"He's going to do whatever in Canada, clean up, get his money situation straightened out, and then he'll send people after his sister and me or come himself," I choked out. "He's not gonna let it go, let us go. He's much too thorough."

Everyone was silent.

"How did he get out?" Ian asked.

Oliver sighed. "He had a ruptured appendix and was transported to the hospital to have the surgery, but—"

"He didn't actually have an appendix since he'd had that out years ago," I finished for him, chuckling under my breath. "Damn, that's impressive."

"How did you know he had his appendix out?" Wojno asked, his tone sharper than it needed to be.

"We talked about it," I told him, meeting his gaze only briefly. "We talked about a lot of things when I went to see him. He had it out when he was twelve, and he was pleased that his father had insisted that a plastic surgeon be on call so that there was no scar. He'd always been sympathetic that there wasn't one on call for me the night he put that chef knife into me, more sorry about the scar than his actions."

"Well, it was missed in his records," Rohl informed me. "When they were prepping him for surgery, apparently the guard stepped out, thinking Hartley was already under, but the anesthesiologist was an old college friend of Hartley's, and she helped him subdue a nurse, get out of the handcuffs, and then kill the officer guarding him."

"Is she still alive? His friend?"

"No," Rohl answered. "They found her in the parking lot at the hospital. The official cause of death was an overdose of morphine."

"At least she didn't suffer," I said sadly. "Damn nice of him."

Ian took a breath and turned to Kage. "What's the plan?"

Kage moved over to the edge of the table, close to Ian and me. "You two are going on loan to a task force out in Phoenix until the Marshals Service and the FBI deem it safe for you to return here to Chicago."

Of course. Because there was a madman on the loose, I had to suffer. Again.

"Both?" Oliver asked. "Why would you send—"

"Because Doyle is his partner," Kage explained curtly, and I watched as Oliver recoiled from the hard, brittle tone of my boss's voice. I was always surprised when anyone talked back to him. He was so big, so imposing, and whether it was his sheer size or how cold his stare got, I couldn't say, but people knew on some primal level that tangling with Kage would be bad. I had told the others on my team that I was sure it had been a factor in all his promotions: he just looked like how you'd imagine a chief deputy would—plain old mean.

"I in no way mean to imply that I would question your decision, Chief Deputy Kage, but—"

"They're both going," Kage retorted before turning back to us, eyes on Ian. "Unless you'd rather not, Doyle."

Ian cleared his throat. "No, sir, I want to go."

Kage nodded. "Okay, so then you're in Phoenix until Hartley is recovered, shot, or his precise whereabouts can be confirmed."

I nodded even as I thought about what I could say to Kage to make him keep Ian at home. The very idea of Hartley coming through the man I loved to get at me made me nauseous. The only safe place for Ian was far away from me. I had to figure out how to get a moment alone with my boss.

"Here's the thing," Oliver began carefully, glancing at Kage, not frightened, but wary. "If we can get eyes on him in whatever nonextradition country he surfaces in, then we can have a team extract him. As it is now, without knowing where he's landed, your safety cannot be guaranteed. Your continued presence could put other lives in jeopardy, as Hartley could become a threat to any witnesses in your care."

Or to someone infinitely more dear.

"We know he could become volatile."

Could? More like *would*. Hartley would murder anyone between him and me when he was finally ready to make his move.

"Listen up," Kage directed. "I've made arrangements for you both to remain on active duty but in Phoenix, under aliases. Only those in this room will be aware of your new assignment and the duration."

"So," I exhaled sharply. "How did Hartley's friend know that he was going to the hospital? How did she know that he was sick?"

"We're looking into that," Oliver answered curtly.

"Basically, you have no idea," Ian surmised.

No answer.

"So is it safe to say that you have a leak?"

"We don't know what we have, marshal."

Ian nodded. "Is that why you made the number of people who know about our assignment to Phoenix so small?"

"We're keeping it on a need-to-know basis," Kage answered curtly.

That was a yes.

"Arrangements need to be made for our dog," I told everyone.

"You do that," Kage agreed. "And also, you need to pack for a month, keeping in mind that you're going to Phoenix."

He lost me.

"Check the weather; it's a bit warm there."

Ian's derisive snort let me know that perhaps "warm" was an understatement.

I TOLD Ian I had to take a piss, and since we were in *our* building and it was like Fort Knox in there, he didn't worry and sat in the office and yelled at the Feds. I ducked into the hall, doubled back, and texted Kage, asking him to meet me for a quick word at the water fountain.

"Yes?" he asked as he came striding toward me, looking even bigger than usual as he closed in on me. "What do you need, Jones?"

It was his height and his build, the way his clothes fit, which sort of outlined the breadth of his shoulders and chest, and how crisp and polished he was. He had the same perpetual squint Ian did, but whereas on the man I loved it was sexy, on my boss it was cold and hard and scary. I had a tough time reconciling his humanity a lot of the time.

"Jones?" Only my boss could sound *that* irritated *that* fast. I wondered if I was the only one who ever got to hear the long-suffering tone.

I cleared my throat. "Sorry, I—sir would you please keep Doyle here instead of sending him to Phoenix with me?"

Normally I would have built it up first, used different words, better ones, not gone right in and asked for what I wanted, instead feeling him out first to try to get a read on him. Talking to Kage usually required great tact, but I didn't have time. Ian would come looking for me any second and I needed this fixed before then.

"I'm sorry?" he inquired, his tone sharp.

"I would prefer Marshal Doyle remain here in Chicago, sir. I don't think he should be placed in harm's way, and he most certainly would be."

He nodded. "So, Doyle, you're saying he doesn't know anything at all about handling threats to his life?"

"No, sir," I sighed. "The man's a Green Beret, so clearly he—"

"And in circumstances like this one, he would be a liability?"

"No, sir, but—"

"So, then?"

I took a breath.

"This request is personal," he laid out for me just in case I was confused.

"Yessir."

"And you don't want him to go because you're worried he'll be compromised due to his relationship with you."

Oh. Yes. That was good. "Yessir," I agreed eagerly.

"And because of that relationship, he could sustain injuries that someone who is not romantically involved with you would not be prone to."

"Precisely."

His eyes narrowed, and I felt like he was studying me under a microscope.

"Sir?"

"I'll rescind his orders, Jones. Doyle stays here."

I wanted to weep. My scary, logical, hard-as-nails boss was on my side. It was a Christmas miracle and it wasn't even Halloween yet.

"Unless," he amended quickly. "You change your mind."

"I'm sorry?"

"*If*," he began, his voice low, "you change your mind and want the guy who has your back every single day there with you... you let me know."

I felt like he was talking about something else, making a point I was missing. "I won't change my mind, sir."

"All right."

"Thank you, sir," I croaked, my voice faltering. "It means everything to me."

He grunted.

"I really appreciate—"

"Go collect your partner, Jones, and get home to pack. You're on a plane in the morning."

I realized that just because he saw things my way didn't mean we'd had a breakthrough and were going to be friends.

I turned and left him as fast as I could but miscalculated the corner at the end of the corridor and clipped my shoulder. It hurt more than I expected, and I had to wonder where my head was. I might have been just a bit overwrought.

THE PROTOCOLS for being on loan to another district were daunting, and even more so when going in undercover, so we had to sit with Kage and basically go through a binder of paperwork. I felt bad for Ian because it was a huge waste of time since he wasn't going to end up going, but there was no way around it. Kage would talk to him alone; that was the way of it. Ian couldn't argue with Kage over the phone, but he could in person. Kage would wait until we were home to call.

Once we were finally done, I made a call about Chickie. Aruna was, of course, giddy to have the werewolf stay with her, and when I drove him over to her at one in the morning, even tired as she was— full-time mom plus working from home—she was cognizant enough to explain to me yet again that if Ian wanted to gift her with his dog, he could come over and see Chickie whenever he wanted. I ignored her, told her to stay away from our Greystone for any reason, and promised to call from the road.

"Why can't I go by your place?" she asked as I stood in her doorway. She'd hugged the daylights out of me, as usual. For a teeny little thing she was really strong.

"Because I'm telling you not to," I ordered. "It's not safe. My place will be under surveillance."

"Surveillance?" She was instantly suspicious and her eyebrows furrowed dangerously.

"Don't worry about it. Just stay clear."

She nodded, biting her bottom lip. "You'll be safe, right?"

"Of course."

"You're a godfather now," she reminded me. "For crap's sake, Miro, you need to stay in one piece."

"Come on, don't get all—"

"Miroslav Jones!" she yelled, whacking me on the arm for good measure.

Ugh, my full name. "Sorry, sorry."

"I need you to be careful!" she insisted, adding a foot stomp.

"Yes, dear, I will," I promised and then left before she could interrogate me any further.

When I finally got home again, at all of 2:00 a.m., Ian was packed, sitting on the end of the bed and texting someone.

"Who're you talking to?"

"Kowalski and Kohn," he said, chuckling. "They want to know how much luggage you end up leaving on our reassignment with."

"You're not supposed to tell anyone where we're going," I snapped.

He was scowling as he looked up at me.

"Shit, I'm sorry," I groaned, realizing that I'd just lectured the black ops guy on keeping a secret. "Where'd you tell them we're going?"

"I didn't," he said with a shrug. "Kage told them we're going undercover, and that's the end of it."

I hadn't thought of it like that, but really, that was all anyone needed to know. Whenever Ian was deployed, I never questioned him.

"What?"

I glanced over at him, unsure what he was talking about.

"You made a noise."

"Oh, sorry."

"Don't be sorry, tell me what you were thinking," Ian demanded.

"Just that I guess it's easy for guys like us to disappear for no reason, and no one would be the wiser. It would make it really easy to cheat."

"That's where your mind goes?"

"Small brain."

"Clearly," he agreed, his attention back on his phone.

"So what's with Kohn and Kowalski?"

"They have a bet," he snickered. "Kohn says four bags, Kowalski says six."

"I'm sorry, what?"

He laughed at me. "A month away, M. I mean, I'm a little curious myself."

Flipping him off, I walked into the bathroom.

"Wait," he said, laughing, following me in. "Don't get all—"

I rounded on him. "You should stay here."

"Because I'm giving you shit about what you're taking to Phoenix? Am I being grounded?"

"No, I—I don't think it's safe, and the longer I think about it, the more worried I get."

His glare was dark. "What're you talking about?"

"If Hartley comes for me, I don't want you in the way."

He nodded but said nothing, and after a few moments of the lingering silence, I understood that he was thinking.

"What?"

"Nothing."

"Ian, come on."

"Okay, well, I'm just trying to decide if that's the stupidest thing you ever said to me or the second stupidest. I'm weighing it out."

"Ian—"

"No!" he exploded, drilling a finger into my collarbone. "The only place I want to be is with you, and getting between you and Hartley is my entire plan."

"I don't want you to get hurt!" I yelled back.

"Then don't do anything stupid and make sure you fuckin' protect me," he growled. "There's no way I get hurt with you watching my back."

We both went silent, eyes locked on one another.

He had such faith, and I realized it was the same I had in him. "I'm—" I took a breath. "I'm scared, is all."

"I know," he said, stepping into me, into my space, hands on my sides, over my ribs as I wrapped my arms around his neck. "But it's gonna be okay. I'm not gonna leave you."

"That's very comforting, marshal," I said before I kissed him.

His arms slid around my back as he leaned into the kiss, his tongue seeking entrance that I happily conceded.

The doorbell ringing was the only thing that kept us vertical. It bothered me that, on the way down the stairs, Ian drew his gun and called through the door instead of just opening it. I hated that we had to be on guard in our neighborhood, in our home.

"It's clear," Ian let me know as he opened the door. "Finish packing."

I did as I was told, and minutes later Ian thumped up the stairs, chuckling.

"What's funny?"

He lifted his head to look at me, and I was struck by the sight of my beautiful man and his crinkly-eyed smile. Sometimes he simply took my breath away.

"Your alias," he said, laughing, holding up the ID for me.

"Smith?" I read indignantly.

"Because you're Jones now!" He broke into raucous laughter, finding the whole thing much funnier than it was.

"Who has the small brain?" I asked pointedly.

He would have responded, but his phone rang. I went back to packing while he answered, realizing it was a bit more difficult than I'd thought it would be. After a second I caught a scrap of the conversation.

"I'm sorry. Would you repeat that, sir?"

Kage.

Shit.

I swallowed quickly and then turned to Ian. Even from across the room, I could see him staring daggers at me.

Fuck.

"I understand, sir," he said as his free hand balled into a fist.

I really wouldn't have to worry about Hartley anymore, because Ian was going to be the one to kill me. He pivoted to face the wall and drove his fist into it like a sledgehammer. It rattled the armoire beside it.

Slowly, as to not arouse suspicion because I didn't want him to run after me, I started backing out of the room. As I heard him wrapping up, I quickened my pace.

"Miro!" he roared the second the call ended.

It was not a "run for cover" yell or in any way cautionary. He was pissed.

I decided the better part of valor was to lock myself in the bathroom and was actually impressed that the door held when he kicked it. Although all the doors in our place were solid wood, so I should have had a bit more faith.

"Open this fuckin' door!" he demanded, kicking it again for emphasis.

"Why're you mad?"

"Because you talked to Kage and asked him to make me stay here!"

"As I said," I replied softly, hoping that if I sounded calm, he would become so. "All I was thinking of was you getting hurt, and it kills me even to think about."

He banged the door. "The only time I don't wanna be around you is when I'm deployed, yeah? Otherwise, asshole, I wanna be with you."

"I feel the same," I said, loud enough so he could hear me from where he was on the other side.

"Well, then," he coughed, "stop trying to ditch me."

"But that's not what we're talking about," I qualified. "I cannot, will not, have you hurt, and I don't see how you expect me to change that."

It got quiet, so much so that I would have thought he'd walked away if I didn't know better.

"Miro."

Even through the barrier between us, I heard the change in his voice. He wasn't mad anymore. The emotion was gone, replaced by something else altogether.

"Love, open the door."

Love.

It was crazy. Every drop of air should not have left my body just because Ian Doyle called me something that wasn't some part of my name.

And mean it—*love*—because he did.

I heard it in his tone; it was gentle and possessive and I knew I was being oversentimental and vulnerable because a psychopath was after me, but still… Ian called me his love, and it was dear and sexy and very, very hot.

It was a wonder I didn't combust.

Love.

God, who knew I was such a sap?

"Please."

The growl with just a hint of delicious, seductive evil, the languorous timbre of curling smoke and slow-poured whiskey made me whimper in spite of myself.

"Please, love, open the door."

"You're not playing fair, and since when?"

"Since when what?" he answered, his voice so decadently gruff that it was no surprise at all that my dick responded before my brain kicked in.

"Love—" I repeated, "—I doh-don't—" Shit. "You're not—you… no endearments." I gave up. Talking was not happening at the moment.

"I'll call you whatever I damn well want to. Now open the door."

"Ian," I managed to get out, fingers splayed on the wood as I tried to focus on what I was trying to do and not what I wanted.

"Do you know what it'll do to me if you keep me from going with you?"

That had actually never occurred to me. I'd been so wrapped up in wanting to keep him safe that I had not considered how he felt.

Not once.

"What if—"

"Is that what we do?" he pressed, and I heard him bump the door. "We sit around and think about what could happen?"

No, we didn't. That would be the death of us as lovers, partners, marshals—everything. Worrying led to a life of static and I didn't want that for either of us.

"So because you're scared, we'll be apart." It was a statement, but the sound of him, seductive, silvery, sent a throb of need rushing through me. "And on top of everything else, you'll miss me, and it'll be you deciding, finally, what I will or won't do."

I wanted to see him, but I didn't dare open the door. He had me if I did. "That's not what this is."

"Oh no? Because it feels like you exercising power over me."

Shit.

"And you're not like that," he concluded softly. "How could you be?"

"Ian—"

"It's how I know you really love me," he said, clearing his throat. "You don't try and change me."

I scoffed.

"Except for that one thing," he chuckled.

I smiled wide, alone in the bathroom because, yeah, I wasn't about to let the marriage thing go. "Okay," I agreed. Being without him when I didn't have to be was just plain stupid. I was a lot of things, but not that. Plus, saying no to Ian had always been next to impossible.

A moment ticked by.

"You gonna open the fuckin' door?"

"Don't sound so smug," I shot back.

"Open the door," he demanded. "I wanna kiss you before we gotta catch the red-eye."

I couldn't say no to that, either.

CHAPTER 9

"HOLY SHIT," Ian groaned as we got off the shuttle that had taken us from the airport terminal at Sky Harbor International in Phoenix to the one where all the rental car companies were. It was only a circle of pavement, a stone sidewalk, and a glass building, deserted at this time of the morning. We were the only ones out there after the shuttle dropped us off. It was also hot, and I was surprised the temperature was already so high. "This is like fuckin' AT out in Twentynine Palms all over again."

I chuckled. "I have no idea what you're talking about, and what is AT?"

"Annual training," he muttered before he put on his aviator sunglasses.

"And Twentynine Palms is what?"

"It's a hellhole in California towards Nevada, but the Marine Corps Air Ground Combat Center is there, and that's the important thing."

"Oh, you train there with them."

He nodded. "Sadly, yes."

"So, what, the temperature reminds you of it?"

"Everything does," he grumbled. "The dirt I can see over there, the rocks, the cactus—God, I hate the fuckin' desert."

"You didn't have to come."

"The hell I didn't," he retorted.

I threw an arm around his shoulders, pulling him toward me, and sank my fingers into his hair. "It's not that bad, and it's really not that hot."

He muttered something about me needing a psych eval, and I couldn't stifle a laugh.

"We're in the shade and it's hot," he complained. "It's like standing in an oven all day."

"If you hate the heat so much," I teased him, nuzzling my face into the side of his neck, "you seriously should have stayed home."

"I already told—what're you doing?"

I was always looking for that one scent I would love and wear forever. I spent money on cologne. It wasn't like I was forever haunting the mall, but if I was there, I checked. Ian, on the other hand, used stuff he picked up in Chinatown that was dirt cheap, that he bought off the shelf at some place that also sold supplements and herbs and seasonings. He didn't buy anything to make him smell good. That didn't even blip on his radar as something he needed to consider. He only bought the essentials—shampoo and conditioner, that had no English anywhere on either bottle—and something that he slathered on after he shaved to keep his face from hurting. I suspected it moisturized, but I would never tell him that. The thing was, his hair stuff plus the product—singular—he put in his hair, all of it together cost fifteen dollars. I knew because the last time he ran out of everything I'd gone with him to buy more. The man was stunning, so whatever he was using worked great, but the best part was the mixture of scents.

Holy God, he smelled good.

Whenever I got close to him I inhaled citrus and vetiver with hints of sandalwood and amber, cedar, and leather. All of it together made me want to lick him all over.

"M?" He chuckled as I breathed him in at the same time I sucked the spot behind his ear.

"You smell so good," I almost mewled.

"I smell like sweat," he grumbled, but I could hear the begrudging rumble of happiness. Me wanting him turned him on big-time. "Come on. Let's go get the car so we can first report in and then figure out where we're staying. We need a bed."

We did, it was true.

Half an hour later, we had the Toyota Sequoia and Ian drove us out of the parking garage, heading toward the street. The temperature on the dash read 101, but I was pretty sure that was because the asphalt was absorbing all the heat. I was interested to know how people drove in the summer and wondered if they slipped on a pair of oven mitts to be able to touch the steering wheel.

"Where are we going?" Ian asked irritably.

"Okay, so right now we're on East Sky Harbor Boulevard, and you're gonna want to take a right onto I-10 in like a minute."

"Then what?"

"Do you know that in the summer they cook eggs on the sidewalk out here?"

"Shut up. What do I do once I'm on the freeway?"

"Oh, are you there already?"

"This is me driving."

True. "Okay, so then you're gonna take the 7th Avenue exit, which is exit 144."

"Roger that—now what?"

"Okay, now you're gonna take the 7th Avenue ramp south, and you're staying on that until you take a left onto Jefferson. It says the courthouse is on Washington just east of 7th, and by the way, it's dubbed the 'Solar Oven.'"

"Oh fuck you," he growled.

I cackled. "In the summer, they let people who work there, security and stuff like that, wear short-sleeve shirts."

"They do not."

"They do, but now it's not as bad."

"It's a fuckin' blast furnace out here," he complained, gesturing to the temperature displayed on the dash. It read 92 degrees. "It's October, for crissakes."

"Yeah, but look, it already dropped nine degrees from when we got in the car."

"You think your body can actually tell the difference between ninety degrees and a hundred degrees?"

Perhaps not. "You know, Kage told me before we left the office that when he was on a task force here once that he and the other guys said it's like a giant greenhouse from hell."

Nothing for a moment before he turned to me. "Are you fucking with me?"

The look on his face was priceless.

"That's what he said?"

"He says it's like being in the devil's terrarium."

Ian groaned and I died.

Died.

I laughed so hard I couldn't even breathe.

"Can you please pull your shit together?"

It took several minutes, because having to leave home because there was a psychopath after me was scary, but Ian was with me, so it was sort of like a vacation. All in all, I was feeling a bit unbalanced.

"He said"—I wiped at my eyes, still chuckling—"that it's all glass when you walk in, and in the summer it's like being in a sweatbox, and it's not much better in the winter."

"That's because during October here, it's still ninety-two fuckin' degrees!"

"I bet it doesn't cool down at night, either," I mentioned. "Look at all this concrete."

At first, we didn't find parking anywhere near the building. It was all blocked off. But Ian finally saw what looked like a gated area and drove around behind it, and sure enough, that was where the people who worked there parked.

We had to stop and show the guard our badges and IDs before we were finally allowed into the atrium. And our boss was right: gorgeous building, all steel and glass, and hotter than hell. Outside, it was like standing in the blast of a blow dryer set to crispy, but inside, for whatever reason, it was hot and humid.

"This is like Chicago in July," Ian moaned.

"And yet back outside, it's a dry heat."

"I wanna go home."

The people working the coffee kiosk and some others wore shorts and T-shirts—some even in tank tops—and I got it, I did. If they were dressed like most people you saw inside a federal courthouse, they'd melt. It was hot inside the atrium, and I wondered if, as winter rolled around, it got cold inside and held that temperature too?

At the security station, we got out our badges and IDs again, passed the guns over, and were finally admitted. Before we could head up to the second floor, though, one of the deputy US marshals we had just spoken to made clear that we were supposed to report to the security director of the court and that he was in the Central Court

Building, which was *not* where we were now. We needed to go back outside and walk a bit.

"I don't think so," I told him. "We're not reporting to Security Administration & Operations. We're reporting to a task force."

"Oh." He seemed startled. "You don't do court security?"

"Not as our main job," Ian said. "We're not security officers, we're inspectors."

It was a gray area.

Kage had us both coded as deputy US marshals, but technically, as neither of us supervised anyone and because we worked with WITSEC as well as with the organized crime units and drug enforcement, we were inspectors. It was only important when we left home, because it let other marshals know what we could be counted on to do.

"Oh, okay," Padgett—his name tag read—was still surprised. "I didn't know we had any openings currently."

"You don't," I said quickly. "We're on loan, we're not here to stay."

He seemed relieved, and I understood. If you were in court security, you wanted to move up, to get into the field, to be Tommy Lee Jones in *The Fugitive*, even though the issues with that flick were endless. It was the same with all kinds of TV shows and movies; it was impossible to get every little detail right. I had dated a sailor once who explained in excruciating detail all the things that were wrong with *The Hunt for Red October* and he thought that I should turn it off and hate it on general principle because of those inconsistencies. He went home and there was no second date. I loved what I loved, and whether or not it was wrong changed nothing.

"We're going to the second floor, right?" Ian asked, returning my thoughts to the task at hand, that of us finding out whom we reported to. We had a name, Brooks Latham, and that was all. "That's what we were told."

"Yeah, you can take the elevator or the stairs," Padgett replied amiably.

Amazing how nice people were when they knew you weren't after their job.

As soon as we reached Latham's office, I realized considering all the people in the room, all the different white boards, and the configuration of the clustered desks, that we were looking at not a single task force, but many.

"Help you?" a man asked as he strode over to us where we stood beside a cubicle wall.

"I'm Morse," Ian said quickly, "and this is Smith. We're supposed to see Latham."

"Commander Latham," he corrected.

"Commander Latham," Ian parroted.

"Let me get him."

We would not be invited into the main area until we had passed muster. And while I understood, at home we were never all about who had the biggest dick. We were a warm, welcoming bunch. Except for Ian.

There was a shrill whistle, and we both looked up as an older man gestured at us from an office in the back.

Ian groaned under his breath. "I love being called like a dog."

"At least it's air-conditioned in here," I offered, pointing out a plus.

He was not impressed.

Latham held the door open and closed it behind us, not moving, staring, taking us both in.

"What kind of background do you guys have? I haven't had time to read your sheets."

Ian described how we'd both been marshals for three years, told him I had been a police detective and that he was Army Special Forces.

"You a Green Beret?"

"Yessir."

He nodded, clearly in awe. "So you're used to doing things by the book."

I was so proud of myself for not laughing my ass off.

Latham turned to me. "The detective piece will help. This is a highly transient state, so running down people fast is important."

"We'll do all we can to help, Commander," I affirmed.

"Excellent," he responded, offering me and then Ian his hand. "Now let me tell you a little bit about how we work."

Brooks Latham was in charge, and we would report to him, but he was simply a senior inspector, not a chief deputy like Kage.

"Normally here you're not going to be with the same partner every day, or even on the same team. We tend to mix things up, depending on individual strengths and what's needed on a certain op."

We were both silent, waiting. He was not saying anything either of us liked so far.

"Are you guys partners in Chicago?"

"We are," Ian told him.

"Great, that helps. I've had some trouble matching people up."

"Not an issue with us," Ian assured him.

He gave us a smile. "You guys hungry at all? I could feed you lunch before I give you the rest of the tour. You like Greek?"

We both did.

Crazy Jim's was close to the courthouse, and since it smelled fantastic as soon as we walked in, my appetite jump-started. We both had pita subs—Ian a steak picado and me a chicken feta—and we shared a goat cheese salad that got hoovered down in no time.

"You guys always eat like this?"

Ian and I exchanged glances. "Normally we eat way more," I clarified. "But since you were buying, we figured we'd go easy on you."

The fact that he laughed was a good sign.

OUR TEMPORARY housing was close to the downtown Willo Historic District, a neighborhood Latham had called a "cottage community."

"Which means what?" Ian asked as he took a right onto a small, quiet tree-lined street.

"I think it means they don't have any apartments. It's all homes."

"That makes no sense," he told me. "If you look in that envelope he gave us, there are key fobs in there and directions for where we're supposed to park our car. There's no way we're staying in some house. It's gotta be an apartment."

"It's so beautiful here," I commented as we passed a Tudor-style home and then a Craftsman bungalow, a Spanish Revival, and many others. Each was different, and that was interesting to look at. The homes and the landscaping told me the neighborhood was old, yet immaculately kept.

"I wanna go home," he growled.

And I knew he did. "Let's just find the house, all right? The sooner we get there, the sooner we can dump our crap and get to work."

"But that's what I'm saying, M. I don't think we're looking for a house."

It turned out he was right. The condo on the fourth floor of the enormous complex we would be staying in was actually adjacent to the historic district on Vernon Avenue.

After we parked the car and Ian grabbed his duffel out of the back, I got my garment bag, duffel, and the wheeled suitcase currently full of shoes out of the trunk.

"May I help you with that, sir?" Ian teased.

If looks could kill, he would have been *dead*, but clearly I wasn't that scary because he only snorted out a laugh before grabbing my garment bag. He lifted it easily, even though it was the heaviest of the three pieces of luggage, and started toward the elevators.

The apartment was 1,700 square feet of boring: one master bedroom, two smaller ones, two bathrooms, fireplace—though only God knew why—a laundry room, and a tiny patio. It made me think of my first apartment when I was going through the police academy. It was sparsely furnished, very clean, and utterly adequate.

"It's fine," I assured Ian.

"It sucks," he judged vehemently.

I understood his hatred. He had left a place with the same lack of character that was totally forgettable not six months before. This felt like backsliding.

"We don't live here," I reminded him as we both dropped the bags. Moving into his space, I kissed him, tenderly, lightly, before nipping his lower lip and stepping back.

"Where ya goin'?"

"We promised we'd be back there in an hour. It's almost been that."

"Fine, but tonight we find a place where we can drink, and then you promise to come home with me and fuck my brains out."

"You don't have to get me drunk first—no alcohol required, marshal."

He chuckled, and the sound of him, all husky and seductive, made me want to rethink the plan of getting back to work.

"Too late," he announced, already using his cop voice. "Let's get going."

No amount of talking was going to get me laid at the present moment, and I had no one to blame but myself.

CHAPTER 10

IT WAS different in Phoenix. And while I was getting the hang of how they did things, Ian was not. Simple things, like other marshals stopping him from putting a guy down on the pavement or up against the side of a car, drove him nuts.

"What the fuck," he growled at me.

I winced at the volume. "The ground is hot; so is the car."

"I hate it here," he lamented.

I had to nag him not to turn off the car and leave people inside, and he had to get used to carrying metal cuffs again—their budget was different in Phoenix, so he couldn't stuff his TAC vest with plastic ones all the time.

"Why?" he asked irritably, holding the cuffs up as he held a guy over the open trunk of the white Mercury Marquis.

I made the snapping motion for him again because he'd locked them... again. "You gotta flip it open and then sort of flick it around their wrist."

He didn't have either the snap or the flick down. It got to the point, after the first week, that they were always my cuffs on the suspects. But I had years of practice on him because I'd been first a patrolman and then a police detective. Ian's background was all military combat, never as an MP, so he didn't have my cuff technique.

"And why are they suspects?" Ian fumed as we took a guy into the office for processing. "They're fuckin' fugitives, for crissakes. That's what we do—we pick those fuckers up!"

Latham was all about being PC, and that included what his team called the people we brought in. He was very concerned about public perception and how his office was viewed. I had never seen so many outsiders allowed to ride along, shadow, and interview team members. I was glad that Ian and I were sort of wild cards, that he didn't know us well and so kept us out of the limelight.

We were on a bust with another team and one of the reporters tried to film Ian and me capturing a suspect. After he put on a pair of latex gloves, Ian took the phone right out of the guy's hand and dropped it down a storm drain. That time we didn't get hauled into the office because it was his word against ours and the reporter was apparently kind of a douche. But it became a daily occurrence for us to be sitting in front of Lathan's desk for *something*.

Excessive force. Inadequate force. Why did we grapple with suspects instead of simply pulling our firearms? Why did we run warrant checks on everyone at a particular location when we had the person we were there for in custody?

After the second week, Ian started stopping in the middle of putting his foot in some guy's back and yelled over to me, "Can I do this?"

And I'd nod yes or shake my head no. One of the things frowned upon was taking a guy at the Scottsdale Fashion Square in front of the food court. Ian flew over a table and tackled the guy, picked him up, and flung him back down onto the tile. The "suspect" didn't move after that. We both had on baseball hats and sunglasses, and when the mall cops showed up, I flashed my badge. As soon as we got back, we were in Latham's office.

"You should have waited for the suspect to exit the mall," he lectured us.

"Write that down," Ian directed me right before he was suspended for a day.

"I'll put it in a memo," I advised him, and that did it, I was suspended too.

We spent the whole Thursday in bed ordering delivery and napping.

"Maybe we should have just taken vacation time," I whispered as I lay on the floor in the living room—the coolest room in the apartment—with Ian draped over me in a sated, sticky sprawl.

He grunted his agreement before tipping his head back to lick up the length of my throat. That was all it took for me to roll him to his back and fuck him again.

Later, while we were lying poolside, a beautiful dark-tanned dark-haired woman who looked like she could model if she wanted walked over and asked Ian if he'd like to have a drink with her later.

"A drink?"

She chuckled. "If you're not busy, uhm...."

"Ian," he supplied.

Her smile was wicked, and the way she bit her bottom lip, alluring. "Ian," she repeated, her voice as seductive as her body. "I'd love to show you the sights. You're new in town, right?"

He nodded.

"Yeah, I figured. I haven't seen you around, and I would have definitely noticed."

It was a nice line.

"I can't," he replied, sitting up on the lounge chair, tipping his head back as he looked at her from behind his aviators. "But I'm very flattered and I appreciate the offer."

"Why can't you? I don't see a ring."

It took everything in me not to pounce on him and yell "Ah-ha!"

Ring. The magic word. She would have stopped and never walked over if she'd seen a ring on his finger.

Fucking Ian.

Getting up, letting him handle the situation he found himself in, I took off my White Sox cap and tossed it on the chair I'd just vacated. After walking to the edge of the pool, I jumped in and let myself sink to the bottom.

It was quiet and calm, and I sat there for as long as I could, eyes open, taking in all the blue before surfacing slowly.

"You're such an asshole."

Looking over my shoulder I found Ian, glaring down at me, arms crossed, sunglasses hanging on the collar of his T-shirt.

I swam backward, away from him.

"Really?"

"Aren't you going for drinks?"

He shook his head. "You're ridiculous."

"Why not? You can go."

"M."

"You got no ring and all," I couldn't help adding.

"Just get outta the pool. I'm hungry."

Instead I did a few laps, and when I finally got out, he was right there with a big fluffy towel to wrap around my hips.

"What're you doing?"

"You can totally see the outline of your dick when your shorts are wet."

I shrugged.

He growled. "Don't be an ass. I told her I was with you, all right?"

I squinted at him.

Turning, he waved, and when I followed his gaze, I saw the woman and her group, all of whom were sitting in the shaded area beneath huge ceiling fans, return the gesture.

"See?"

I nodded and went to move past him, but he stepped into my path.

"Ian," I said softly.

"Stop," he ordered gently as he took my face in his hands and stepped closer, into me, into my space, leaving no room to guess what we were to each other. "I know what you need, M."

"Yeah?"

"I do."

I liked the way those two words sounded on his tongue.

"Gimme time."

Whatever he wanted.

THE FOLLOWING day we were inside the AJ's Fine Foods in Glendale because when we went to arrest a fugitive in a house off of 67th Avenue, I had run after him when he took off.

"Ya good yet?" Ian asked, putting the ice pack that the very nice woman in the deli had given us on the back of my neck.

"He needs to drink more water," Courtney Quinn, another deputy, explained to Ian. "And next time you should fuckin' listen to me, Smith."

If I answered her I'd say something shitty, so instead I drank the Gatorade that Lucas Hoch, yet another deputy, gave me. He'd twisted the cap off, which was damn nice of him since I was still seeing spots.

"Nobody runs in the heat," he reiterated to me, as he had for the past half an hour.

I'd done what I always did, bolted from the car, and this time, it was Ian following. But the chase took a good twenty minutes, up over walls, through backyards, around the sides of houses, across streets, and finally when I caught the guy in a flying tackle on the manicured front lawn in a quiet upper-middle-class neighborhood, I didn't get back up. I couldn't. I could barely breathe, I was so hot.

Ian managed to get cuffs on the guy—we'd been practicing at the apartment, in and out of bed—and told him to stay still before he checked on me.

"Jesus, M, you're really red."

There was only heat and my skin felt like it was burning.

The homeowner, a beautiful blonde housewife dressed immaculately and sporting a diamond ring as big as my thumb, came out immediately, her friends waiting in the doorway, to see if she could offer any assistance.

"No, ma'am," Ian said quickly, clearly worried about me. "I just need to get him off your lawn and hydrated."

"Exactly," she agreed. "You need to get him inside and push fluids. My kids get like that if I don't watch them like a hawk."

"Yes, ma'am," he said affably.

"Do you want to bring him in here?"

We were never, ever, supposed to involve civilians in anything if possible.

"No, ma'am, but thank you."

When I looked up at her from my prone position, she smiled and nodded.

So Ian found the AJ's and dragged me inside to sit in the a/c and drink water.

"We don't run," Quinn expounded. "Not until after Halloween, when it cools down."

"It doesn't cool down until Halloween?" Ian was flabbergasted.

"Yes, marshal," she teased, and I saw her pupils dilate as she looked at him—easy to see she found him very appealing. "You have to wait a bit longer."

Letting my head fall forward, I bumped his thigh with my shoulder.

"When we do AT like I was telling you about out there in Twentynine Palms, this shit happens all the time," he said, trying to reassure me as he put his hand in my hair, scratching my scalp before gently moving the ice pack. "Big strong guys drop all over the place."

He was trying to make me feel better about being a dumbass, but it wasn't helping.

"You still feeling light-headed?"

"A little."

"You'll be okay."

"This is lame."

"It's gonna happen in this kinda heat, M."

"You wouldn't have nearly passed out."

"No, 'cause I've trained in this bullshit," he insisted, squatting down in front of me, his hands on my knees to look at my face. "And I know you hafta hydrate and limit what you expend energy on."

I couldn't shake the embarrassment or the memory of the looks from Quinn and Hoch implying that I was a lightweight.

Of course, fifteen minutes later I had the sunstroke headache, and Ian and I had to pull into a Circle K on the way back downtown and get me Tylenol, more Gatorade, and a 64-ounce Thirst Buster cup full of Dr Pepper because I needed both the caffeine and the sugar, he said. As I held the gigantic plastic-handled cup in my hand, I asked him why.

"'Cause you're gonna need it."

"I have to hold it in my lap or between my feet. It's too big for the cupholder."

"Just drink it and shut up," he grumbled. "And get in the car."

After we ate again, between the food, drugs, caffeine, and staying cool, I was back to myself, feeling better, ready to chase down more bad guys.

When we reached a task force site out in Tempe, close to the university there, we saw all the usual suspects, plus DEA agents. Ian and I vested up, he strapped on his thigh holster—which held his spare SIG P228, because only having the Glock 20 we each carried wasn't enough—and we headed toward the cluster of men.

"Where are you guys going?" Hoch asked before we got far.

Ian pointed toward the staging area.

"Not yet," Quinn told us. "We wait until they tell us where they want us."

I glowered at her. "I thought you said this was our grab. Is it a fugitive capture or not?"

"It is, but, you know, Latham always says we wait for direction."

"Even on a warrant that we're serving?"

They both nodded.

"Oh." I shouldn't have been surprised, the procedure in Phoenix a constant learning opportunity. "So even during those times when we're supposed to take point, you guys run the support agenda?"

"Yeah."

"Huh," I said, turning to Ian.

He crossed his arms. "Are you fucking with me?"

I checked on Hoch and Quinn, and as they both appeared confused, I returned my focus to Ian. "No, I don't think so."

When I was hired, Kage had made clear that in his office, we went for the jugular each and every single time. He was always in charge; he expected his men to carry themselves that same way in the field. It was lucky that Ian had ended up working for Kage, as he was not the guy who waited and said *please* and *may I.* Ian kicked the door down and God help you if you were behind it when he did.

"We hang back and wait," Hoch reiterated, in case Ian and I were slow.

"Okay," I agreed, because it was not my call.

"Fuck no," Ian growled, and when he stalked away, I was committed to following, as it was basically in my job description.

Two hours later, as we sat in Latham's office listening to him yell again, for like the hundredth time in a three-week period, I realized Ian and I were on thin ice. We'd be lucky if we had jobs when we got home.

"We never lead!" he bellowed at us. "We take our cues from the other law enforcement on site so it can never come back on us!"

Latham's team didn't breach, they didn't tell everyone else to fuck off; they took custody only when it was time or when they were asked to. It was a completely different dynamic than we'd been operating with since we became marshals but really, was probably the one with a lot fewer incident reports.

"And you went in without even pulling your guns. What the *hell* was that?"

I cleared my throat. "We were walking into an area with a high number of civilians, sir, and so until the threat presented itself, we didn't want to draw our weapons."

"There didn't need to be an escalation of force," Ian seconded. "We try not to draw our weapons unless we're going to use them."

"You were on a task force!"

"Close to a college campus," I enlightened him. "It wasn't necessary."

"We were able to collect the fugitive without trading any gunfire," Ian stated in case Latham hadn't been informed.

"But it wasn't your call to make!"

It had been, in the end. Ian had seen the guy and the two of us had walked over to his table and taken him, fast, easy, shoving his face down into his nachos. He was cuffed and ready for transport before the DEA douche bags were even ready to move.

"I hate those guys," I muttered.

"You shouldn't!" Latham shouted. "Because you work for them!"

Ian scoffed, which didn't help Latham's blood pressure even one bit.

"You two need to take the rest of the day and get yourselves right," he snarled. "We'll try this again tomorrow."

We were halfway to the elevator when a guy yelled out our names. Turning, I found a tall, handsome man striding toward us. When he stepped in close, he offered me his hand first.

"I'm Javier Segundo," he greeted me, smiling, squeezing tight, before facing Ian. "I didn't get to meet you guys yet 'cause me and my partner Charlie Hewitt were assigned to SWAT all last month up until yesterday, heading up a Fugitive Task Force."

"A whole month?" I was horrified. "Why?"

"How else do you pick up guys fortified in their homes?" he asked with a shrug.

"No, I get going in with SWAT for those, but how many can you have?"

"This is Arizona," he said, chuckling. "We've got a ton of survivalists and doomsday preppers, and everybody's got an arsenal on their land."

I myself had noticed quite a few firearms in plain sight.

"Just so you know, we get loaned out to SWAT so we have backup. It's basically for our safety since we don't wear body armor."

We had body armor back home because we worked tactical operations upon occasion because of where our office was located. Other pieces of possible marshal duties, like Asset Forfeiture or

Judicial Security, Ian and I didn't do, though Kage supervised other marshals who did. But to hear that Segundo and his partner never wore armor was a surprise. When it was a full breach, when it was us picking up a fugitive someplace where there could be heavy gunfire and God knew what else, all of us, the whole team, went in suited up in our tactical gear. The only way to tell us from SWAT was by the letters on our backs.

"Never?" I pressed, because it was so odd.

"No. Have you guys?" Segundo asked.

I tipped my head giving him a maybe without committing before I got in trouble for oversharing. That, too, was an issue with Latham. Without meaning to, Ian and I ended up going on and on about how we did things in Chicago. It was not endearing us to our current boss. And I understood, I did, no one liked to hear how they were not measuring up in comparison, but if the information could be helpful and the job could be done better, how was that not a good thing? Ian said the Army was just like that. Heaven forbid someone wanted to make a change so things ran more efficiently. "So where's your partner? I'd love to meet him," I said to change the topic.

"He got paperwork duty, but he'll be done shortly," Segundo answered, putting a hand on my shoulder.

"Well, we're on our way out, so we'll catch up with you guys tomorrow," I said, trying to extricate myself.

Ian's scowl had been immediate. He was not a big fan of new people putting their hands on me. Even before we were anything, he'd been very possessive of my space.

"Hey," I said to my partner. "We better go find some place to eat before we both pass out from hunger, right?"

"Yeah," he agreed quickly, reaching out and taking hold of my bicep, easing me forward to stand beside him. "I'm starving.'"

We didn't make it to the elevator that was not even five feet away.

"Hey, you should let me and Hewitt take you guys out to one of our favorite places. We can swap war stories, eat, and get our drink on."

I wanted to go to the store, get food, and go back to the condo and veg with Ian, but it was not the smart thing. We needed to bond with the people we were working with, and Segundo seemed like a good guy. Even more importantly, I didn't want to sit around and talk to Ian about Hartley and he didn't want to share the reasons... again... why he didn't want to get married. We were sort of talked out and if we weren't alone....

"Yeah, sure, just tell us where it is," I agreed quickly, drawing a frown from my partner. "We can meet you there."

"We can actually walk it. That way no one has to drive if we overindulge."

"But it's a school night," I teased.

"Work hard, play hard—isn't that the marshal motto?"

I didn't think it actually was.

THE CULINARY Dropout at The Yard was on 7th Street, a few blocks from the courthouse. I had thought to drive because normally it was cooking outside, but at the time of day we were walking, right around six, it had cooled somewhat, down to the high 80s, so it wasn't horrible. Without humidity, strolling, not running, it was almost nice.

Usually when we went out to eat, we went home first and changed out the Glock 20s so we were both carrying our secondary weapons. Ian had a SIG Sauer P228 semiautomatic, and I had a Ruger SR9C Compact Pistol with laser and stainless-steel slide that I could keep either on my hip or in an ankle holster. He'd bought it for me after hearing me say enough times that, unbelievable as it was, I did own only one weapon. Ian found that whole idea horrifyingly sacrilegious—he owned three, counting his M1911 that he took with him when he was deployed. So he remedied that when he moved in with me. I got the gun, which he liked and found both dependable and easy to conceal, in a beautiful wooden box with my initials carved in the top right corner. Kohn had given him crap about it, not understanding why it wasn't a nickel-plated Desert Eagle or something, but Ian being Ian said it was the man carrying the gun, not the gun itself that made it badass.

It felt odd to be walking around with my duty gun strapped to my hip when I was off for the night, but everything about Phoenix was weird, so it was simply one more thing in a long list. I had also wanted to change out of my undershirt and button-down and trousers, but it wasn't in the cards. In Chicago I would have made certain to wear a jacket, but it was just too hot here to even contemplate. Ian looked a bit less miserable in his Dockers and denim shirt, only the AMI Alexandre Mattiussi Black Chelsea boots he had on dressing up his outfit at all. Of course, Ian had no idea what was on his feet. I bought shoes, put them in his side of the closet, and he wore them. It was probably good that he didn't know the prices of any of them.

We sat on the patio away from where you could play shuffleboard and ping pong, on couches around an unlit fire pit. Apparently in the winter—mid-November, December—it got cold enough to use it. I couldn't imagine.

Ian got a beer—they had the Dogfish 90 minute IPA he liked—and I had the Green Flash they had on tap, plus water for both of us because really, hydration was important in the heat. We let Segundo do the ordering, getting us appetizers, meat, and cheese, and though he suggested the prosciutto deviled eggs, since I was not a big egg eater outside of omelets, I had to put the kibosh on that. It was nice that his partner, who had not made the walk over, finally caught up and joined us.

Hewitt was the exact opposite of Segundo—blond-haired, blue eyed, with a golden tan and a lean, long muscled frame. Segundo's body was gym-toned, cut and hard, and between that and his deep, dark brown eyes and thick black hair, I was betting that he had never in his life been starved for female companionship.

"It's about time I get to meet the guys who are giving our commander an aneurysm," Hewitt greeted us happily as he stood and leaned over the table, offering us each his hand one after the other. "I hope you're planning to stick around for a while. I'm looking forward to seeing his brain explode."

Segundo snorted out a laugh. "He really don't like you guys."

I knew that already.

"Please tell me you both like to play pool," Hewitt said hopefully.

"Who doesn't like pool?" Ian asked quietly, but I heard the edge in his voice as he bumped his knee against mine and let it rest there.

"Well, then, we should go after this. I know the best place."

I was going to say that we'd see, that if we were vertical we could decide, because the two of us were operating on zero sleep and I knew from experience that the less rack time—as Ian called it—he had, the more on edge he would get. And not like cranky the way I got, or prickly and generally a dick. Ian had occasional night terrors that the shrink who regularly cleared us all for duty said was mild PTSD.

Kage made us all go talk to the staff psychiatrist every six months. I hated going, made sure to smile a lot and give answers so he'd think I was simple. More than likely Dr. Johar knew I was bullshitting him, but he was nice enough to never call me out. But my partner was another story. Dr. Johar had concerns about Ian and his bad dreams, which could wake him up in the middle of the night in a cold sweat, panting for breath. Since he'd moved in with me there had been none, but he confessed that he got them when he was deployed or if he slept somewhere else other than with me. Lately, being overly tired all the time, sleeping so hard when he finally did, he'd been having nightmares. I had planned to get him to bed at a decent hour, sometime before midnight, and so playing pool seemed like a bad idea.

"Sure," Ian agreed, leaning back on the couch, taking hold of my sleeve. "I'm a shark, right, M?"

I looked over my shoulder at him. "Definitely."

After the one beer, Ian and I both stuck to water, so by the time we left two hours later, we were the sober ones. Both Segundo and Hewitt had pounded down drinks, easily two an hour, so since they were stuck walking the rest of the night, we were as well.

The pool hall Hewitt took us to wasn't his favorite, he said—that one was out in Mesa—but the family-owned place downtown would suffice until the weekend, when he'd take us to his spot. On our way in, I noticed a little boy standing outside an alley on the opposite side of the street, and as we waited in line to get into the pool hall, he tried to get the attention of people walking by. No one stopped to listen to him even though once or twice he even grabbed for the clothes of those passing him by. I couldn't hear what he was saying, but between how scared he looked and the way he wrung his hands, head turning left and right, I could tell he needed help.

"I have Cardinal tickets for a couple weeks from now," Segundo said, draping an arm around my neck and squeezing gently. He was obviously one of those guys who you got a few drinks in and got all touchy-feely. I didn't mind, he was harmless, but Ian's glare was getting icier with every passing second. "You and Morse should come with us."

I made a noise of agreement, still distracted.

"You don't like football?" he asked with a belch, pulling me in tighter. "Come on, man, everybody likes football."

"No, I... hold on," I said, easing free, checking both ways on Central Avenue before darting across to the little boy.

The way his eyes lit up when he saw the badge on my belt, you would have thought he'd won the lottery. He bolted over to me, and as I dropped to one knee so we were closer to the same height, he fisted his hands in my shirt.

"Hey, I'm Deputy United States Marshal Miro Jones," I said without thinking. "Who're you, kid?"

The tears came fast and as I wiped them away quickly, he hit me with a stream of Spanish I could not hope to follow.

"Shit," I groaned, before looking across the street, seeing Ian on his way, Hewitt and Segundo following. "Hey, Javier, you speak Spanish?" I called over.

"Why?" he yelled back. "Just because I have a Spanish name?"

"Yeah!"

"That's racist, man!"

"Do you or not?" I spat, annoyed.

"No, man, and fuck you."

Returning my attention to the little boy, I realized he was shivering as he cried. I put my hands on his arms to calm him. "Mi nombre es Miro. ¿Cómo te llamas?"

Big gulp of air. "Oscar."

"Oscar," I repeated, really pissed at the moment that I had not remembered much Spanish from college. I needed to remedy that at some point. "¿Ocupas ayuda?" I asked, even though it was clear that he did, in fact, need help.

"Sí," he answered. "Mi hermana está en problemas."

Sister. Okay. "¿Dónde?" I said, which I was pretty sure meant where.

He slipped his hand into mine and tugged.

"What're we doing?" Hewitt asked.

"The boy needs help," Ian declared, stepping in close to me. "So we're helping."

"No, no, no," Hewitt said, waving his hand. "We've all had a few, it's late—just call the police and let them handle it."

I scowled at him before turning back to the little boy and gesturing for him to lead me. "Show me where your sister is."

He pulled on my hand and we would have taken off running, but Segundo moved around in front of me. "This is a mistake," he insisted angrily.

"We help. It's what we do," I said levelly, stepping around him.

Oscar yanked on my hand again, and when he went from a walk to a jog, so did I, and when he started running, I kept up easily, with Ian beside me. Hewitt and Segundo followed after us, each explaining why what we were doing could go wrong at any second.

We passed several side streets and a parking lot, went up and over a six-foot chain-link fence and across a vacant area full of cigarette butts and beer bottles, and finally came to another street that we crossed to reach a three-story apartment building that looked abandoned but, the closer we got, was clearly not.

We went around the side and down a short alley to the back, where dumpsters stood shoved up against the wall. There was a small laundromat directly across from them on the left-hand side. Five men hovered near the door that led into a building, and when we got closer, Oscar pointed, like that was it: inside was where his sister was. It was fortunate they were busy talking, smoking, and drinking and didn't notice us. The way we were standing in the shadows didn't hurt either.

"Okay," I told the little boy as I grabbed his shoulder, walked him around a parked car on the street, and crouched down beside him. I think he thought I was going to let him go in with me, but that was certainly not going to happen. When he tried to follow, I lifted my hand, indicating for him to stay. He nodded and then lunged at me, wrapped his arms around my neck, squeezing tight and shivering. He pointed at my gun and then at the men, and I understood. Letting him go, I rose, patted his head, and returned to Ian and the others, still standing in the shadows away from the group of men.

"And?" Ian prodded.

"Those guys are strapped."

"Of course they are," he said, grinning and pulling his Glock. "What else would they be?"

"Oh, fuck no," Hewitt cautioned, putting a hand on my chest. "None of us are wearing vests. We can't run in there. We have no idea how many there are!"

"Right," Ian agreed before he stepped into the alley where they could see him if they noticed, arm behind his back, and began his walk toward the door.

"Call for backup," I directed, immediately following Ian.

"Fuck," I heard Segundo growl behind me a moment before he touched my shoulder. "You and Special Forces over there better know what you're doing."

I grunted to let him know I'd heard him, but I was laser focused on the men we were approaching.

Normally, we had vests on, dressed up as something else: homeless men on the street, tuxedos like we were coming from a black-tie affair, or suits if we were going as drug dealers. Whatever the op called for, we had an outfit. But no subterfuge here, because we had no good reason to be in that alley. It was really deserted, we were far from the rest of the nightlife downtown, and all the surrounding buildings were dark but for the laundromat and some stairwells.

When the first man finally saw us, he shouted at the others and they all pulled their guns fast.

It was actually pretty frightening to watch the speed with which Ian dispatched people. He shot three, and I took out one and Segundo the other.

"Holy fuck," Segundo gasped from behind me.

Ian ran around the fallen men and stopped at one's side. Bending quickly, he holstered his Glock, took a Heckler & Koch P30L fitted with a compensator off the body, checked his pockets for extra mags, found two, and then went to the entrance.

Ian was listening as he made sure the new gun was loaded, stuffed a mag into each of his pockets, and reached for the knob to open the door.

"Why would he take that?" Segundo whispered, tilting his head at the gun in Ian's hand.

"Because it's a good gun," I replied quietly. "With the recoil compensator attached, when he shoots a lot, the barrel won't lift like it usually does. It makes your shots more precise."

"How many people does he plan to kill?" Segundo asked cautiously.

"Anyone who shoots at us," I answered, following Ian in as he threw open the door and darted through the opening.

He had run right so I went left, fanning out, Segundo following me as we faced not a large space with apartments, as I'd imagined, but a hall with a stairway at the end. There were four doors, and at that moment I really hoped Hewitt had called for backup. If we were at home, any other pair from our team would have made me feel safe. It was whoever-went-through-the-door-last's job to call Kage. Our boss always sent everyone when we called for reinforcements. I had no idea who would show up here.

I moved in beside Ian but was ready to turn and fire at anyone who came out with guns blazing.

Ian kicked in the closest door and ran through, announcing himself as he went, "Federal marshals! Everyone out!"

I stayed in the hall, covering his back, praying there was no one in the house with a shotgun or an Uzi, and he flushed a couple from that room—early twenties, Caucasian, I was guessing meth addicts from their ruined complexions of telltale blotches and sallow skin—who explained quickly that this was a flop house and nothing else.

"You see any kids here?"

The guy coughed, loud and wet. "No, man, we—"

"I think upstairs. I heard someone crying a while ago," the woman said.

"Go back inside," Ian ordered, and they scrambled fast to obey.

It wasn't an apartment building at all, we discovered after we went through each of the remaining three doors, but instead an enormous house with individual rooms and connecting Jack and Jill bathrooms.

Except for that couple, the floor was vacant, so with Segundo covering us from the back, I headed for the stairs. Ian stopped me with his hand, like he would have if I was in the front seat of the car, splayed across my chest.

"What're you—"

"Me first," he demanded.

"Why? Did you become bulletproof and didn't tell me?"

If looks could kill, I would have been in trouble, but as it was I got the Green Beret death stare before he turned to sprint down the hall and start up the stairs. I was right behind him, with Segundo following.

As soon as we hit the hall on the second floor, we drew gunfire.

"Fuck!" Segundo yelled as I ducked back behind the corner of the wall, then leaned out for a second so I could see where everyone was before stepping out and laying down cover fire as Ian dove through an open door, rolled to his feet, and shot whoever was in the room.

Retreating for a moment, unnerved because I couldn't see Ian, I yelled for Segundo. "Cover me so I can cross the hall!"

"What? Where the fuck are you—"

"There," I yelled again, pointing at the first room on the right.

He gave me a quick nod, and I rushed across the hall, hitting the door with my shoulder before exploding into the room and falling to a crouch.

Five men were inside—two armed, who immediately fired at me. They missed, having aimed too high, not anticipating the textbook maneuver we were all taught upon breach. I returned fire, dropping them both, and then faced off with the other three who were standing around a naked girl who couldn't have been more than twelve tied to a bed.

"On your knees!" I roared, hearing gunfire around me as well as Ian's familiar shout of "federal marshals" before the pop-pop-pop of what had to be his gun.

The men were exchanging nervous glances, deciding what to do, so to help that along, I moved closer, twisting my body just enough so I was sure they could see the star on my belt.

"Federal marshal, get on your knees," I snarled. "Hands on your head!"

Ian had the *stare*—the scary military one that made people understand he'd seen worse and done worse and they wouldn't live too much longer if they didn't comply with whatever order he was giving at the time. I didn't have that stare, but what I did have was my hard, muscular physique, and I could make myself look pretty damn intimidating. Me there with the gun in a small space, my weapon already drawn and none of them even having their hands close to their holsters became the deciding factor.

All three went to their knees as the door flew open behind them, and Ian came through, gun out, blood spray on his shirt and face and in his hair.

"Clear," he reported even as he saw the girl.

"You got them?" I asked, moving slowly to the side of the bed.

"I do," he responded woodenly, and I saw how scrunched up his face was, how pained. He put them on their stomachs and pulled guns off all three.

"Make sure the two I hit are down," I ordered, not wanting them to get up and shoot at me, Ian, or the girl.

He darted over, checked for a pulse on each, and then shook his head. "They're both gone."

"Okay," I sighed, resigned to what I'd had to do.

Moving to the bed, I holstered my gun and tore off my long-sleeved shirt, covered her, then unbuckled her wrists and ankles. Scrambling to get up, she clutched at me, threw her arms around my neck, and plastered herself to my T-shirt–covered chest, trembling. I felt her intake of breath, and then came the high-pitched howl of a terrified, wounded animal.

"Fuckers," Ian swore, his voice dangerously low.

"Police!" I caught from somewhere in the house before I heard Segundo identify himself from the stairs. Then the sound of thunder, of several boots climbing before I was looking at SWAT, automatic rifles pointed at us.

"Federal marshals," Ian said, explaining who we were, raising his ID and letting them see the star on his belt.

In that moment, I realized that was why Oscar had trusted me, why his sister would not let me go: the star. Sometimes it was nice to be reminded about the badge you wore and why being one of the good guys was so very important.

CHAPTER 11

HER NAME was Sofia Guzman, and her little brother, Oscar, lost his mind when I carried her out of the building. He let out a shriek that startled everyone, crying in that way little kids did where they ended up almost heaving out sobs. I sat with them in the back of the ambulance, my arm around Sofia and Oscar holding my hand.

The EMT was a very pretty woman—Collins Bryson, long bouncy ponytail, enormous robin's-egg blue eyes, and a sprinkle of freckles across her nose—who spoke gorgeous flowing Spanish. She asked Sofia question after question, always nodding, always soothing with her tone as she checked the scared girl over.

"She wasn't raped," she said gently to me, not raising her voice. "That was supposed to happen next."

I took a shaky breath and squeezed Sofia's shoulders.

"They were going to film that," Bryson said with a cough, her voice trying to even out. "They filmed her naked. You should alert the others."

But I couldn't leave the kids, so I yelled for Segundo, who was standing with Hewitt and a couple of police officers. Ian, on the other hand, was talking to the SWAT commander, two other officers in plainclothes, I was guessing a police sergeant, and several others. He was the epicenter of the storm, and as I watched, he handed over the gun he'd used to one of the policemen, dropping it into an evidence bag along with one unused mag. He'd reloaded at some point. That was disconcerting because that meant there had to be, at a minimum, fifteen more than likely dead men in the house.

"Whose shirt is this?" Bryson asked, drawing my focus to her.

"It's mine."

She nodded. "I figured."

"I tried to look for her clothes, but she just wanted out."

"She'll never put on those clothes again, marshal. The shirt is good."

Sofia was, in fact, holding the collar over her nose, so I guessed whatever trace of my cologne was on the shirt smelled better than whatever else she had been forced to endure. Oscar shivered and burrowed into my side.

"They both have to be transported to the hospital, marshal," she pronounced. "Are you riding with them?"

"Marshal Morse and I are, yes," I responded.

"Better call him, then, because we have to go."

"Ian!" I called, and when he turned to find me, I gestured for him. He joined me at the ambulance in seconds.

"She wasn't raped."

His relief, the slight tremble, the droop of his shoulders, and the way he visibly relaxed, calmed me as well.

"They filmed her, though, so collect cell phones and find everything—any laptops, I mean, you know the drill. I hope nothing got e-mailed or... make sure they take this place down to the studs because we need to be sure there's no video of her anywhere."

"I'll question the witnesses myself. I'll find out."

"Okay, I—"

"Do we know if these kids are illegal?" the other EMT—Treschi, his name patch read—asked Bryson. She shrugged.

"Why does it matter?" Ian flared angrily. "Either way, she has to go to the hospital. What the hell?"

"Don't get all defensive, marshal, I'm one of the good guys," Treschi told my partner. "There are just hospitals that care, and some that only want the bill paid and will make long-term arrangements. If the kids are illegal, we'll pick one of those that cares."

Ian grunted, conceding nothing. "I see. Okay."

"You gotta know all the ins and outs."

"Yes, you do," he agreed but still didn't apologize. It was not his way.

"Sorry," I offered, "we're both new here to Phoenix."

Treschi moved behind me to put a butterfly bandage on the cut on Oscar's head that he had cleaned earlier, ruffling Oscar's hair when he was done. "No, you go right ahead. After the night you guys put in, you have every right."

All at once new lights, new sirens, and a stream of big black SUVs invaded each end of the alley.

Ian's glower was dark. "What the hell is the FBI doing here?"

You could always recognize Feds. While marshals tended to swagger a bit, the FBI always walked into any situation like God himself had arrived, so now things could be handled correctly. And while normally the pompous act grated on me, with the local cops there and the federal representatives outnumbered, I felt myself warming to their presence.

The suits were endless, and after only moments in the cluster of police along with Segundo and Hewitt—who had clearly done his job and called for backup—they were directed to Ian and me and so headed over.

Ian stepped in front of me, protectively, as he always did.

"Marshals," the first man said as he closed in on us, pulling a badge that clearly identified him as being with the State Department. "Do we have Sofia and Oscar Guzman?"

"We do," Ian informed him, moving sideways, no longer barring the path between him and me and the kids.

The State Department guy turned and signaled to one of the cars, and all four doors opened. A man and a woman, an older boy, and three other people climbed out and came running. All were dressed immaculately. The woman was in what I knew was Chanel from all the times I'd bought suits with one of my girlfriends; the man I guessed was Sofia's father appeared polished and crisp in Dolce & Gabbana; and the teenager was in slacks and a dress shirt with a sport coat on over that. I knew I was making assumptions about who they were, but once Oscar looked up and screamed, "Mama!", there was no question.

She was not a big person, Oscar's mother, but everyone got out of her way as she tore over to the ambulance. I would have moved, but Sofia still had a death grip on me. Oscar leaped at his mother and she grabbed him so tight, so hard, it looked painful.

"Sofia!" the older man yelled, and when she heard his call, she lifted her head off my chest and looked around for him.

There was no missing the bruises or the bloodied lip, or the haunted look in her eyes as tears welled up in them. But the relief on her little face when he was finally right there in front of her, at the rear of the ambulance, was the most heartbreaking of all.

"Papa," she whispered as she climbed into her father's arms.

When he grabbed her, the shirt rode up a bit, and I leaned over and patted Mr. Guzman's arm to direct his attention to the fact.

Instantly he turned to the other boy, who had to be her older brother, and I watched as he pulled off his sport coat, wrapped it around his sister's waist, and tied the sleeves together tight, making sure it couldn't come loose.

Sofia was telling her father everything; I heard the rush of words and my name—and Ian's, which she had asked for—and then more words that cut off when she started to cry.

After a few moments, Mr. Guzman handed Sofia off to her mother, who wrapped her daughter up in her arms and rocked her and hugged her and kissed her over and over. Mr. Guzman then scooped up Oscar and crushed him to his chest, whispering to his son, crooning his name as he kissed him.

It was a very sweet reunion, and eventually the older boy took his sister and brother in his arms, and then both parents wrapped up all their kids. Not wanting to intrude, I hopped down out of the back of the ambulance and put my hand on Ian's shoulder.

"Good job, marshal," I sighed, moving my hand to squeeze the back of his neck.

"Can we go back to the condo after this?"

I chuckled. "Why marshal," I teased. "Are you tired?"

"Fuck yeah," he grouched. "And I'd like to point out that it's still like eighty degrees or some shit out here. I hate this crap."

"You didn't have to—"

"Yes, I did," he growled. "Where you go, I go."

"And vice versa," I agreed, so wanting to kiss him, needing to. "You should be more careful when you're the first one through the door."

"I was," he assured me. "I didn't run into the room as soon as I kicked the door down."

It was as good as I was going to get.

"Miro!"

I turned and Sofia was there, banging into me, arms around my waist, Oscar following, same action on the other side. Bending, I curled over both of them and rubbed their backs.

"Marshal."

Lifting my head, I was faced with Mr. and Mrs. Guzman.

"My son says that you were the only one who stopped to help him," Mr. Guzman said.

I had no idea what I was supposed to say to that. It was a real concern, the fact that lots of people didn't stop to help kids anymore because they were afraid of being accused of child molestation. And as it happened, Oscar *had* needed help, because pedophiles were already preying on his sister.

"You have my enduring gratitude, marshal," he said gravely, glancing over at Ian. "Both you and your partner."

"I only wish we'd gotten there sooner," Ian told him.

"You responded as soon as you were apprised of the situation by my son," he said, inhaling quickly. "I could not ask for more."

Mrs. Guzman flung herself at Ian, hugged him tight, and though surprised, he gave her a quick squeeze back before she turned and grabbed me.

Mr. Guzman offered me his hand, enfolding mine in both of his, giving me a truly heartfelt thank you before doing the same with Ian.

"Your son was very brave," I told them. "He had to go a long way for such a little boy, had to remember where Sofia was and be out alone until he found help. He was amazing."

"Yes," Mr. Guzman agreed, pulling his phone from the inner breast pocket of his suit jacket. "Please, I would like both your full names and who I should contact on your behalf."

"Oh, that's really not necessary," I assured him.

His eyes lifted from the screen of his phone to my face. "Oh, but it is, marshal."

Ian coughed. "You should include Marshals Segundo and Hewitt as well," Ian suggested. "They were our backup."

Mr. Guzman cleared his throat. "Though my son does not yet speak English, only French in addition to Spanish and a few others thus far—"

"Thus far?" I chuckled. "Christ, what is he seven?"

"He's six," Mr. Guzman replied, smiling at me. "I was most recently assigned to Paris, and of course my family was with me, so my son, who has already mastered Portuguese and Italian, as well, was just beginning his English studies."

"Holy crap, he speaks four languages already?" I was in awe. "I can barely speak English!"

Mr. Guzman chortled over that, squeezing my arm as Sofia drew away from me and went to Ian. She'd watched him throw one of the men who'd hurt her down the flight of stairs when he tried to bolt after Ian told him to walk with his fingers laced behind his head. On the ground, Ian had put his foot on the guy's throat and asked him if he would and could follow directions from that point on. The man peed his pants when Ian pulled his gun and asked a second time. Sofia had watched the man cower before Ian, and so, in his arms, I knew, she felt safe. I was of the same mind when it was me there.

"My son," Mr. Guzman continued, "understood that the other two marshals were not as inclined to help him as were the two of you."

"There's protocol we violated," I disclosed. "And come tomorrow—we're gonna be made to understand the scope of that, sir."

"No," he said quickly, squinting to try and keep his eyes from filling, the battle quickly lost. "You will not."

I got a second handshake from him as I rubbed his son's head.

"What is your supervisor's name?"

I cleared my throat. "We're actually not from Phoenix, sir. We're from Chicago."

"Oh," he said, exhaling quickly. "I love Chicago. My kids particularly enjoy the Lincoln Park Zoo."

My smile was huge. "Me and my partner live maybe two blocks from there."

His sudden squint caught my eye and I instantly knew what I'd said. But he'd been talking about his family, so I talked about mine, and that included a werewolf currently eating my friends out of house and home and the man standing beside me.

"It's beautiful there," he commented and that was all.

"Yes," I agreed. "We hope to be home before it starts snowing."

He grinned at me. "You like the snow, marshal?"

"I didn't use to, but a month here has me rethinking my entire opinion on snow, sir."

"Really?"

I threw up my hands. "It's 85 degrees right now. Are you kidding?"

"It's hot," Ian chimed in irritably.

Mr. Guzman laughed at us, and that was good, better than standing there slowly coming apart because he had not been there when his kids had been assaulted by monsters.

"Spell your name and your partner's," he instructed.

I exchanged glances with Ian, but he just shrugged. There was only so much we could do.

"It's Miro, sir," I said, and I spelled both my first and last, giving him Jones and Doyle instead of the fake ones, because for starters, he deserved the truth, and secondly, Segundo and Hewitt were too far away to overhear.

"And what is your supervisor's name in Chicago?"

I cleared my throat. "His name is Chief Deputy Sam Kage, sir."

"With a K," Ian chimed in.

"Excellent," Mr. Guzman said.

"How did your son get away, sir?" I asked, because from the bits and pieces I could decipher, I knew Oscar had told him the whole story.

He took a breath. "His sister shoved him out of the car as soon as it stopped and she ordered him to run."

"Smart."

"Yes," he agreed. "She was brilliant for keeping him safe, he was good for listening to her. For once."

"It's fortunate they didn't go after him."

"They would have never caught him unless…."

No one wanted to consider what *unless* could have meant.

"I need to make sure that every cell phone is accounted for," Ian said into the sudden silence. "We can't have any pictures of your daughter leaked."

Mr. Guzman nodded.

"I'm going to follow up on that now, make sure the FBI is made aware."

"Please," he murmured.

Ian gave Sofia a last hug, turned her over to her father, made quick eye contact with me, and then jogged back to the gathered suits, all the FBI and police still talking.

"We're ready to go to the hospital," Bryson announced.

Sofia and Oscar did not want to leave me, and when it became apparent that it really would not happen without tears, I agreed to go with them and their mother to the hospital, Banner Good Samaritan Medical Center, which was not far away.

I went to find Ian first. I took hold of his bicep as I excused us both for a moment from the discussion with the LEOs.

"What?" he asked, his gorgeous blue eyes softening the moment his gaze met mine.

"Listen. I have to go to the hospital with the kids, but I'll be—"

"No," he directed in his *I know everything and it's all decided* voice that he pulled out upon occasion. "Just stay there, and I'll meet you as soon as I can."

"So stay put until you come get me?"

"Yeah."

I was exhausted, my adrenaline had bottomed out, I was responsible for killing people, and I had to turn over my gun to the Phoenix PD for processing, so now I was without a weapon until I got back to the apartment. Ian was not because he hadn't shot anyone with his Glock, but I felt vulnerable and that was not helping.

"Because I'm what, five?"

He stepped into me, close, crowding me, in my space, and while it could be mistaken for him trying to impart privileged information, it was also, very clearly, a display of dominance and possessiveness. "Just fuckin' wait for me," he growled.

My hands itched to touch him, to slide up under his shirt and caress his skin. I breathed out slowly in an effort to calm my racing heart as I watched his pulse beat in his throat. I wanted to lean in and kiss that spot, the need nearly overwhelming.

"Don't stand here and make me beg, simply do what I ask."

"Okay," I agreed, voice weak, realizing that being the entire focus of his attention was making it hard for me to breathe.

"I'll see you," Ian said before gently squeezing my elbow.

Watching him leave me was harder than I thought it would be. The only upside was that I got to ride in the back of the ambulance going to a hospital and for once I wouldn't be on the verge of death on the way. It was really sort of novel.

CHAPTER 12

GRUELING WAS the word of the night, very early morning, and then late morning. Ian never got away to collect me because he was stuck there, recounting what had occurred to the FBI and Phoenix PD, and I was at the hospital with Greg Hollister from the State Department and Efrem Lahm from Homeland Security.

"You understand how sensitive this is, marshal," Hollister said patronizingly, giving me a serious look with furrowed brows, narrowed eyes, and the knowing nod. "We needed to determine what kind of attack the Guzmans suffered because as a cultural attaché who works at the Spanish consulate, what the FBI first thought was a kidnapping and ransom ended up being a run of the mill abduction for the purpose of filming child pornography."

It was surprising that it wasn't me who lost my temper. One second I was parsing what had just come out of Hollister's mouth, and the next he was pinned to the wall outside of Sofia's hospital room with a forearm across his throat.

"Are you fucking kidding?" Lahm, blond-haired, green-eyed, and pretty Lahm, whom I had taken for easy-going, lost his shit and slammed Hollister back hard enough to make him yell. "That just happened, right? Those kids were just put through something horrific, and you just used the words *run of the mill* when you described it?"

Hollister squirmed against the wall like a trapped insect on the end of a pin.

"You better put some respect in your tone and your verbiage, Agent, or you will be treated to my displeasure."

Hollister was rapidly turning gray.

"Do you understand?"

Hollister nodded and Lahm moved fast, like coiled snake fast, and in the next moment, the man who had seemed so full of himself bent over and threw up.

I stepped back—I was wearing my Alexander McQueen black monk strap boots, and I didn't want vomit on them, after all.

"Okay," Lahm said calmly, like Hollister hadn't just bolted down the hall, looking, I assumed, for a bathroom. "Here's what we—"

"That was great," I interrupted. "You sticking up for the kids."

He crossed his arms like he was bored. "Most of those guys are pretentious pricks," he informed me. "And they're so used to dealing with heads of state, they forget how to talk to regular people."

I nodded.

"Okay, so, here's how it went down." He described how the kids' bodyguards had taken them to Bookmans over on 19th Avenue to trade in some of Oscar's PlayStation games and for Sofia to pick up more manga. Because it was such a routine outing—the kids loved the store and went often—only one member of their protection detail accompanied them. On the way back they stopped at a Circle K to get drinks, and Sofia had asked to use the bathroom. On her way out, she was grabbed and taken out the back, away from the car where the now fired bodyguard had been waiting. The man who carried her informed the clerk that his daughter was sick and had thrown up. The clerk insisted that Oscar resisting, screaming and crying while being dragged out, was a temper tantrum when he had to explain to the FBI why he'd done nothing to help the little boy who was clearly, from the video surveillance, terrified.

"Jesus," I whispered, feeling bad for Oscar all over again.

"The FBI has spoken to three of the men who lived through you and your partner's siege on the house —"

"Oh, no, it wasn't just—"

He lifted his hand to shut me up. "It looks like the plan was to move Sofia to Mexico within the next few days and sell her to a whorehouse. If Oscar had showed up without backup, he would have suffered the same fate. Clearly this has nothing to do with Homeland Security, as it was not, in fact, an act of terrorism."

"Why was the State Department here?"

"They had to make sure that the attack was not made specifically against the Spanish consulate or Guzman."

"Oh, I see."

"Once they determined it wasn't, they're off the hook too."

It was nice of him to stand there and explain it all to me.

"What the heck is this?" an orderly asked as he stopped at the puddle of vomit a few feet behind Lahm.

He glanced over his shoulder at the man. "Some drunken frat boy, man. I'm sorry."

"I'm so sorry, gentlemen," he said quickly. "I'll be right back to clean this up."

"No worries, it ain't like it's water. No one's walkin' through that."

Once the orderly was gone, Lahm turned back to me.

"So this is all the bureau now. They'll follow up on whatever the bigger picture is here, how big this operation is or isn't. You and your partner did a very good thing, marshal. You should be pleased."

I nodded as he offered me his hand.

"So," I said as he turned to go. "You think you're gonna get any crap from Hollister for putting him on the wall?"

"And he would say what? I was talking smack about a couple of kids and Lahm took offense?" His right eyebrow arched evilly. "I think not."

"Okay."

"And besides, you'd back me up, right? I just have to get out there to Chicago and track you down."

I wasn't really surprised. He was Homeland Security, after all. "You like living here in Phoenix?"

He scoffed. "I live in Washington DC. I wouldn't make it here on the surface of the sun."

I liked him. I knew we could be friends if we lived anywhere near each other. "Have a safe trip home, Agent."

"You, too, marshal," he said as he walked away from me, down the long hall.

"Miro?"

Turning, I found Oscar.

"Hey buddy," I greeted him.

He gestured for me, so I followed him back into the room.

It turned out that Sofia's left wrist was sprained, but other than that she was in good shape. Oscar was dehydrated, but other than a few cuts and bruises, he too was fine. Once Mrs. Guzman heard that, I got kissed and hugged all over again.

"I know you're the reason that both my children are still with me, Miro."

"I can't take all the credit," I assured her, because I knew that without Ian giving me backup—as always—I wouldn't have been able to save both of them.

"Yes, I know," Mrs. Guzman agreed, smiling sweetly at me, like I was dear to her. "Marshal Doyle will be in my prayers along with you for the rest of my life."

I grinned. "I appreciate that, you know. I can always use the help."

She sighed deeply as she hugged her kids.

When I finally had to leave to join Ian at the office, Mrs. Guzman took my information and put it in her phone so if she felt like it, she could call, e-mail, or text me. It was the only way the kids would let me out of the room. Their mother would have kept me had six bodyguards not shown up. They all shook my hand, and as I surveyed them, I was really glad I meant the family no harm. The men were enormous, tall and muscular, and each one carried some kind of firearm. I wouldn't have wanted to mess with them. I left knowing Mrs. Guzman and her sweet kids were in safe hands.

The FBI sent a team to pick me up and take me back to their field office where Ian, Segundo, and Hewitt waited. We were joined by Brooks Latham, who was explaining to Supervisory Special Agent Zane Calhoun that his men had followed all procedures and that Ian and I were incorrigible. He'd disciplined us yesterday afternoon for a different incident, after all, and he was very concerned that with the clear lack of discipline we were used to operating under that—

"Hold up," Calhoun said, smiling, having raised a finger to get Latham to shut up. "You think that Chief Deputy Sam Kage is soft on discipline?"

"I—"

Calhoun's snort of laughter sounded funny coming from such a serious-looking man. "I so wish we could get on a plane tonight so you could tell him that in person. I would pay good money to see that."

"I—you know their boss?"

I was interested in that answer myself.

"I do," he replied, nodding, "and if I told you how many times I wanted to break protocol when we worked an op together and how many times he recited the book to me.... Except for once," he added, like he was remembering something before he was back, present and focused. "You'd pass out. That man is a walking manual, so I suspect that Smith and Morse here are very well versed in the procedures of being a marshal."

"Yes, but begging your pardon, I think—"

"Tonight's incident was a special circumstance," Calhoun said, glancing from me to Ian and back to Latham. "And I have a remedy for the situation in either case."

We all remained quiet as he turned toward a knock on the door. In came two men with sealed plastic bags. Ian, me, Segundo, and Hewitt were all given one, and inside the bags were our guns.

"These have all been processed, gentlemen, and your accounts of who you shot at and why are now in the record. While it will take another few days for you to all be cleared, your weapons are being returned at this time."

"That's fast," Ian commented.

"We're the FBI," Calhoun said smugly.

A woman came in then, walked over to Ian, and delivered the Heckler & Koch P30L he had used last night.

"This isn't mine," Ian stated.

"You used it," Calhoun told him, "and we ran ballistics on it and it's clean. The serial number is gone, burned off with acid, so the gun is completely untraceable. I'm giving it to you because it will play well undercover for what I'd like you and your partner to do. At the conclusion of the op, you'll return it to us and we'll have it destroyed."

"I'm sorry?" Ian asked.

"What part of returning the gun didn't you—"

"No, sir, not that," Ian expressed quickly. "You said undercover?"

"I spoke to Sam Kage, and he gave me permission to move you onto my task force with the DEA. You need to collect your things because I need you two in place and ready to go tomorrow morning."

I was going to bitch... DEA... *no*... but Ian shot me a look to shut me up.

"You—what?" Latham sounded panicked.

Calhoun pivoted to face him. "I'm taking these two marshals off your hands, and as our office has, as you know, taken over the Guzman case"—his arms crossed quickly, daring Latham to speak—"you can go back to work tomorrow, business as usual."

Latham opened his mouth to protest.

"That will be all, marshal."

Latham was excused, and whereas my boss—and me and Ian, for that matter—would have never taken shit like that from the FBI, I wasn't sure if Latham had any idea what he did and didn't have to put up with. Not that he cared, though. In his opinion, Ian and I were clearly trouble—better to not have to deal with us. I was sure he was pleased.

"Sit down, gentlemen. We have a lot to go over," Calhoun said and then told one of his aids to bring in Orton Taggart from the other room. "And I want you to meet your new fake boss."

Combined FBI/ DEA drug ops. Had to love them.

THE FEDS had a lot of cars at their disposal, and Ian finally decided on a 2012 Cadillac Escalade ESV because, as muscle, we needed room to carry lots of people in a little higher-end car to make the story stick. It seemed like a good choice to me.

"Latham hates you both," Kage told us over the phone on the way to the JW Marriott Phoenix Desert Ridge Resort & Spa. "And I trust Calhoun. It sounds like a simple op in cooperation with the DEA, undercover on a drug dealer as bodyguards. You're basically just following the front man in."

"We met him," I replied. "Taggart. He seemed okay."

He was young, was what he was, but he was supposed to be playing flashy, punk, from big money, used to dealing with the Mexican cartels bringing drugs across the border into Texas. The background was put in place, but it didn't need to be too deep; it wasn't a two-year or five-year deep-cover op. It was set up as a quick bust because DEA had caught the real drug trafficker, Chris Bello, and to skip jail time, he rolled on all his friends. So now they were introducing Brock Huber—Taggart—as a new player on the scene with a solid reputation because he had people the Feds had leaned on to vouch for him. More importantly, his bank account was huge.

"It's a straightforward op," my boss continued. "Calhoun just needs new faces to go along with his agent. You guys fit the bill."

"Yessir," I agreed for both Ian and me.

"I told Calhoun that you could start tomorrow. I can't imagine you've slept yet."

God bless him, sometimes he was actually human.

"And you can't run in the heat, Jones."

Of course they'd told him about that. "No sir."

"Pull your head out of your ass and hydrate. You're in Arizona, gentlemen."

I took it back—he was the devil.

"Touch base with Calhoun when you get to the hotel so he knows you're there, get some food, sleep tonight, be ready to go in the morning."

He didn't wait for me to acknowledge him or agree, he simply hung up. I turned to look at Ian. "His communication skills are seriously fucked up."

He snickered. "So are yours, M."

"Mine?"

Ian stopped the car on Lincoln Drive, pulling off the road into the dirt under the shade of several trees. He turned and cupped my cheek in his hand. "I want to be alone with you so badly my skin hurts."

There was a time when he would have never admitted to that. I was so pleased it had passed. Being told I was needed and wanted was so much better. "Me too."

He grinned. "Tell me what's wrong."

I squinted. "Besides feeling like my life is on fast forward and that we're stuck in an oven on broil because a psychopath is after me?"

"Yeah."

I took a breath. "Can I wait until I sleep a little?"

He shook his head.

"Why not?"

"Because whatever it is, is making you weird and I don't like it."

I was hesitant to say.

"I know you want to get married," he said, defaulting to what the issue had been for months. "But I'm just—"

"It's not that," I sighed.

"Oh?"

"No," I said, my voice rising in panic. Ian never got to think that I didn't want him. "I mean, clearly I want that, but that's not what's eating at me."

"Then speak."

"It's not that big a deal."

"Fine, if it's not important, then just tell me," he whispered, moving his hand, stroking the nape of my neck.

"Okay," I said on an exhale. "A long time ago, I fucked Wojno."

He made a face. "Yeah, I know that."

I was surprised. "You did?"

His shrug with the accompanying curl of lip made my stomach clench as I took hold of the front of his shirt. "Sure."

"How?"

"This was from when you were a cop, right? When you first put Hartley in jail? You were working with the FBI then."

I nodded.

"Yeah, so when we first became partners, that was still going on, and he called a couple of times," he revealed, eyes on my mouth. "And when I asked him what it was about, he said he just needed to talk to you and to tell you not to blow him off."

"Yeah, but that could have been about anything."

"Not with how persistent he was," he apprised me, leaning into my space, his lips hovering close to mine. "When you need something, cop to cop, if someone isn't helping you out, you call their boss. With how many times he called your desk and your cell and not one call to Kage—I knew what it was about."

"You're very clever," I said before I pressed my mouth to his.

He tipped my head back and attacked me, his tongue invading, tasting, rubbing as he kissed me, hard and thorough.

I lost myself in his hunger, in his urgency and taste, his hands all over me as he tugged and yanked until my shirt was rucked up and my pants were open. "What're you doing?"

"Stupid fuckin' question," he growled before he bent over my lap and took me down the back of his throat.

"Ian!" I cried out, back bowing, jolting under him and burying myself in the liquid heat of his mouth.

He made the suction powerful, his lips stretching around me, and the sounds that came out of him as his mouth slid up and down on my shaft, along with the bruising grip on my thigh, were overwhelming.

"I can't—Ian!"

A shiver raced through my body as I came, frozen for a moment, my hand palming the back of his head as he swallowed.

"Jesus," I moaned as he laved me clean, finally rising, his tongue at the corner of his mouth, licking away the very last drop of me. "Come here."

His smile was wicked as I claimed his lips, hands on his face, keeping him still. One kiss becoming another and another until he was squirming in my grip.

"We should—" He gasped as I got into his pants and wrapped my hand around his hard, drooling cock. "—go to the hotel."

"Tinted glass," I reminded him. "Get in the back."

He didn't hesitate; he scrambled between the seats and dropped to the floor in front of the next row that thankfully had been pushed all the way back, giving us room.

"Take everything off."

"No, we—" He grunted, rolling over on his stomach, lifting to his hands and knees. "Just fuck me like this so—"

"Are you in charge?" I asked angrily, my voice thick with desire. "Tell me if you are."

He exhaled sharply and got to his knees, pulled the Hattington wingtip boots off his feet—they were mine—and then stripped. Only his socks stayed on, and that would have made me smile if I was not so caught up in looking at him.

Sometimes I examined all the many scars that crisscrossed his olive skin, and my heart hurt. I wanted to hunt down and kill everyone who had scarred him. But other times, the marks made me that much hotter, as his power and survival instinct right there on display was sexier than anything.

"Miro," he rasped as I reached over him to the seat for my bag, digging into the side pocket and retrieving the lube.

"Open your legs for me," I demanded, "and hold on to your thighs."

Immediate compliance. The sight of him, ready, his hooded eyes, panting, flush on his chest and neck as he waited for me, made my mouth dry. How in the world I'd ever gotten Ian Doyle to not only see me but want me was mind-blowing.

He caught his breath when I was naked, too, and when my slick fingers slid over his puckered opening, he bucked off the carpeted floor of the SUV.

"Gonna go slow," I promised as I curled over his hard, muscular body, wanting his mouth and his warm skin on mine.

"No," he whispered, wiggling under me, notching his entrance with the head of my cock. "Fuck, no, Miro, I need you now."

I kissed him hard at the same time as I pressed inside the tight, hot passage, not stopping until I was buried in his body.

The garbled noises he made as he held himself spread open for me, his groans hitched, caught on the sharp edges of his short gasps, and his muscles flexing around my length all urged me to move, but instead I waited, remained still, letting his body get used to me.

"Make me," he husked. "Miro—fuckin' make me."

After easing free just a fraction, I thrust home, pounding down into him, pegging his gland, making him shudder with the sensation and howl my name. He made me feel ridiculously powerful, and my smug rumble was loud in the small space.

"Pleased with yourself?"

His voice was hoarse, and I liked the sound, gravelly and deep. "Yeah," I answered, dragging myself from his channel this time, and then again, in and out, screwing him slow so he could feel me.

"Miro, could you just—fuck!"

I pulled out and rolled him to his hands and knees before I pistoned back inside, using him as hard as he craved.

"Don't," he warned me, and I understood. I was taking a chance with my life if I stopped.

"Ian, I can't... you feel too good."

"I want you right here," he pleaded, his voice barely registering. "It feels like I can't—like you're pulling away."

And I had been, little by little, scared to death of him coming between me and Hartley. We had resolved the geography issue because yes, he was here with me, but emotional distance was a whole other thing. Because I loved him, the idea of him getting hurt was making me instinctively guarded, and I was distancing myself without even meaning to.

For instance, normally I would have insisted that we go home alone after a rough day, but just the night before, I'd wanted a buffer in Segundo and Hewitt. We would have eaten together, it would have been intimate, but I didn't do that at all. I was filling up our time, taking him to restaurants with me when he wanted to veg on the couch on the off chance that I'd start to worry. But now Ian was telling me he felt it and he wouldn't have it. Not ever.

Neither would I.

Pressing along his back, hand on his shoulder so I could drive into him and hold him still at the same time, I ordered him to grab his dick and jerk off.

"Miro—"

"Now!" I roared, demanding his submission.

I felt his inner walls clamp down, ripple around my length as he came, violently, semen splattering the carpet beneath him. I plunged deep, climaxing just as hard before collapsing on top of him and then lifting his hand from his dick to my lips so I could lick clean each of his cum-coated fingers.

"God, Miro, that's so fuckin' hot."

I loved the taste of him.

He turned to look at me over his shoulder, and I kissed him, long and slow, sucking on his tongue, tasting him all over again.

His whole body thrummed beneath mine, the shudder that ran through him causing his muscles to spasm, squeezing me almost painfully tight once more.

Finally easing free of him, I went down on my back, ready to fall asleep right there in the parked Cadillac, the air conditioner thankfully still running full blast.

"No, don't lie down," he cautioned me softly, twisting around to straddle my hips, hands splayed out on either side of my head as he bent forward to stare down at me. "You'll never get up."

"Drive to the hotel and carry me to the room," I mumbled, my eyes fluttering shut.

"No." He snickered. The sound was so joyful I opened my eyes to see his smile, the wicked one that curled his kiss-swollen lips and arched an eyebrow.

He was so beautiful—sometimes just looking at him took my breath away. "You walk to the room, I'll order room service. We'll eat and sleep and do this again."

"We could swim," I suggested. "I hear they have a nice pool."

"I think they have, like, eight or something."

"Eight's too many," I said to be contrary.

He leaned over and kissed me. "Whatever we do, you gotta put your clothes on first."

I made a noise somewhere between a groan and a purr.

He trailed kisses along my jaw to the side of my neck. "The quicker you get up, the faster we can be eating and sleeping."

That got me moving.

CHAPTER 13

I DIDN'T see the pools. I didn't see anything but exactly what Ian said: I saw the room, the guy who brought up room service, the shower, the bed, and a great view of the mountains. That was all.

I listened as Ian talked to Calhoun, and after I ate and cleaned up, I pulled on sleep shorts and passed out in Ian's arms. His breath on the back of my neck, his strong arms wrapped tight around me, and his thighs pressed to the backs of mine was all I needed. I slept hard, but when Ian woke me in the night, rolled me to my back, slathered my cock with lube, and rode me, I came alive for that.

Holding his thighs tight, I watched him above me, bathed in moonlight, head back, eyes closed, lips parted as his breath started and stopped, and I knew that whatever I had to do to keep him for the rest of my life, I would.

"You're so fuckin' stuck with me," I told him.

"Yes," he agreed, spurting over my chest as he came. I followed seconds later, filling him up, much to his happiness. He loved it—it grounded him somehow, showed ownership, and he craved that. For my part, I was simply happy. I almost had everything I ever wanted; now all we had to do was hope they found Hartley soon. After close to a month, I was so ready to go home.

Ian was in the shower when I woke up to the sound of knocking. I ducked into the bathroom, told him someone was at the door, and shut it before answering. Standing outside in the hall was our contact, DEA Agent Orton Taggart, posing as Brock Huber, high-profile drug dealer from Dallas.

He came in and I closed the door behind him, taking in his surfer-cut blond hair, the navy blue Hugo Boss suit, and his black wingtips.

"No tie?" I asked.

"I'm keeping it casual," he said, patting my abdomen as he moved in closer to me. "Hey, man, I'm counting on you and Morse to keep me alive on this op, right?"

Hey, man? Christ. "No worries," I assured him, hopefully keeping the annoyance out of my voice. "So where are we going this morning?"

"The guy we're meeting is Luis Cano, and he's sending guys to pick us up in the bar in twenty minutes. Are you and your partner ready to go?"

"Always," I assured him.

He squinted at me. "Is that what you're wearing?"

"No," I said irritably, since I was in my sleep shorts and a T-shirt. "Obviously not."

"Well, let's go, man."

It was way too much familiarity and trying to sound street.

In the bar lounge twenty minutes later, I was having coffee and scarfing down a croissant along with Ian, and Taggart was smiling.

"What?" Ian asked.

"You two clean up nice."

Ian did look stunning in his brown Gucci suit with a brown pinstripe dress shirt underneath. He looked uncomfortable, as he always did in anything but fatigues or jeans, but he wore it well and that was all that mattered. According to him, the best accessories he had on were the two gun holsters—one under his jacket, the other around his ankle.

"You look better than he does," Taggart said, smiling at me, leaning forward into my space. "What is this, Armani?"

I was wearing my gray three-piece suit with a white dress shirt underneath and, unlike Ian, I had on a tie. It was yellow, as was the pocket square, and I knew I looked good because my boyfriend had made that noise in the back of his throat when I came out of the bedroom to head down to the bar with him and Taggart.

As we were leaving the room, Ian let Taggart out and then closed the door before I could follow him. I turned and he'd stepped in close, bumping his nose along my jaw, inhaling me.

"Yes?"

"I should take you places where you wear suits more often."

"Why's that?" I fished.

"You know why," he said, his voice husky, coaxing.

"You like what you see."

"I do." He took a step back, his gaze running down my body. "Very much."

"I'll leave it on 'til you take it off."

"Yeah, that'd be good," he said, coughing, opening the door right before Taggart knocked.

"What the fuck are you doing?" he huffed at Ian.

"Following you," Ian growled back, and because of the ice in his tone and the chill in his gaze, Taggart shut up, pivoted, and walked away. It was the smart choice.

"Smith?"

I came back sharply to the present. "Sorry. What?"

"Is this Armani?" Taggart questioned again.

"Yeah."

"So, Smith, you—"

"Oh, here we go," Ian interrupted as two men stepped up to the table.

Eventually we would meet with Wilson Roan, but before that his second-in-command, Cano, had to vet us to make sure we were who we said we were.

We were greeted by the men who were clearly bodyguards, like Ian and I were pretending to be, and then escorted outside and put into a Maserati Kubang SUV that was roomier inside than I thought it would be for one made by a sports car company.

They drove us to Paradise Valley, a stunning area full of million-dollar homes, finally turning onto E. Caballo Drive and rolling through the enormous wrought iron gates of a house I could never hope to afford unless I won a lottery.

"Holy crap," I said under my breath as we all got out of the car.

"This is how the other half lives, M," Ian teased, bumping me with his shoulder as we trailed behind the others.

"This is incredible," I went on, glancing around. "Are you seeing this?"

He huffed out a breath. "I'd rather have the townhouse with you."

"Ian, come on." I prodded him, since we were walking well behind the others. "Are you looking at this? I bet they have like twelve thousand square feet or something."

He shrugged. "I don't care. I don't need a house like this. I have what I need, what I want. Don't you?"

I did. "Well, yeah, but it's still nice to dream."

"I did dream, now I live in it."

Fucking Ian. "Why you gotta say shit like that when you know we're here and I can't do nothin' about it?"

He shrugged. "'Cause it's true."

God.

"Man, could you go for some pizza or what?" he grumbled, breaking the spell.

"One month and you're already going through withdrawal?"

"One month?" he repeated like I was nuts. "I've been dying for pizza since we fuckin' got here."

I chuckled and we followed the others inside.

It looked like a resort.

Hardwood floors, vaulted ceilings, a formal dining room, a living room that opened out onto a palatial patio that descended into an enormous sand entrance pool with two fountains and a waterfall that looked like it belonged in some Roman temple. A bar/lounge and a wine room, all of it open, with misters and ceiling fans. It was simply the most beautiful home I'd ever been in.

Ian was squinting in the way he had that let you know he was not impressed, was a little bored, and mostly was ready to go. What was funny was that it fit the stereotypical bodyguard image he was supposed to be presenting.

"You're really in character," I baited him.

"Shut up."

"So where is he?" Taggart asked the two men who brought us to the house. "Where's Cano?"

"Here," a man answered as he rose out of the pool.

Luis Cano was a very handsome man. He was tall with a swimmer's build and lean muscles, and his skin was tanned a gorgeous golden brown. Dark eyes and hair made an impression as he smiled at Taggart.

"Welcome to my home, Mr. Huber. May I offer you and your men some refreshment?"

"Whatever you're having," Taggart answered solicitously. "And just for me, nothing for my men."

Cano nodded and then gave both his guys and Ian and me a dismissive wave. "Please, gentlemen, take a walk around the pool. There are things to see. I keep my house stocked with all manner of delights."

I didn't want to know, so I took up a position between the sitting area where Taggart was standing and the patio, and Ian went to the opposite side.

"Really, gentlemen," Cano directed with deliberate sternness, "go for a stroll."

I couldn't argue, and since Taggart seemed reasonably safe, I walked around the pool toward the cabanas, and Ian went in the opposite direction toward the women sunbathing on padded lounge chairs. I watched them all check him out as he walked by, and I would have called him over to me—because I really had not yet learned to not be jealous when others openly leered at him—but a blast of laughter caught my attention.

Moving around the side of one of the cabanas, I found a woman in a bikini being held down and groped by a man as five others stood around and watched. She was struggling and the men were laughing and the guy on top of her was trying to take off her bottoms.

"Get off her," I commanded, moving quickly over to them.

"Oh, no, man, it's okay," one of the others told me. "She's for us, like the others. That's how it is here."

"The hell it is," I barked, reaching out and grabbing the guy on top of the girl by the hair and wrenching him sideways so I could drag her off the futon with my other hand.

"What the fuck?" Another of the men yelled as I shoved the girl behind me, shielding her.

"Ian!" I called, less concerned with the number of them than with my ability to keep the girl safe. "Step back," I cautioned them.

"It's just fun, asshole," another guy said. "She likes it, they all do."

"Fuck that," I said flatly as Ian appeared at my side, gun drawn— the new one, compensator already attached.

They all put their hands up at the same time the curtain shielding them from the patio was pulled. Cano and Taggart and the men who had brought us to the house all stood there.

"What's going on here?" Cano asked me icily.

"No, Luis," the girl said as she walked out from behind me, reaching for the man who had been groping her.

He took her hand, kissed it, and drew her into his arms, where he hugged her tight. They both then turned to Cano.

I was at a loss.

"What the fuck is going on?" Ian asked as he holstered his gun.

Cano turned to the woman. "Tell me."

She pointed at me. "He came right in, didn't wait, didn't let anyone explain, just got Emilio off me and put himself between me and the others."

"And the other?"

"He came when his partner called, no question, ready to shoot, to help him and save me."

Cano exhaled quickly and then gave Ian and me his attention. "I apologize, gentlemen, but I've had nine men come to my home like your boss here, Mr. Huber, to try and help me move my product in the US. The issue is, the men who come with those who would do business with me are not honorable."

He was testing us, but I was confused as to why.

"I have had my sister, Marisol, and her fiancé, Emilio, play out this scene many times, and sadly most men who have come to my house have wanted to join in on the rape, have wanted to have her when Emilio was done, or have suggested much worse." He put up his hands, gave us a smile. "I have no issue with any act people agree to willingly, but I cannot have men in my employ or do business with men who would lower themselves to the mindset of a pack of dogs."

It made sense to me.

"So," he announced, turning to Taggart, offering his hand. "Your men have passed my test, you have cleared my background check, and guys I trust vouched for you. So tonight I'll take you to see Wilson so you two can talk business."

"Excellent," Taggart agreed. "What time would you like us here?"

Cano squinted at him. "You're already here. We'll spend the day together and then go for dinner at his place out in Cave Creek."

So he trusted us… just not enough to let us out of his sight.

"That sounds fantastic," Taggart said gamely, rubbing his hands together. "I didn't get breakfast. Can we have some brunch?"

Cano seemed very pleased with "Huber" being so agreeable.

IT WAS easy for Ian and me to cover our lack of eating and drinking and flirting with the fact that we were on duty.

"My men are also here to protect me," Cano said suggestively. "You need to loosen up and partake." He was offering food, alcohol, pot, and blow. "Only you two are sitting here ready to shoot."

"Begging your pardon," Ian explained, "you live here, sir. Our boss does not."

Cano nodded, the logic was sound. "You look like ex-military to me."

Ian scoffed. "Do I?"

"Yes, and I know the breed well. I have many of them working for me at home."

Ian had an opening, but to ask any more questions, to say *oh, so where do you call home* would not have been received well. There was no such thing as an informal chat with a drug dealer.

We spent the day watching people swim, drinking bottled water, and refusing lines of blow, highball glasses of whisky, and frosty mugs of beer. Cano passed out joints, and to not get busted, Taggart had to smoke one. He also had to imbibe a few drinks to keep his cover in place. The good news was, he had taken the pills to help keep him sober and focused, but it was up to Ian and me to watch his back. Neither of us took our eyes off him.

We caravanned out to Cave Creek about six; turned off on 26th Place, twisted and turned down other roads I couldn't see the street signs for, and finally hit a private paved road before arriving at open gates guarded by men armed with AK-47s. A guy in a suit with an iPad looked like he was checking names on a guest list. I really hoped that the tracer Taggart had somewhere on his body was working.

"Here we are, gentlemen," Cano announced as the car stopped and the driver rolled down the window so words could be exchanged.

It seemed so serene and quiet at the gate, but once we reached the house, it was lit pools and an enormous bar outside, and strobe lights and a dance floor inside. A bar stood at each end of the ballroom we walked through.

"It's like a Roman orgy in here," Taggart commented loudly, laughing and clapping, Cano's arm slung over his shoulder as they moved through the crowd together.

Then we filed out one of the doors to another pool and a quieter area, then through an underground grotto that emptied out into a private area.

Ian and I kept pace with them, and when we were finally at the end of our quest, I was not surprised that the man himself, Wilson Roan, was sitting with a small group of men watching three very beautiful women have sex. Now I understood what Sodom and Gomorrah had probably looked like. It was definitely as close as I would ever get.

As we neared, Taggart was obnoxious—as he was supposed to be, it was the part he was playing—and catcalled and clapped. It changed the ambience from sultry and sensual, more art than fucking, to flat-out porn. The women themselves were clearly not amused.

Roan was older, handsome, with lines on his weathered face and sun-bleached hair shot through with strands of silver. He was clean-shaven and wore a gorgeous black bespoke suit with a black dress shirt underneath. He was sitting between two younger men, and as we approached, he glanced up, saw Taggart, saw me, saw Ian, and then returned to Taggart, the guy he was supposedly ready to do business with.

They made small talk as Ian and I took up flanking positions on either side of Taggart, and as soon as Roan clarified that the drugs were on the property and ready to go if the money was, in fact, also in play, Ian turned the dial on the dive watch he was wearing, triggering the signal for the breach.

We had been wanded and searched when we entered the compound, our weapons had been confiscated, and we had been patted down just on the off chance someone missed something—which they had. Everyone watched a lot of TV and actually thought the bad guys were as well equipped as the good guys. It was really not the case. Government to government, that was problematic. Had Ian and I been sneaking onto some base in Moscow or in Beijing, they would have caught us. But this operation was not high-tech. It looked like an episode of *Miami Vice*—not that any of us were cool enough to be Don Johnson from back in the day.

So Ian twisted the bezel on the Rolex Submariner he'd been given as a prop, and in so doing, made it rain DEA agents, FBI, state police, Phoenix PD, and SWAT personnel twenty minutes later, just as Taggart and Roan had begun toasting.

We did our parts, got down on our knees, fingers laced behind our heads, and accused Roan and Cano and everyone else of setting us up. As we were cuffed and led away, Taggart blasted both Roan and Cano, swearing that neither one of them would last a day in prison once his father found out what had happened. He then started screaming that he himself would not serve a day behind bars.

It was impressive; he never once fell out of character, even when the state police officers were rough with him. The only people who knew we weren't criminals were the FBI and DEA agents, and they were too busy taking Roan and Cano into custody to care what was done with us on the way from the house to the cars.

As Ian was being dragged away in cuffs after Taggart, I realized I was going in an opposite direction.

"Hey, what the fuck?" I snarled at the officers walking me toward a van. "I'm supposed to go with them."

Ian heard me, strained to turn around, but only succeeded in getting a club to the abdomen as he and Taggart were thrown into the back of a government-issue black-tinted–window SUV. Once he was in there, I couldn't see him anymore, and so, figuring my night had just gotten really long, I stopped fighting and let them take me to the scary stalker van, the one every woman in every police drama was kidnapped in.

As the door rolled open, I was surprised to see Agent Wojno.

"What the hell?" I asked before I was shoved hard and fell face-first onto the floor of the van. Rolling over quickly, sprawled at his feet, I glared up at him for a moment until I realized how horrible he looked. "Cillian?"

I had not used his first name since we'd gone to bed so very long ago, but it snapped him out of whatever was wrong with him.

"What's the matter and what're you doing here?"

He squinted. "I'm so sorry."

"About what?" I asked as the van door rolled shut behind me.

"Me."

Jolting, I twisted around, and there hovering over me was Dr. Craig Hartley. I didn't even see anyone else and definitely missed whoever shoved a needle into my thigh.

"He's sorry about me," Hartley said, tipping his head and smiling. "Because, my dear Miro, he's the leak."

I tried to process that, tried to yell, tried moving at all, but everything sort of ran like raindrops streaming down glass windows. Everything dripped and was simply lost in a smear of color before I saw nothing at all.

CHAPTER 14

WHEN I read about waterboarding, and even when Ian described it to me, how it was done, I had always kind of thought it was mind over matter. I figured I could take short gulps of air, breathe shallow, and not get too much liquid in my lungs. I'd never been so wrong about anything in my life. What was in my head and what actually happened were night-and-day different.

I never fought so hard in my life.

When water poured down my nose, when I was drowned and held down at the same time, I screamed myself hoarse.

My brain said I was drowning. I heaved for oxygen, my throat was raw, my coughing wet, and the terror of it—that I was dying, that I could not hold my breath another second—was a total mindfuck.

They did it over and over, and even when I inhaled to breathe, it felt like the soaked towels were smothering me.

When they finally let me up, I was dumped sideways off the cot and down onto the icy cement, sprawled there in my water- and urine-soaked dress pants. I'd never thought I'd be the type to piss myself, but the panic and adrenaline were too much for my bladder. I rolled over quickly and vomited until there was nothing left but bile, then curled into a fetal position. I wasn't surprised when I started retching again moments later.

They never even asked me a question.

WOJNO SHOWED up after I was stripped naked, hosed off, and shackled to the ceiling of a small ten by ten cell. There were bars above me, so the only place to see anything but concrete was if I tipped my head back and looked up.

I was having trouble focusing on him, so I knew something funny was running through my system. "What'd they give me?" I asked, my words slurring when I spoke.

"Some lorazepam to calm you down and—"

"No. Before, to knock me out," I insisted, wanting to know.

"It was hydroxyzine pamoate," Hartley said as the cell door swung open and he came in. "But don't worry, Miro, I would never give you anything bad."

He was wearing a patterned three-piece suit that was a mixture of brown houndstooth and nailhead on a cream background with a six-button vest, paisley tie, and a pale blue shirt. He looked like he should have been on his way to the opera or some other high-class endeavor.

"Oh no?" I said, trying to keep my voice level.

The scalpel Hartley had in his right hand was terrifying.

"No," he assured me, walking over and stopping beside Wojno. "I'm actually the only one here who doesn't want to do something despicable to you."

His hair had been cut since he was in prison, back to the way it had been on the outside: thick blond hair with short sides, the longer top combed back and slightly to the side. He had always looked like he should have been on the cover of a romance novel.

"Like?" I asked.

He came forward, close, and then slowly reached out and put his hand flat on my chest, over my heart.

"Hartley?"

He cleared his throat as his hand slid down my abdomen. "Some of them wanted to rape you."

I squinted and tipped my head to the side in disbelief, causing him to make a face like he'd smelled something horrible and then shake his head with a tsking noise for good measure.

"I know, can you imagine? Me? Raping anyone or allowing anyone to ever be raped in my presence?" He shuddered. "Horrible."

At least there wouldn't be that. "What else?"

"Well, apparently the cot that you were on the first day, when they put the water down you—if we clipped battery cables to it, we could send great currents of electricity through your body."

"But you didn't like that idea?" I hoped.

"Your heart," he said, like we were at dinner somewhere, his voice mild as he reached down and took gentle hold of my flaccid cock. "I don't want to accidentally put you into cardiac arrest. That would be devastating."

I worked hard to remain calm even as my skin felt like it was crawling with ants.

"I will not have anything harm the inside of you, only the outside."

That was not comforting.

He smoothed his hand back up to my abdomen. "Your skin is so smooth, do you know that? And you keep your body in exquisite condition, marshal."

I stayed quiet as he walked around behind me, trailing his hand over my skin.

"Agent Wojno said you're good in bed. I asked him."

My eyes flicked to Wojno, who looked pained.

"I wanted to know what kind of lover you were."

"Why?"

"Because one can tell quite a bit about another by how he treats the strangers he beds. Don't you think?"

"I guess," I answered levelly, even though his hand slid down my spine to my ass and gripped it tight.

"This is so hard and firm," he whispered, caressing me. "You never let anyone have it?"

I cleared my throat because it was filling with swallowed phlegm again, the lingering effects of waterboarding. "No."

"Not even Marshal Doyle?"

I was silent.

"Oh, come on," Hartley said, hand on my shoulder, still behind me. "I know you two are an item. Agent Wojno says he's going completely out of his mind as we speak."

I pinned Wojno with my stare. "Why?"

He gestured at Hartley. "You know why."

"Are you blackmailing him?" I asked Hartley about Wojno, even as I felt the needle in the side of my neck. I should have known he had more goodies in his suit jacket.

"Of course," he said as he traced a pattern on my back. "Tell him."

Wojno took a breath. "I told him you were being transferred to Phoenix."

"No," Hartley husked as he shifted to stand at my side.

I was having trouble focusing, and my head fell forward so that I was looking at Hartley's Cole Haan Brogue Medallion Double Monkstrap brown shoes. "Huh," I grunted.

"What?" Hartley asked, sounding interested.

"Those are like the ones you wore in court that time."

"Yes," he replied delightedly. "They are. I wore them for you, as we share an interest in tasteful footwear."

I tried to nod, but I couldn't lift my head. "Yeah, we do."

"That pair of Jo Ghost boots you had on when I took you were lovely."

"Thanks," I slurred out.

"How do you feel?"

"How do you want me to feel?"

"I want you numb before I have you beaten."

"Why? And why the waterboarding?"

"You were a bit high-handed with me upon occasion, so, like a dog, you have to learn your place."

"So... beating," I murmured.

"Yes."

"But you don't want me to feel it."

"Of course not."

I scoffed. "That makes no sense."

"To you."

"To anybody."

He stepped forward again, and I felt the pressure of his lips on my shoulder before his teeth. I saw his pristine shoe between my two bare, dirty feet. The large drop of blood that appeared a moment later contrasted beautifully with the deep brown tan color.

"Did you feel that cut?"

"No." I answered truthfully because I suspected that without the drugs, whatever he was doing would hurt.

"That's excellent, because I need something of yours."

"Like?"

"A token, really, but it must be wholly your own."

I coughed.

"Try not to move," he cautioned me.

"You're gonna get your shoes dirty," I mentioned as the droplets began to rain down and Wojno retched hard.

"I don't mind," Hartley assured me as a door opened and another man walked in with a tray of surgical tools. "I just need a saw for a moment."

It got quieter in the room as the floor blurred, going in and out of focus. I felt detached from my own body, only loosely tethered. "Am I dying now?"

"Oh, not at all, I promise you."

He was a surgeon, after all. "Okay."

"Did that hurt?" He was checking on me.

"I feel... pressure."

"Excellent," he said before he repeated whatever he was doing.

The sound of Wojno puking was the last thing I heard.

I WAS stiff when I woke up, and my head felt like it was wrapped in gauze. Everything was muffled and I was on my stomach on the cot, head turned to the right, arms and legs back in the straps.

"Try not to move," Wojno said, and the metal frame of the cot creaked as he perched on the edge beside me. His hand moved in my hair, and even though it was him, the guy who'd betrayed me, it was comforting, and my eyes fluttered shut. "You lost a lot of blood when he operated."

"Operated?"

"It was fast. Are you in pain?"

"Where?"

"Rib cage?"

I couldn't tell. "Something's in my arm," I managed to get out even though my tongue felt like it was swollen too big for my mouth.

"Yeah, you've got antibiotics in one arm and glucose in the other. He really doesn't want you to die."

"Until he's done," I concluded.

"Yeah... until then."

"Did he cut my back?"

"He cut *into* your back."

"For what?"

"I don't—he made sure you stopped bleeding. He used that surgical glue."

It was hard to think. "He's… biting me."

"Yes."

"Did he have me beaten?"

"Yes."

"I bet I look like tenderized meat."

"You peed blood earlier."

"Well, you take enough kidney punches and that'll happen."

"Yes," he agreed sadly. "God, I hope the bites don't scar."

I chuckled. "They won't have time. I'll be dead before they do."

He sounded like he was about to cry. "I don't—things could—"

"Just don't let me be dead and missing, all right? Don't do that to Ian."

His breath caught. "You're in love with him."

"No," I lied. Because we were not friends and I would not have him tell Hartley, who would go after Ian as well. "But he's my partner. Hartley's got it wrong. We're not together."

"Yeah, but—"

"Please, whatever happens, make sure you find me and tell him or make sure he finds me. I don't wanna be missing."

"Okay," he whispered.

I rested for a few minutes. Just that much talking and I was ready to pass out.

"You didn't ask me why."

I knew why. He was being blackmailed.

"I'm the one who told Hartley's friend when he was coming to the hospital. I'm the one who got her killed by getting him out."

Of course he had. He was the leak.

"Okay."

"Don't you want to know why?"

He needed to confess.

"Yeah, tell me."

"I covered up a case when I was a cop in Chicago."

"Go on," I got out, wanting to stay awake, afraid to fall asleep and him not be there to talk to when I woke up again. It was terrifying to imagine being there alone.

"There was a rent boy that used to work for Rego James, you remember him? James?"

"I remember James—he died in witness protection." Some guy had realized who he was, just some random guy from his past who passed him on the street, and followed him home, broke in, and ended up stabbing James to death with a knife from his kitchen. We could account for our own witnesses in WITSEC, but we didn't run every name in an entire town when we placed someone. It simply wasn't possible.

"I didn't know that part. I used to go to James's club downtown when I was an off-duty patrolman, and one night I went to see this kid I liked, Billy Donovan, and halfway through the trick, Rego comes busting in with this other kid I'd seen around."

He took a deep breath, like maybe he was having trouble telling the next part, and began carding his fingers through my hair over and over.

"So he throws the kid I don't know down beside Billy on the bed and shoots them one after another."

I could imagine Wojno there, frozen, terrified, with blood splatter all over him.

"And then it hits me that James isn't alone, and that's when I first met Hartley."

The story came together.

"And right before James is about to put one in me, Hartley stops him and tells him I'm a cop. Apparently the first one James killed, the kid who I kept seeing around, was undercover with vice."

"And what did you do?"

"I moved both bodies, made it look like Adams—that was the cop—and Billy were a thing and Adams shot Billy and then himself."

"But?"

"But there were cameras in every room of James's place, and I guess he gave the tape to Hartley for safekeeping."

"Why would he do that?"

"I dunno. Maybe James had something on him as well."

Perhaps he did.

"If it ever came out, I'd be finished in the FBI."

"You'd go to prison," I told him. "You know that. You were an accessory."

"Yeah."

I knew why he'd told me. I was a dead man. There was nothing to fear.

"Why did you bail on me after just the couple of times?" Wojno asked.

Now *there* was a time to talk about closure—when the person you wanted it with was cuffed naked to a cot. "No," I answered.

"No, what?" he asked, leaning over me, his lips close to my ear.

"No, we're not having a talk. Fuck you."

"I—"

"For the record," I said, my voice bottoming out, tears welling up in my eyes. "I would get you out of here. I wouldn't leave you to die here."

He stood up fast. "There's nothing I can do. He'd kill me if I tried to set you free."

"Okay," I replied, swallowing my tears. "We know where we both stand, then."

"You're an idiot. I could give you some comfort."

"I don't need any," I snarled as I heard a door open.

"What's going on?" Hartley said accusingly, his dress shoes clipping across the cement floor, the leather bottoms rubbing over the grit so it made a loud scratching sound when he stopped beside the cot. "Why are you in here?"

"I wanted to explain things to Miro."

"He doesn't need anything from you," Hartley assured him, "and I need to see him."

Wojno left quickly. Hartley squatted down beside the cot and tipped his head sideways so we were sort of eye to eye.

"They broke your nose when they beat you, but I reset it, so you shouldn't have any trouble breathing."

"Okay."

"I splinted your ring finger and pinky of your left hand because one of the men broke two of them before I realized what was happening."

"Thanks," I said, trying desperately to remain calm. I was close to having a panic attack—I remembered what they were like because I had quite a few when I was younger. It had been years, but the signs were there: the nausea, my racing heart, feeling overheated and freezing at the same time, and the spots in front of my eyes. If I couldn't catch my breath, I was in real trouble.

"I drank some of your blood yesterday and ate a piece of flesh from your shoulder the night before. I apologize about the divot."

Jesus. "It happens," I replied, swallowing down the revulsion and fear.

"Originally my plan was to pull off all your flesh, but it's much harder than skinning other things and would take far too long."

My stomach rolled ominously.

"I of course have pentobarbital and thiopental on hand and would have put you into a coma before I did any of that."

"I appreciate that."

"You know, I think the lorazepam I'm giving you—"

"What else is that called?"

"Ativan or Orfidal."

"Ativan," I repeated, "that's the word I know."

"Yes, well, I think I might be giving you too much. You're a bit too calm. You're not scared at all, are you?"

"I'm resigned," I mumbled, even though I wasn't. If I saw any glimmer of a chance to get out, I would take it in a heartbeat. The problem was, between the beatings and the sedation, I couldn't really feel my body and wasn't altogether sure what was working.

"Well, that's no good. I want to hear some begging."

"I'll beg now," I told him as he straightened his head and curled over me. I felt his lips between my shoulder blades. "Please don't get rid of my body when you're done. Leave something for someone to find."

"Of course," he assured me as he slipped his hands around my neck and squeezed.

I held on to consciousness as long as I could.

CHAPTER 15

IT WAS one of those things. After the guys beat me so hard that my
entire body throbbed and I could only see out of one eye, I was left
hanging there, feeling like a side of meat, and that's when I noticed the
door.

It was open.

Not hanging ajar, not enough so you'd notice—enough like
someone had meant to close it behind them but had not hung around
long enough to hear the click. And no click meant it was not locked.

I had to gauge my motion, because after nothing but glucose
and saline for I wasn't sure how many days, my body was not mine
anymore. It was ravaged. He had me full of drugs, I'd been beaten,
bitten, strangled... tortured... the baseball bat to the ribs had gone
on for what seemed like days on end, and now... now I needed to
move.

I needed to lift the chain that bound both wrists to the hook above
me up over the end, drop down, and run. When I'd first gotten there, I
would have been able to do it easily. It was a dead lift up, and I could
have managed that, but now, I wasn't sure. And if I did it and that was
all I had, then what? Once I was out of the room, where did I go? There
were so many variables and I had so very little energy.

It was so much to imagine and—

Ian.

It was *everything*, a whole universe of sound and images and
smells and all of it assaulting me and pummeling my brain and then—
quiet.

Ian.

There was only his face and the curt nod I used to get that I knew now was special and arrogant and the way he was with only me.

He'd worked so hard to keep himself away, and then when he simply couldn't, when I'd broken through and held him, kissed him, loved him... all that puffed-up macho pride became clear as what it was—his desire. Ian wanted me, and I was the first person he'd let down that wall for. I would not be responsible for him locking himself away again. Even if I died, he'd know I'd been trying to get to him, and that would tell him he was worthy of love and so he would someday love again. It was my hope, anyway.

I had to try. There was no way out of that.

Every muscle in my body screamed that it could not do what I wanted. My heart pounded, I shook like a leaf in the wind, and sweat poured off me. I lost the grip on the hook three times—gripping, pulling, and then falling back down. But on the fifth try, on the one I was going to quit after, I heaved my body up, pushed through a pressure in the back of my head that felt like someone was driving a spike through it, and fell hard to the concrete floor.

I heard my left ankle snap, and the pain was instantaneous. If I'd had my regular strength, I could have compensated for my descent. But as weak as I was, I slipped, and it was over. I crawled to the doorway because I wasn't ready to put any weight on it.

Hearing voices, I rolled sideways and waited.

"You get the water. I'll go call the doc and tell him that he's ready for him."

"Good."

Only one man reached the door and noticed it was open. He pushed it open and leaned in. "Dr. Hartley, are you already in—"

He went down hard when I grabbed his left ankle and tripped him face forward. But even with how hard he hit, he still had his gun out when he rolled over. I took that easily; I was trained for the contingency, but in so doing, I missed the spear-point knife. It was only five inches long, but when it was buried in my right shoulder, it hurt like hell. When he shoved on it, making the cut longer, I threw an elbow to his face, and that time he hit the ground with enough force to knock him out. I sat there for a long moment before I searched his pockets and came up with my salvation. Not an Uzi or more mags for his Beretta 92FS, but instead, his iPhone.

I couldn't get Ian because the phone was password-protected, but as I struggled to my feet, checked the clearance on the gun and the mag, and leaned against the wall, the call to 911 went straight through.

Quickly, efficiently, I rattled off my badge number, explained I was a marshal, and went on to say that I was critically wounded and needed help at my location.

"Stay on the phone with me, marshal," the operator ordered.

"I can leave the phone on, but I have to put it under my arm so I can have both hands on the gun."

"Okay."

"Normally I can shoot with one hand," I told her.

"Of course."

"But I'm shakin' kinda hard right now."

"Yes, I would suspect so," she said, taking a breath.

"So you might hear armpit noises."

"That's quite all right."

"Are you sure?" I teased and realized I was bordering on unhinged.

"Yes, marshal," she answered, her voice soothing. "I wish you could put me on speaker."

"So do I."

As if on cue, two guys came hauling ass around the corner, and I dropped them both with shots to the legs and shoulders. I had them throw aside their guns and their phones, and after slowly moving over to them, dragging my fractured ankle behind me, I put the muzzle of my stolen Beretta to the forehead of the closest guy and asked him which way was out.

I was worried I was in some underground bunker or an enormous abandoned warehouse or God knew what, but it so happened that I was being held in a trailer like they had on a construction site, just much bigger, with the bars built into the top of one room. Apparently sheet metal and pipes and other things were usually stacked in them, straight down and then pulled up through the roof for use. What I had thought was a torture chamber was merely functional.

All of that I found out once I was outside in the dirt. I had to thank God it was Arizona. If I was home in Chicago, I would have gotten hypothermia. As it was, at eighty degrees or so at night, I didn't freeze my balls off, even naked as I was, waiting for the cavalry that the lovely Gloria—the 911 operator—told me was coming.

When I saw lights in the distance, because I heard no sirens I moved faster, hobbling, and after Gloria confirmed that her guys were still ten minutes out—I was up in the foothills somewhere—I got down on my hands and knees and crawled as fast as I could. I didn't care how much it hurt with the rocks cutting into my skin because nothing was as bad as putting any weight on my ankle. I got torn up scrambling over rocks and between bushes and through thorns and branches, and it was dark out there in the desert. I would have used the flashlight app on the phone, because who didn't have that, but I was still on the emergency call, so it was me feeling around blindly and soon bleeding. Again. More.

I fell down a short ravine and decided to wait there. My adrenaline was shot, my muscles were done, and I could barely get any air moving in my lungs. At least I still had the gun, so whatever got near me I could kill, even a rattlesnake or wild boar or whatever other kind of animal was out here waiting to prey on me, and that included the kind that walked on two legs. I really hadn't meant to pass out.

AFTER ALL the trouble I went to to get out of the trailer, I was horrified when I woke up with lights in my eyes and Hartley greeting me.

I jolted hard, struggled against the hands helping him hold me down, and shouted at him to let me go.

"I'm not him, marshal! Please," the voice gasped, and it hit me that maybe we'd been going over this more than this one time I was aware of. "You have to believe me! Open your eyes! Please! Open them!"

If I could just get up....

"Marshal Jones!"

My name... not the fake one, the real one.

"Open your eyes!"

But what if I was dreaming?

Someone brushed my side and the pain was excruciating. I couldn't hold in the scream.

"Let me in!"

I instantly stilled because I thought I heard—

"Move!"

I was straining to hear, trying to smell him if I could, anything to not open my eyes.

"I swear to—fuckin' move!"

"Ian!" I shrieked.

After his frustrated roar, I was released. Everyone let go at once, and I would have fallen off the cot or whatever I was on if Ian hadn't been there to take my face in his hands and kiss me.

I had no idea that one simple kiss could warm my entire body so thoroughly and fast.

His lips pressed to mine before moving to my cheeks, nose, eyes, forehead, and then made the quick trip back. I wanted to put my tongue in his mouth; I wanted to taste him and remember everything that had been taken away in the past few days.

"I'm so glad he didn't hurt you or—"

"Quiet now," he ordered.

"Ian," I whined, my hands on his wrists, holding on for dear life as his breath mixed with mine.

I opened my eyes a slit. I *had* to see him.

He was tired, I could tell. There were dark circles under the red-rimmed blue eyes I loved; the normal stubble would be better described as a beard given a couple more days, and his hair was a riot. It was clear Ian Doyle had missed me terribly. It was all over him.

"I need you to stay still so they can check you out and run a tox screen and see what the fuck is under this bandage on your side."

"He bit me."

Ian cleared his throat. "I can see that."

"And he choked me."

"I know."

"And he operated on me, too, I think."

Ian bent close to me. "M—"

"It was Wojno, he was the leak!"

"Yeah, the Feds figured that out already."

"They did? How did—"

"Could you please stop talking and let these nice people do their jobs."

"Yeah, but you won't—"

"I won't what? Go?"

"Yeah."

"*No*."

"But what if you get a call?"

"Deployment call, you mean," he said solemnly, leaning in close to me, nuzzling my cheek, my ear, and kissing along my jaw.

"Yeah."

"I will not move from your side."

"Promise."

"Oh yes. Not on your life."

"Okay."

"Good."

I had to ask, as much as I didn't want to. "Did they catch him?"

"No, love, he's in the wind."

I took that in. "How long was I with him?"

"Four days."

It had felt like so much longer.

"Breathe," he whispered.

I nodded.

"I'm here now. You know I'll protect you. I'm not going anywhere."

It was good enough for me.

IT WAS later when I heard him speaking soft and low, the tone lulling and resonant, and it wasn't enough. I wanted to see him so I opened my eyes slowly, carefully because I wasn't sure what the light situation would be. But the room was dim, it was dark outside and there was only a small bedside lamp on. Ian was at the window looking out as he spoke on his phone.

I watched him, appreciating the strong lines of his frame, the T-shirt he was wearing clung to his broad shoulders and the sculpted muscles in his back and biceps. The faded jeans hugged his lean hips, ass and long, powerful legs. My breath caught as I stared because yes, I knew all about his heart and that made me love him, but the body on the man made my pulse race.

He turned at the sound I made and the smile lit his face.

A throb of arousal rolled through me and I was so glad that everything still worked. Responding to Ian in such a primal way, a physical way, made me feel like me again.

"He's awake," he said into the phone, "I have to go, but I'll send my report later tonight." And with that he ended the call before crossing the room quickly to me.

I lifted a hand toward him and he took it gently when he reached me, bending to kiss my knuckles before leaning in further to kiss me.

The need for more was instantaneous but he pulled back to look at my face. I wanted him closer, on me, in me... and that was new. Not that I had never thought about Ian topping before but for whatever reason, at the moment, the idea was almost overwhelming for how much I needed him to.

"What's going on?" I tried to ask, but my voice wasn't working all that well.

"I think you need some water," he concluded, turning to the pitcher on the nightstand to the left of him. He filled the cup with the straw and made sure I could drink easily, watching me intently. I drank slowly, and when I'd had enough, I leaned back and cleared my throat.

"Hi," I said hoarsely, smiling at him.

"Hi back," he sighed, trailing his fingers through my hair, pushing it off my forehead, over and over, languorously, seemingly content to do nothing more.

"Who was on the phone?"

"Kage. I've been giving him hourly updates."

"Is he mad? I bet he's mad."

"Yeah, I don't see either one of us—or anyone who works for him—on a FBI or DEA task force in the near future. Only ops we run that are secure."

Ian had shaved, and his hair in its usual tapered crewcut was no longer standing on end. He still looked beat, but he was smiling rakishly at me, the lines in the corners of his eyes were crinkling and his lip was curled dangerously, and listening to him talk, with the rumbling growl, was making my body heat. Oh, I needed to heal faster.

"M?"

I cleared my throat. "Yeah, but no op is completely secure. Even when we're in charge of them, shit can happen."

"I wouldn't try and play devil's advocate with Kage right now. He's kind of pissed at everybody and you don't want to be on his list."

"Point taken," I agreed, taking hold of the hem of his T-shirt, tugging just a little so he moved closer. "So tell me what happened to Hartley."

Instant scowl. "He was gone when the FBI got to the place where you were held."

"There were others guys. Did they get them?"

"Everybody was dead when they went in."

"Oh shit."

"But we figured that, right? I mean, Hartley, he's not the forgiving type, and they let you get away. They were dead the second you went out the door."

It was true.

"What about Wojno?"

"He wasn't there."

"Okay. So what's the next—"

"Enough," he said gruffly. "There's marshals and the FBI and the state police and Phoenix PD all out looking for Hartley and Wojno. You and I can't do shit about that."

"Yeah, but—"

"I don't wanna waste time talking about them. I have something else to say."

Whatever it was couldn't be good, from his irritated expression, the squint, the frown, and the clenched jaw. "Okay."

He took a breath. "You gotta marry me."

It took me a moment, because even though I'd heard him, and what he was saying was amazing, I was also very concerned that he'd lost his mind. "I'm sorry?"

"Yeah, yeah, I know," he grumbled, moving his hand to my cheek, stroking over my skin. "But listen, there were decisions that had to be made about you."

My throat hurt and my mouth was dry, but I was afraid to ask for another sip of water because I didn't want him to stop talking.

"And they had to get in touch with Aruna," he said, his voice cracking just a bit. "I was right here, but what I thought, nobody gave a shit about."

I nodded.

"You want another drink?"

"Yeah," I croaked.

He poured more water for me, then maneuvered the end of the straw to my lips and watched as I took several sips. Taking a breath after he replaced it on my nightstand, he slipped his hand into mine.

"So will you?"

Could he have looked any more miserable?

"M?"

I chuckled softly. "Listen, I know you were scared, but—"

"No, that's not it."

"Ian—"

"Just say okay, you'll marry me."

"No."

His head turned sideways a little, like he wasn't sure he'd heard me right. "No?"

I couldn't hold back my smile. "You wanna marry me so you get to say what happens to me, and I get that. But you don't have to—"

"No, I—"

"We can get a power of attorney and—"

"You wanted to marry me before you were kidnapped," he said defensively.

"And you didn't," I pointed out.

"Yeah, but now I do."

I shook my head. "You wanna have a say—*the* say—and I'm telling you, you can have it. You don't have to put a ring on my finger just to be the guy who's in charge of pulling or not pulling the plug."

"Miro—"

"It's okay," I soothed him, lifting my hand to his face. "God, I'm so glad to see you."

He closed his eyes a moment, leaning into my hand, and then sighed deeply as his gaze met mine. "I thought the marriage thing was stupid."

"I know you did, and do."

"Yeah, but now I'm thinking I don't know."

"Well, let's put this whole discussion on hold until you figure it out, okay?"

"But I wanna be… closer."

"Oh, marshal, you have no idea how much I want that."

It took him a second. "I'm unburdening my heart and you're being pervy."

I didn't want to laugh because it hurt. "Ow-ow-ow... stop."

"You're thinking about sex."

"What?" I teased innocently.

"Jesus, only you."

"Come here and kiss me," I mumbled, my energy level dipping, making it hard to keep my eyes open.

"I think you need to rest."

God, I was tired. "Yeah, okay," I agreed, hearing my voice crack as I closed my eyes. "But kiss me first."

His lips brushed my forehead.

"Not what I mean," I yawned in conclusion.

"I know," he agreed huskily, pressing his lips to my temple. "Sleep now."

"You're staying, right?"

"Yes, love, you don't have to worry."

And I didn't. It was Ian after all.

THERE WERE things that surprised me and things that did not. Like I was not shocked to find Ian passed out on one of those recliners beside my bed when I woke up, but I was surprised that one of my best friends, Dr. Catherine Benton, was standing there hovering over me, resembling a wrung-out old mop.

"You look terrible," I commented, my voice scratchy, full of gravel.

"Well, you're not looking so hot yourself," she volleyed, never missing a beat.

"Why're you in scrubs?" I asked, wondering why she was there.

She stepped closer, brushed my hair back from my face, and then bent and kissed my forehead. "Because I just operated on you," she answered when she straightened.

"How come?"

"That man took a rib out of your body and I wanted to make sure there were no sharp edges left inside," she said flatly.

I grinned up at her. "Who called ya?"

She lifted an eyebrow.

Shit. "Aruna," I answered my own question.

"Yep. She's your emergency contact; she's who they called to ask what to do."

"And she called you like a second later."

"As she should have," she answered.

"Is she okay?"

"She's worried, as were we all."

By *all* she meant my coven, Catherine and the three other women who had been my family since college. "But you told them I'm okay."

"And they all agreed to stay home as long as I made the trip."

"Thank you."

"Of course," she murmured, glancing over at Ian.

It was ridiculous, but I sighed deeply. "He's pretty, huh?"

"Gorgeous, yes."

"I think he loves me."

"Yes, I would agree."

I dropped my voice to a whisper. "I wanna marry him."

"You already got him moved in. I think you're on the right track."

Thinking for a moment, I looked down at the hospital gown, the cast on my left leg from right below the knee down, and then returned my gaze to her face. "I'm kind of out of it."

"Yes, I know."

"Is that why I'm so calm?"

"Uh-huh."

"I think I'm stoned."

She waggled her eyebrows at me.

"Hartley gave me drugs when he had me too."

"He certainly did."

"It's why I didn't die from sepsis or something when he took the rib, right?"

"I refuse to give that psychopath credit for anything," she replied, her voice icy. "I don't even believe in the death penalty, but in his case… I'm ready to make an exception."

"No, you're not."

She went quiet a moment, thinking. "No, I'm not. I'm sure I could think of many more creative alternatives to death."

I reached for her hand and she grabbed it tight. "Siddown."

She perched beside me, and I finally noticed how tired she looked. "My fault, I'm sorry."

"For what? Being kidnapped? Really?"

"You really do look terrible."

"I know. Normally I'm stunning."

She was right, she normally was. With her long, thick black hair swept up into a side braid with a low bun, her eyelashes so perfect they appeared fake, and the slightest blush to her cheeks, she was a goddess in the flesh. Even in pale blue scrubs she was usually quite alluring, and now that I was really studying her, I could still see her innate beauty, but her concern, her worry, her fear... for me... had changed her appearance. Furrowed brows, lips set into a tight line, dark circles under her eyes, and how pale she looked all worked together to show me a picture of grief. I'd scared the crap out of her.

"Forgive me."

"Stop," she said simply.

"You're beautiful," I croaked.

She covered our entwined hands with her other before her gaze met mine. "Stop talking, you're not strong enough yet."

"You, then."

Quick inhale of breath. "He took out your number twelve rib, what's called a floating rib, and if you have to lose one, that's the one I'd pick."

"Okay."

"It's called a floating rib, or a false rib, because it's attached only to the vertebrae, not to the sternum or to any cartilage of the sternum."

"So?"

"So it's not like you snapping the ones near the top, this one is small."

"It was the best one to lose."

"Right."

"And so why'd you open me up?"

"I told you already—I wanted to make sure he did it right and that you were okay, nothing punctured inside, nothing bleeding, and nothing left behind. I needed to see for myself."

"You couldn't just do an MRI or something?" I prodded. "You had to open me up again for fun?"

"Yes," she said dryly. "I did it for fun. I'm a sadist, I thought you knew."

I scoffed. "And?"

"And it looks fine and two other surgeons agreed with me."

"Okay."

"I won't even guess why he needed your rib."

"Best not to."

"You had to have been in shock afterwards because the pain would have been unbearable."

"He gave me lots of drugs."

"I saw—he had quite the cocktail going."

"But nothing that could hurt me long-term, right?"

"I think it messed with your memory a little, but other than that, no."

"What else is wrong?"

She explained that my left ankle was broken, as were the ring finger and pinky on my left hand—that Hartley had already told me about. I was covered in scrapes and bruises; I had a concussion. I'd been stabbed in the shoulder and it had required nineteen stitches to close, but her dear friend, Gavin Booth—who was some kind of miracle-worker plastic surgeon who worked in Scottsdale—had come when she called and sewed up everything on me that needed mending.

"The scarring should be very minimal," she informed me.

"I don't care."

"I do," she retorted sharply. "It's bad enough this animal had you. I won't allow him to leave any marks."

"He took a rib."

"And no one can see that from the outside, but scars they could," she said adamantly, and I could see how upset she was getting. I really had scared her to death, and she hated that. She liked things she could control; it was why she was a neurosurgeon. "Now it's your story to share or not, as you see fit."

"Okay," I soothed her, squeezing her hand tight.

We were quiet a moment.

"So how come they let a neurosurgeon operate on me?"

"Because I'm good," she snarled.

"Okay, okay." I chuckled "So am I gonna live?"

"Of course," she assured me with a glare.

"Good," I sighed as I closed my eyes. "Tell me before you go home, okay?"

"Yes, dear."

I felt her lips on my forehead again before I fell asleep.

SHE STAYED three days and then had to go home to her job and husband. It was for the best; she was driving my physician bonkers and annoying the crap out of Ian. Catherine had a way of getting under your skin, and even though she was really trying with him, she blamed Ian for not being with me on the op. Had he been closer, maybe I wouldn't have been taken. It was nuts because it was no one's fault, particularly not his, but she needed someone to blame and he was handy. But really, he blamed himself enough as it was, not missing even one opportunity to berate his own actions.

"So," I began, because my friend was gone and we could talk freely. "Any news on Hartley?"

"He's still at large," he answered woodenly.

"Ah."

"You like that? It's how the FBI announces shit. Dr. Craig Hartley is still at large."

"And?"

"He's considered very dangerous though not armed."

"I see."

"You know how we know he's not?"

"Not what?"

"Armed, idiot."

I snorted. "Tell me."

"Because your gun was recovered at the scene."

"No shit?" I was happy for some ridiculous reason. "You have my gun?"

He nodded. "I have your gun."

"Why is that such good news?"

"Because it's one more thing he didn't take."

Exactly. "Yeah."

He stared at me a moment and then stalked over to the window. "You know this whole thing... Phoenix—" Ian fumed as he turned and paced my room, "—was a disaster from the beginning. We should have stayed home."

"Which would have worked if there was no big-ass scary leak the size of Cleveland in the mix," I countered.

"This is the furthest from funny that something could be." His voice was dark and the accompanying snarl warned that he should not be teased.

I went ahead and baited him. "You didn't have to come."

"This is fuckin' serious."

"I know."

"You could have died!"

"I know," I agreed, waiting for him to get closer.

"You were—I couldn't—" he rasped, pacing closer to the bed. "You were gone. You just disappeared. It took a minute to lose you."

"I wasn't lost. I was taken."

"Don't you think *I know* that?" His voice got big.

"You didn't have to—"

"Don't say that to me," he warned.

"You didn't have—"

"I'm not kidding!"

"You didn't—"

"Miro!"

"You—"

"This is *funny* to you?" He was incredulous, and it showed in his flushed face, furrowed brows, and hands balled into fists.

I shrugged with one shoulder, since the other one was covered in bandages and tape.

He moved fast and hovered over me, hands on either side of my head. Up close, I saw the pain in his eyes, how puffy they were, raw and red, and the slight tremble in his lower lip, the muscles cording in his jaw and neck. I heard how rough his breathing was.

"Miro," he rasped.

I slipped my hands around the sides of his neck and slowly lifted toward him.

"It's not—I can't—you're not replaceable."

"I know," I said, smiling as I brushed my lips over his.

"It's not funny."

"No," I agreed, coaxing, my voice husky as I kissed him again, longer the second time, my tongue running over his bottom lip.

He shuddered, the full body kind, and I felt the roll of desire tumble through me. His need was obvious; he had to be shown that I was okay, and me holding him down was necessary. The problem was, at the moment, I couldn't.

"I was gonna give up," I confessed, and when he leaned back, I saw how focused on me he was, listening. "But then I thought, that's not me. I don't do that, and Ian, you, would miss me. I'm not just your partner at home, in bed. I'm your partner on the job and I have your back."

He nodded slightly.

"So there was no choice. I had to get back to you."

His eyes filled. "There was nothing I could do."

Oh, he was hurt down deep. "Are you sorry?"

"What?"

I had to dig it out of him or it would fester and become something we couldn't get past. "Are you sorry you started up with me?"

He squinted, obviously lost.

"If you *didn't* love me, it wouldn't have felt like that."

He searched my face.

"But... if you didn't *love* me," I repeated, slower, "it wouldn't have felt like that."

It took him several breaths to answer as I petted the sides of his neck and kissed his left temple and his right cheek and nuzzled the corner of his mouth. "Yeah."

I lifted both eyebrows, questioning. "Yeah, what?"

"Yeah, it's worth it," he growled. "Yeah, I felt like I couldn't fuckin' breathe, but—I wouldn't change it or... even if I could go back, I wouldn't."

"You could change it now," I apprised him. "We could go back to being—"

"That would be easy for you?"

"That would fuckin' *kill* me," I swore, gripping him tighter. "But you have to know what you can do, what you can gamble on and what you can live with. I do it whenever you're deployed. I hold my breath the whole time you're gone."

I saw it hit him, the reality of what I was telling him, the truth of it. "Oh shit."

"Yeah," I said, letting him go. "You think it's your job and it sucks being away from me and your life, but for me—it's like that."

"'Cause you don't know."

I nodded. "I never have any idea when you'll be back."

"Or if."

"I don't do 'if,'" I retorted, suddenly annoyed. "I never do 'if.'"

We were silent, staring at each other.

"Okay," he finally said.

"Okay, what?"

"Don't be so quick to offer me an out next time."

"There won't be a next time."

"Make sure," he grumbled as he leaned in and kissed me, tipping my head back and opening my mouth.

Dominant Ian full of hunger was a huge turn-on, and my dick noticed, hardening fast.

"Miro?" he asked before he kissed me again, continuing his lazy, decadent assault, each drugging kiss becoming another and another, sucking on my tongue, feasting on my lips, pressing me down, his warm hand on my chest. When he tried to pull back, I fisted my hand in his Henley and held him where he was. "Oh, you want me," he said arrogantly, breaking the kiss to grin at me, bumping my nose with his.

"Could you—" I had to swallow hard to get my voice back. "Get in my lap?"

His chuckle was deep and sexy, and I couldn't stifle my groan. "I'm sorry, what did you need?"

I squirmed on the bed, which made him smile, and to see it with how wrecked he looked made me deliriously happy. It was clear that Ian Doyle loved me very much. I could see it all over him.

"Just lay there and be good and don't tease me. You have at least three more days until you're even out of here, let alone ready to engage in any sexual intercourse."

"What if I get a note from the doctor?"

He shook his head. "That fuck took a rib out of you," he finished, and I saw the pain flicker across his face.

"No-no-no." I stopped him, hooking my hand on the collar of the Henley and trying to yank him down to me. "Stay hot for me. Focus on that, focus on me."

"M—"

"Ian," I begged, hand around the back of his neck, slipping up into his hair. "Don't get so caught up in what could have been that you lose track of what *is*."

"No, I know."

"I'm here, right?"

"Yeah."

"And you're happy?"

"That's a stupid fuckin'—"

"Tell me," I demanded.

He took a shaky breath. "Yeah, I'm happy."

"Well, then," I said before I drew him down to me.

I made enough noise after he ravished my mouth, with endless pleading and suggestions about how he could draw the curtains and lock the door, that he had to stuff a pillow over my face to get me to be quiet. It wasn't my fault. I really wanted to go home.

CHAPTER 16

WE FLEW home on Sunday, and by the time we made it to the townhouse, people were there.

"Shit," I grumbled, and Ian snickered behind me.

"I don't know why you're laughing," I said as I followed behind him on my crutches. "You ain't gettin' laid either."

He laughed harder, and when he opened the front door, Chickie came bounding over to me and tried to take the crutch away. I waved at the crowd crammed into our living room as they all applauded.

Aruna was holding her daughter, Sajani, and when I reached her, I stopped before hugging her because I got distracted with what was going on in front of me. Having been shooed away from me, Chickie was now sitting patiently in front of Aruna, his entire focus riveted on the baby in her arms. Sajani was squealing, kicking her feet, and cooing down at the dog.

"What happens if you put her on the floor?" I asked.

"Oh Miro, you're home and—"

"Lemme see," I interrupted, smiling because Chickie's tail was thumping so hard and fast that it sounded like a motor.

Aruna rolled her eyes and put Sajani on the floor, much to Chickie's obvious glee. He danced a few feet away, turned, crouched down, and whined at her.

Sajani was laughing as she crawled over to him. The second her teeny hand gently brushed his nose, he repeated the motion, darting away, but not far, got down and waited again.

"She crawls now?" I was amazed.

"Quite well, yes," she sighed, leaning into me, arm around my waist, head notched underneath mine. "And she loves that stupid dog."

"So what do you do when they're doing that?"

"I sit on the couch and eat Godiva," she said snidely.

Hurt or not, I was treading on thin ice. I knew she was a new mother who now also worked from home. "I'm just giving you shit."

"Yes, dear," she said, kissing my cheek. "I know."

Minutes later, I flopped down on a corner of my sectional, and the members of our team were fast to take the other spots: Kohn on my left, Kowalski on his, then White on my right, and Sharpe on his. Becker and Ching sat on the rustic, industrial coffee table, which I was lucky was very sturdy, and Dorsey and Ryan hovered beside them.

"So, you good?" Ching asked what no one else seemed able to.

"Yeah."

He pointed at me. "He took a rib?"

I nodded.

He leaned forward. "When we catch him, I'll take one of his."

It meant a lot coming from him, and when I patted his knee, he covered my hand for a second before nodding.

"Did they tell you about Wojno?" Becker asked me.

"Miro, I made shepherd's pie. I'm serving you some!" Aruna called from the kitchen.

I twisted in my seat to look over at her. "Do you even know how to make that?"

Her gaze could peel paint.

"Oh, for crissakes, I'm sorry."

"Liam's mother taught me, you asshat," she snapped at me. "Just sit there and look pretty, will you?"

I threw up my hands, much to the enjoyment of my fellow marshals, their peals of laughter making me smile in spite of myself.

"Hey," Becker said, snapping his fingers to get my attention. "Listen."

He then had all my attention, as well as Ian's. He was lingering behind me, leaning on the console table behind the couch.

"Wojno's dead."

"What?" I barely got out.

"Yeah. Hartley—and we know 'cause his DNA is all over the body—he took out his rib cage and left him on the side of the road."

I processed that, everything becoming clear. "That was supposed to be me, right? I mean, that was his plan. I just didn't hang around long enough."

"No," Kohn argued. "He was careful with you."

"Because he didn't want me dead that fast. It was gonna be a long, slow painful process."

"Stop," Aruna ordered as she approached the coffee table, pushing by the men, reaching for my hand. "Get up, come sit at the table and eat and visit and talk to me and your friends. Once I go, you can talk about all the horrors you want."

Kowalski and Becker lifted me to my feet, and Kohn helped me around the couch until I could reach Ian. Putting my hand on his shoulder, I hobbled over to the kitchen table and took a seat on one end of the bench. It was a picnic-style setup, so we never had to go hunting for chairs.

The food was good. Everything Aruna ever made was. The loaded shepherd's pie—apparently Liam's mom gave hers a little kick—grape, avocado, and arugula salad; homemade yeast rolls with cinnamon butter; and chocolate peanut butter brownies for dessert because Aruna knew they were Ian's favorite. Watching her hug him was particularly endearing.

The meal took a couple of hours, and when everyone else was gone and it was only us marshals left, the ten of us, sitting around having beer, Kohn started again.

"I think the rib cage is symbolic."

"It protects your chest, your heart," Dorsey chimed in. "So by Hartley taking Wojno's rib cage, he was taking what was supposed to guard his heart."

"And that's why he took your rib," Ryan agreed. "It was supposed to be the start."

We were all silent.

"Wojno deserved what he got," Kowalski told us. "Just because Miro got away from that fuckin' psychopath doesn't let him off the hook."

"Agreed," Ching said quietly, meeting my gaze. "He would have let it be you instead of him. You can't forgive that simply because Hartley took out losing you on him."

"I don't give a fuck what happened to Wojno," Sharpe announced, getting up to walk into my kitchen to grab himself another beer. "He was dirty, and when you're dirty you get what you get. But the report says he was sliced up his back and the rib cage was cut out of him and that it was done—at least for a few seconds—when he was alive."

No one said a word.

"For that—I'm putting a bullet in that guy's head myself," Sharpe growled.

"I just want him caught, one way or another," Ian said. "I don't want Miro to keep looking over his shoulder."

"Yeah," Ching agreed. "One way or another."

THEY STAYED late—it was Friday night—drinking beer, talking, watching ESPN, and telling us what had gone on while we were vacationing in Phoenix.

"Fuck you all," I groused.

"It's like this giant glass terrarium that they work in," Ian was explaining later as I was chuckling beside him. "I mean, seriously, it's still in the nineties there, and it's fuckin' October."

"You didn't have to go," Kohn mentioned.

Ian flipped him off.

"When do you need to sit with the Feds and talk about Wojno?" Dorsey wanted to know.

"Monday," I sighed. "They're coming to the office to talk to me."

Everyone was quiet after that.

Once we had the house to ourselves, Ian took some Cokes and sandwiches out to the cops in the patrol car sitting on our curb. Until Hartley was caught, they'd be there night and day. It was a shitty gig, and I really hoped he'd show himself soon, because if he was still at large in January, we'd have to let the cops camp out in our living room. It would be way too cold to be guarding the house in the middle of winter in Chicago. No car heater could run that long.

I was turning off the big lights and flipping on the ones we left on at night when I heard Ian come in behind me.

"You're supposed to be using the crutches."

Looking over my shoulder at him, I watched as he closed and locked the front door—we used a key and turned the deadbolt when we went in or out—before darting over to me.

"Did you hear me?"

"Yeah."

"So why aren't you using them?"

"I'm contemplating the stairs."

He chuckled. "Oh yeah?"

I grabbed hold of the bannister on the left, since on the right there was only the wall, looked him up and down, leering, and then took a breath. "Yeah… contemplating."

He swallowed hard, and his voice came out like dried leaves. "What's with you?"

"You. You're with me."

"Yes, I am."

"And I wanna get laid."

His smile crinkled the lines around his eyes. "I don't think you can do that with your surgery and—"

"Yes, I can," I assured him, bracing my arm and leaning so it would take my weight as I hopped.

"Don't do that," he ordered. "You'll tear your stitches."

"I don't care."

"Yeah, but I do," he rumbled, pushing by and stopping in front of me before kneeling, presenting me with his broad back.

It took me a second. "Oh, fuck no."

He didn't even try and hide the snickering. "Come on, M, lemme help you."

"Just move," I grumbled, trying to push him out of the way with my knee. "Kage won't let me out on the street with you if he thinks I can't—"

"Now," he demanded, "or it'll get really embarrassing for you."

"Meaning?"

"I can caveman carry you up, if you're into that."

"With my rib out and all?" I called his bluff.

"It's gone, it ain't broken or healing," he informed me. "It's the ankle and the stitches in your shoulder at this point."

"Seriously, I—"

"And you're not going out with me, you know that."

"What're you talking about?"

He turned and sat down, which meant he had to look up at me even though he was above me on the stairs. "You can't, not until the ankle heals. You're stuck at your desk until the cast is off and until you complete the PT and you get the all clear from the doctor."

"No, I—"

"It's at least six weeks and then however long the physical therapy takes after the cast comes off."

"You think I'm gonna be on desk duty for two months? I'll die of boredom."

"You won't die of *anything*, actually," he growled, getting up and shoving by me, charging back down into the living room.

"Oh, I get it," I said, swiveling around so I could see him at the front door, grabbing Chickie's leash and pulling on the navy knit jacket hanging there, what we both grabbed to wear to walk the dog, at least until it got cold enough outside to layer. "You want me to sit my ass behind a desk where I'll be safe."

"And what the fuck is wrong with that?"

"I'm a goddamn marshal, the same as you. The threat of getting hurt is part of the job."

"I think you've had enough excitement for a while."

"You don't get to decide that!"

"No," he agreed icily. "But your ankle does, doesn't it?"

I was stunned. "You're happy I'm hurt."

"I am not, and that's a shitty thing to say."

"You're happy I'm off the street," I accused.

"And if I am?"

"What the *fuck*, Ian? I'm your partner. Before anything else, I'm the guy who—"

"No!" he roared. "Before anything else you're my *life*, you stupid prick!"

Thoroughly gobsmacked, I just stood there as he stormed out of the house with Chickie in tow, slamming the door so hard I was surprised it didn't splinter.

I sat down on the stairs and tried to put things together.

Us being more than partners was new, but for whatever reason, I was still putting the bulk of my importance to him on the work partnership. And I knew a lot of it was because it was there that I had proven my worth to Ian Doyle to begin with. I was always the first guy through the door after him, and he knew he could count on me. But apparently, whether or not I followed him out into the field, I was still the guy he wanted to come home to.

Getting up, I grabbed the crutch I had left leaning against the stairs, balanced myself as I held on to the railing, and with a sort of rocking motion, up on the right, lift, and lean back to the left, I made it up the stairs.

Earlier in the day, Ian had run garbage bags up to the bathroom and put them under the sink so I'd have them when I took a shower. They would protect the cast that covered all but my toes on my left foot and extended up to under my knee. I secured a bag before I got in the shower. I had to figure out what I was going to wear to work on Monday, since with my boss, sweats and lounge pants weren't going to cut it.

I was drying my hair, towel wrapped around my waist, when I heard the front door open and close. After limping to the edge of the loft and looking down, I watched as Ian hung up Chickie's leash, took off the jacket, and went to the kitchen to wash his hands. The point of taking the dog out was so he could take a crap, so even through two layers of bag, it felt gross. Once he was done, I was surprised he didn't come up.

"What're you doing?"

He walked out into the middle of the room so he could look up at me. "You had to prove to me that you didn't need any help?"

He was pissed I'd climbed the stairs alone. "No, I figured out a way to do it that took little effort, and since I'll have to do it when you're not around, it was good to practice."

"Fine," he said dejectedly and walked back into the kitchen.

"Is that it?" I called out.

"I don't wanna fight," came the reply.

"I don't either."

"Then leave it alone."

"Can't do that, either."

He reappeared in the living room, staring up. "What do you want from me?"

"So here's what I thought," I said softly, done drying my hair and leaning forward on the railing. "If something happened and I couldn't be your partner anymore, you wouldn't want me."

"I'm sorry, what?"

"You heard me."

"Not want you?"

I ignored his tone, how angry he sounded, and the glare. "Part of that is that us being partners, me showing you that I could do the job plus keep up with you—that was how you first started trusting me."

"That was a long time ago."

"But it still matters. It's like the guys on your team."

"We're back to that?" he retorted. "You think I'd let anybody in my unit fuck me?"

"No."

"Then what?"

"You need to know you can count on me."

"I know I can fuckin' count on you! I don't depend on anybody as much as you."

"And why's that?"

"Because you always have my back!"

"Exactly," I agreed. "So what if I can't? What happens then?"

"I don't—" He growled before stomping up the stairs. "Why do you always have to make everything so goddamn difficult?"

I chuckled as he appeared in the loft and strode over to face me.

"So what's in your head now?" he asked, stopping in front of me, arms crossed, muscular legs braced apart, power rolling off him as he stood there and fumed. "If we're not work partners that I won't wanna come home to you anymore?"

"It took you a long time to trust me."

"But I do now," he said curtly. "And I can't even remember a time I didn't. Don't you—it doesn't matter."

"What?"

"Whether or not you get transferred or I do. If you wanted to go back to being a cop or if one of us really wants to move up." He sighed, raking his fingers hard through his hair. "What's important now is that we live in the same house, that we sleep in the same bed, and that we try as hard as we can to see each other all the time."

"Ian—"

"Come on, M, you already deal with me leaving when I'm deployed. I'm gone and you're here and—" His voice broke. "Don't you fuckin' miss me?"

"Of course I miss you! What the hell kinda question is that?"

"Well, then, don't you think when you're not with me all day that by the end of it I'll be dying to get back to the office so we can go home together?"

I had never been particularly good about putting myself in another person's shoes. I really sucked at it, actually. The only thing that had gone through my head was, *If I can't be Ian's partner, do I still get to be his partner in all things?*

"Miro?"

I met his gaze and saw the vulnerability there, as well as the hope. I cleared my throat. "I should know better."

"Yeah," he replied hoarsely.

"So the partner thing—that's just a perk at this point."

"*Yeah*," he repeated.

I reached for him, sliding a hand over his hip and easing him forward, close to me so I could lean in and kiss his throat. He tipped his head sideways so I could reach more skin. "Nothing will change, whether I'm your partner or not."

"Not between us," he said with a soft groan. "But that doesn't mean you get to be anyone else's. You're *my* partner, M. That's how it needs to stay."

Yes, it did.

His breath caught as I sucked on his skin. "Are you sure you— Miro!"

To show him that I was indeed up to the task of manhandling him, I stepped back, wrenched him off balance, and threw him down onto the bed face first.

"You know I could hurt you if you're—"

"Stop talking," I ordered as I came down on top of him, pinning him to the bed, my knee parting his thighs as I wrestled off first his worn denim shirt and then the white T-shirt underneath. Once I had his broad muscular back bared for my pleasure, I lifted off him enough to kiss down his spine.

"You always—" He was having trouble breathing and so took a gulp of air. "—treat my body like it's—oh," he finished with a groan.

"What?" I asked, moving down to his hips, tugging on his pants, kissing lower.

"You have to wait, M. I'm... I... you shouldn't... I need a shower and—"

"You smell like sweat and soap from this morning, and you," I husked, my hand sliding beneath him, working open the button and zipper, tugging the gray chinos down, revealing the round chiseled ass I loved. It was as close to perfection as one could get. I especially loved it when I got to watch my cock slide deep inside.

"Miro," he panted as I put him on his hands and knees before spreading his cheeks and licking over his hole.

He smelled musky and I liked that, but what got me off was the noises he made. The husky groan, the throaty cries, and the pleading where the only word was my name—all of that made me want to see if I could get him to come just from rimming him.

When I pushed inside, tasting, sucking, and took hold of his hard, leaking length, he nearly came off the bed.

"Please," he gasped. "Lay down."

Normally I would have done his thinking for him, because that's how it was for us in bed—what I said had to be followed. But his voice, the sound, so steeped in his own need, made me hesitate.

He scrambled out of reach and then flipped around and tugged the towel from my hips. "Could you.... M."

He wanted me down on the bed, so I quickly complied, loving that he dove for the nightstand to get the lube.

Already painfully hard myself, it was agony when he slicked me fast and then straddled my hips.

"Go slow, okay?" I cautioned, hands on his thighs. "It's been a while and—"

"I need you inside because you're not dead. If you're here, with me, you're safe."

It was not a fast plunge; he didn't impale himself like a porn star. Instead he eased down steadily, slowly, taking his time so I felt every ripple of muscle, every release of tension, and every second that he shuddered against me.

He was so strong and powerful, his skin was like warm silk over steel, and when I was all the way inside him, buried, the second he moved, I felt my body flush with heat.

"You feel too good," I warned him. "I'm gonna come."

"Not yet," he whispered, curling over me, hands fisted in the covers as he started to rock back and forth, rising and lowering, setting a gentle rhythm that quickly increased, eliciting a low moan from deep in my chest. "I need you."

I knew what he needed. "If I can, if it's up to me, I'll always be here."

"Right here," he rasped as his muscles clenched around me, and I saw him visibly fighting to keep his orgasm at bay.

"Yes."

"With me."

"Yes."

"I know we can't promise," he whispered, and I saw his jaw clench, his lips pressed in a tight, hard line.

"No," I agreed, reaching to cup his cheek. "But we'll try as hard as we can."

His attention never left my face even as his movements became frenzied, riding me, not caring about anything but reaching his climax. He didn't touch himself, and I couldn't, capable only of grasping his thighs, holding him tight, my fingers digging into his muscles. When he spilled over my abdomen, lost in the throes of release, I yelled his name as I came deep inside his body.

Before Ian, I'd been selfish in bed. I had tried to make the other person feel good, but in the end, my pleasure was paramount. That had all changed when my partner joined me. With Ian I made sure: I wanted to hear my name in a breathless moan; I loved the smell of him, his taste, but more than anything, seeing him sated afterward, replete, panting beside me, on me, draped in a boneless sprawl… *that* was what I craved. To know that I had cared for him, loved him, made my heart swell almost painfully.

"God, Miro, I better not have ripped your stitches," he said gruffly, rising off me gently, the small gush of fluid running down my cock and balls.

"I don't think so, but who cares."

He bent to kiss me, but I turned my head. "What's with—"

"Think where my mouth was last," I reminded him.

"I don't care, you don't care," he growled, capturing my face in his hands. "I wanna kiss you."

He mauled me until his head finally clunked down over my heart and his eyes fluttered shut, even with how hard he was fighting sleep.

I put my hand in his hair and massaged his scalp. "You should turn off the light."

"You turn off the light," he mumbled.

There was no more discussion after that.

CHAPTER 17

TALKING TO the staff psychiatrist, Dr. Johar, was something I really tried to put off, but two weeks later after lunch on a Saturday—Kage scheduled the meeting himself—I had no way around it. He'd brought me into our meeting room, where we normally talked to people entering witness protection, and had my file, complete with pictures of my injuries in living color, spread out in front of him.

We were quiet for long minutes before I finally asked if he had any questions for me.

"I do," he answered, smiling. He was older, early fifties—I'd never thought to ask—but as Kohn had said on a number of occasions, he *looked* like a shrink, with his mustache and beard, all dark chestnut brown, and his pale blue oxford, charcoal gray tie, and black cashmere sweater. He'd taken off his suit jacket, also black, which I thought he always did to make us feel more comfortable.

"So, normally I don't talk to the other marshals about one another, but in this instance, I needed to know what they thought about you."

"Okay."

"Are you curious about what was said?"

"I dunno."

His grin was warm. "They said you're normally quite the clotheshorse."

It was true, everyone knew that. I'd grown up poor in lots of foster families with nothing of my own. In reaction, I now had too many clothes, too many shoes, and I'd made sure that one of the first things I ever acquired was a thirty-year mortgage on an $800,000 home that had only become manageable after I became a marshal. When I'd first bought the house on my detective salary, my budget had been meager. Now, I could eat, buy clothes, and pay the bank on the fifth of every month.

"Why aren't you dressing up right now?"

I shrugged. "I'm stuck in the office, and with my broken ankle I can't wear any of my good shoes."

"You're wearing one combat boot, I see."

It was Ian's, and since it was already beat to crap, I didn't feel bad wearing only the one. "Yeah. I don't want any of my good shoes wearing unevenly so—gotta wait."

"That's important to you."

"What's that?"

"That your shoes wear evenly."

"Sure," I agreed.

He nodded and was quiet a moment, writing. I wondered what deep truth he had ferreted out of me with my confession about the soles of my shoes.

"So tell me about Agent Wojno."

"What would you like to know?"

"Anything you'd like to tell me."

I thought a second. "He didn't deserve to die like he did."

He stared at me.

"And I'm glad they only told his family that he was killed, but not how."

"Did you know he was married?"

"He was divorced."

"Yes, but that's not what I asked. What I asked was, did you know he was married when you first met him?"

I cleared my throat. "No."

"Did you have a relationship with Agent Wojno?"

"No."

"No, you didn't have a relationship with him?"

"I had sex with him three or four times. It was not a relationship."

"You didn't go drinking together?"

"No."

"You didn't have him over to eat pizza and watch a movie?"

I leaned forward. "No."

"Are you sure?"

I met his gaze. "If we ran into each other and it was convenient, we'd hook up. I went to his place once, there were a couple of bathrooms, and his car, if I'm remembering right. I never had him over and we didn't hang out."

He nodded. "Well, then, please explain to me why you feel so much guilt over his death."

I was surprised. "What're you talking about?"

"Everyone I've talked to, including your boss and your partner, say that you're not yourself. You come in, you go right to the back and sit in the computer room where you answer the phone all day, run searches, and work cases from the desktop."

"That's all I can do right now."

"Yes, it's true, but also, you wear your White Sox cap in every day, you're always in jeans or chinos, you're always in a hoodie and the one boot."

I threw up my hands. "I have no clue why any of that matters at all."

"No?"

"I'm doing my job!"

"Craig Hartley is still at large."

"Yes, I know that."

"His sister is in WITSEC."

"I know that as well."

"Your old partner, the police detective, Norris Cochran, was put on paid leave, and he and his family were relocated for the foreseeable future."

"I'm seriously waiting for you to tell me something I don't know."

"Why don't you go?"

I scoffed. "We tried that. He found me."

"Because of Agent Wojno."

"Yep."

"But the leak is gone now. It won't happen again. You could go to another city and work, and there would be no issue."

"Maybe."

"Maybe?"

"Who's to say? I'd rather be home here where I know everyone, than in another city trying to get acclimated."

"But there are people here that Hartley might hurt to get to you."

I scowled at him.

"Marshal?"

"Did you ever meet Craig Hartley?"

"Yes, I did. We were colleagues."

"Well, then, you know hurting someone I care about is not something he'd do."

"But you cautioned your friend Aruna not to visit your home while you were in Phoenix."

"Because if he was at my house and she stumbled onto him, he'd have to hurt her on general principal, from a witness perspective. But he would never go over to her house for the express purpose of harming her to get at me. He wouldn't see the point of that when he could hurt me directly."

"And your partner—Marshal Doyle? Aren't you worried about him?"

"The same dynamic applies. If Marshal Doyle was protecting me when Hartley was trying to hurt me, that's when he'd get hurt. But hurting Marshal Doyle to punish me or make me suffer is not his way."

"No?"

"No. He's got this huge ego, right? If he's trying to hurt me, it's me he wants."

"So you're only worried about others getting caught in the crossfire."

"Yes."

He studied me a moment, his small sepia eyes taking my measure. "Why do you feel guilty about Wojno?"

"I don't."

"He betrayed you."

"He did."

"He would have let you die to save himself."

"Yes."

"When the joint task force between the FBI and the marshals service went through his personal e-mail, downloaded his calls and other correspondence, they found that Wojno was personally recruited by Hartley to get close to you and sleep with you because Hartley wanted to know everything about you, right up to what you were like in bed."

"I've been briefed," I said sharply because I was so sick of thinking about this, having it all run around day and night in my head, that I was ready to put my fist through a wall.

"Hartley was blackmailing Wojno, yes, but his plan wouldn't have worked if you hadn't slept with him."

"What's your point?" I asked, frustrated, feeling my anger rise, hating that Hartley, even though nowhere near me, was still the one in control. Because of him I was stuck feeling like shit and having to talk to a shrink.

"My point is that maybe your guilt is not from how Wojno died, but that he was in the position to report to Hartley to begin with only because initially you found him attractive."

Since I couldn't deny it, I kept my mouth shut. The truth was, if I hadn't fucked Wojno the first time, he might still be alive.

Maybe.

I couldn't say for certain what would have happened to Wojno. He'd made a mistake and Hartley knew about it, and between the time Hartley found out and the time when Wojno turned me over to him, he'd become an FBI agent. It was naïve to think that Hartley wouldn't have collected his pound of flesh at some point.

As I'd run the last time I'd spoken to him back through my brain over and over, I was at a loss to figure out what I could have done differently.

"Marshal?"

"Okay," I conceded, so tired of all of it, the second-guessing myself, trying to figure out whether if I'd been able to connect emotionally with Wojno, things would have gone differently.

"Okay?"

"Yeah, I feel guilty, alert the media. What the hell am I supposed to do about that?"

He seemed confused. "You stop it."

"Just stop it?" I was incredulous. "This is your sage advice?"

He chuckled. "There is absolutely nothing you could have done to save Agent Wojno. He had to save himself. You were the one cut open, beaten, knifed, and hung up like a slab of meat. You were brutalized, marshal, and it's a wonder you made it out alive. You are in no way responsible for anyone but yourself."

I crossed my arms because I was shaking and I didn't want him to see. "Yeah, but what if, right?"

"How do you mean?"

"If I could have been a bit more convincing, maybe I could have gotten him out too," I whispered, the floor I was staring at beginning to blur. When the tears welled up seconds later, I tried to rub them away fast. Goddamn Wojno, I had no idea why I even cared, other than he absolutely did not deserve to be dead. Rotting in jail, yes, but not dead.

"It's important to you."

"What?" I'd lost track of the conversation, as lost as I was in my own thoughts.

"It's important to you to have saved him."

"Well, of course."

"To do what?"

"I'm sorry?"

"He would have spent the rest of his life in prison."

"But he would have been alive."

"And would that have suited him? Prison?"

"I don't know." I huffed out a breath, letting myself fall back in my chair, crossing my arms as I regarded the doctor. "Again, I think the alive part is key."

He put down his pen and apparently made himself comfortable as well, hands behind his head, legs stretched out in front of him. "You need to stop blaming yourself for something completely out of your control."

"I'll get right on that."

He was back to scrutinizing me. "May I say that your partner, as well as the rest of your team, all think very highly of you, marshal?"

"Oh yeah? Even my boss?"

He was silent.

I laughed at him. "Yeah, see, I knew it."

"He's very guarded."

"Yeah, maybe you should go head shrink him."

"No, I don't think so."

"You scared?" I baited him.

"Perhaps a bit."

I stood up. "You're clearing me for continued service, right?"

His sigh was deep. "I am, yes."

"Thanks," I said, heading for the door.

"You're a very lucky man, marshal. Don't waste your life mired in second-guessing yourself."

"How're you supposed to learn anything, then?"

I didn't wait for his answer. I left before he changed his mind about me.

I STOPPED at Windy City Meats on the way home after seeing the shrink and was amazed at the cost on the beef tenderloin my regular butcher, Eddie, passed me over the counter.

"Holy crap, are you kidding?"

He shrugged. "It's some of the best, Jones. Whaddya want me to say?"

"Is it unicorn? Is that why it costs so much?"

The little girl standing close to me gasped, and if looks could kill, her mother's would have stopped my heart right there.

"Oh, I—"

"Nice, Jones," Eddie groaned, shaking his head. "You want the hot Italian sausage or the regular?"

I glared at him.

"Fine, hot it is. Howzabout the prime bone-in ribeye?"

"Yeah, gimme two."

He snickered as he turned away. "Keep your mouth shut while I'm gone."

I would have flipped him off, but I was still close to the little girl and really didn't want to do any more to piss off her mother.

Once I was done at the butcher, I went to the farmers' market and picked up produce before heading home. After checking in with the cops sitting on my house, I hobbled inside and unloaded everything. Because it was hard for me to walk Chickie with my ankle, Ian had dropped him off with Aruna that morning and had plans to grab him on the way home from his stakeout assignment. I was putting away groceries when he called.

"You're cooking?"

"Yeah. Your choice is between spaghetti or steaks."

"Oh."

It was a weird noise. "What?"

"I was gonna cook."

"You cook?" I was stunned. Since when?

"Why you gotta say it like that?"

"I dunno, because—I had no idea you cooked."

"I've cooked for you before."

"You have?"

"Yeah."

"When?"

He was quiet.

"I would love you to cook for me," I assured him.

"Of course you would," he said smugly, and I smiled at the sound. Ian clothed in his arrogance, smirking on the other end of the phone, was the best thing I could imagine.

"So I'll wait for you to get home and cook for me."

"As opposed to what?"

"You walking through the door at some point tonight and the house smelling like food and me putting a cocktail in your hand as I serve you dinner."

He was thinking again, quiet as he considered his options. "That sounds pretty good too."

I chuckled. "When do you actually think you'll be home?"

"I'm thinking around eight—we're doing paperwork now."

"Oh, you guys picked up Aronson already?"

"Yeah," he grumbled.

"What?"

"Well, guess who's all mobbed up now?"

I could not bite back the snicker. "No shit."

"No shit," he grumbled. "Little Peter Aronson who used to be a CI when he was running with Cantrell and his car theft ring downstate has moved up in—"

"You're such a snob."

"What're you talking about?" He was incredulous. "I'm trying to tell you a story about Aronson and how we have to put that piece of shit into WITSEC and you're giving me—"

"Downstate," I snorted. "Really, Doyle? Everything in Illinois that is not Chicago is what?"

"Crap," he baited me, "and you know it is."

"You should learn respect."

"And who's gonna make me?" I could hear the husky, smoky sound in his voice that signaled his desire to play. He wanted to be home very badly. "You?"

"You're awfully lippy over the phone," I said as I turned toward the front door, having decided I needed to take a quick walk down to his favorite bakery and pick him up a blackberry pie. It was his favorite. "Come home and try and give me this much grief."

"Oh, I'll give you something."

"Promises, promises," I teased.

Silence.

"Ian?"

He cleared his throat. "So if I… if I wanted…."

I'd been waiting for this. Hoping. "Yes?"

"I could—" He took a breath. "—because since you've been home, I've wanted to—and it's stupid, but—"

"It's not stupid."

"You don't even know what I'm talking about."

"Oh, of course I do."

"What?"

I smiled into the phone. "You want to be inside me."

No reply.

"Because then you'll know I'm really here, with you."

"No."

"Yes."

"When we—" He coughed. "Two weeks ago, the first time after the kidnapping, I got that all out of my system."

"What?"

"I felt like you were slipping away, like maybe you thought I couldn't protect you."

"I can protect myself. Me getting kidnapped was on me, not you."

"Yeah, but I'm your partner, your backup. You should know if you can't do something, that I can."

"We've been through this already."

I was not weak. He couldn't protect me from the whole world, and neither did I want him to. Having him put all that on himself, the burden of not trusting me, instead feeling as though he had to watch me when we went out into the field together, wouldn't serve either of us well. We were partners; he wasn't there to be my shield.

"I know, and I don't want to dredge it up because everything got better."

"After we had sex."

"Yeah."

"But now?"

"Now nothing, we're good."

"Ian?"

"You can't think that how we have sex matters to me."

"I don't, but I also think that sometimes you want me but you stop yourself."

"Yeah, so what if I do?"

"Why would you do that?" I sighed. God, getting the man to trust me all the way was going to kill me.

"Because maybe you don't—"

"What did I say?" I demanded, my voice edged with frustration. Why on Earth would I tell him something I didn't mean? It was maddening the way he couldn't tell me what he was thinking and feeling.

"Miro—"

"Ian," I said sternly. "What did I say?"

"I don't wanna go over—"

"Ian!"

"God, you're like a dog with a bone!" he lashed out. "You said that however I wanted you was good."

"And so what, you don't trust me? I'm a liar?"

"No, but—"

"Jesus, Ian, you don't think I've thought about it?"

"What?" He was breathless.

"You don't think I've thought of you shoving me up against a wall or down on the bed and just taking what you want?"

"Stop."

"Your skin all warm on mine," I mused with a groan.

"I'm at work, dickhead."

"Your hand in my hair, the other on my cock," I went on, my voice low and seductive, knowing I was pushing it but loving the idea that I was driving him nuts. "Stroking me until I spill all over your hand?"

"Oh God, now I can't even walk."

I cackled, feeling mischievous and powerful at the same time. "You know, sometimes I think, what would Ian feel like moving inside of me?"

I got only a garbled noise from the other end of the line.

"And I know you, so I know you're worried 'cause you don't wanna be a selfish prick in bed, but think about that a second."

"It's all I'm thinking about at the moment," he rasped.

"You love me."

"I used to, back at the beginning of this conversation."

I scoffed. "Oh, no, baby, I know better," I crooned. "You love me bad. You ache with it, and because of that, I know you will take care of me when I'm under you in bed."

The sharp inhale made me grin like an idiot.

"So Ian, come home and I'll feed you and then you can have your wicked way with me."

"I don't wanna hurt you."

"I know."

"But I think about having you wrapped around me… in every way… all the fuckin' time."

My stomach flipped over and my cock hardened painfully fast in my jeans. "Come home now."

"I swear to God I will be there as fast as I can."

"Looking forward to it, marshal."

"Aww, don't call me—"

"I'm really good at following orders."

"Jesus, Miro, get off the phone before I gotta explain to Kohn why I have a boner in the middle of the office."

I was laughing when I hung up.

SINCE I decided on the way to the sidewalk that pie wasn't going to hit the spot, I got in my truck and headed over to Webster Avenue instead. I wanted to get some cupcakes from Sweet Mandy B's, because honestly, they made these awesome jumbo ones we could eat in bed. I had a one-track mind.

After I got dessert, I headed over to The Silver Spoon near west Armitage and north Halsted to pick up the keychain I'd ordered for Aruna. It was a silver circle I'd had hand stamped with her hubby's and her daughter's names. She'd been taking care of Chickie so much, I wanted to make sure she knew I appreciated her, and that boutique was one of her favorites.

I had parked my truck around back of one of the buildings, and after I hit the alarm and got in, there was a tap on my window.

Jolting with panic, I turned to find a stunning woman in an outfit that looked like she'd walked off the cover of a fashion magazine giving tips for fall layering. The diamond wedding ring on her left hand was the size of a small ice rink. I immediately rolled down my window.

"Can I help you?" I asked, breathing through my nose, calming my racing heart. Gun-shy was an understatement for what I was.

"Marshal Jones?"

Instantly I was on edge. How the hell did she know my name? "Yes."

She took a breath and her eyes welled with tears. "I have a daughter—her name is Saxon and I know, what was I thinking? All the boys are going to call her Sax when she gets older and then it'll be Sexy Saxy and later on Sex instead of Sax but I figured she had time to yell at me, right? She had all the time in the world."

Oh, she was so scared, and the rambling was only half of it. Her hands were shaking, her voice was going in and out, and she was maybe another minute and a half away from hyperventilating.

"Ma'am," I began, opening my door a crack.

She slammed it closed. "No! Ohmygod, you can't get out of the truck! What if I can't get you back in there after or—he'll kill her!"

She was now sobbing, pulling in those great gulps of air, totally breaking down. And I understood why, of course.

Craig Hartley was a scary sonofabitch who made good people do very bad things. It was why she pulled the gun out of her purse and leveled it at me. She really needed me to listen.

CHAPTER 18

EMERSON WENTWORTH Rice was in the kitchen when the back door opened and her husband came through, followed by a man holding a gun on him. Quickly, efficiently, he asked her if she could help him with a serious matter. When she didn't answer, he shot her husband in the stomach. The screaming began then.

"He has my little girl," Emerson said now, her explanation halting because she was still doing the half-crying half-talking thing people did when they were scared out of their minds.

She'd been allowed to call 911 for her husband of fifteen years before she and her daughter were loaded into the BMW SUV and driven away. She had no idea if he was dead or alive. What she did know was that she got to trade me for her daughter, and by God, that was what was going to happen.

"I'm really sorry about this," she assured me as she leaned against the passenger door, both hands on the weapon, making sure that if I twitched she blew off the side of my face. "But he wants you and I want my daughter."

"I understand."

"I need your gun. He said you'd have one."

"Where am I going?" I asked as I pulled the Ruger from the holster under my jacket and passed it to her.

I had to drive out to Park Ridge, and Emerson directed me to Touhy Avenue and then down Courtland. Four blocks south on the left was a large two-story house, and I was told to get out and go to the front door and ring the doorbell. Emerson would be right behind me.

Yes, I could have easily taken the gun from her, but she was terrified for her daughter and I understood that.

"As soon as I have my child, marshal, I will send the Marines back here for you, I swear to God," she promised as we climbed the front steps.

I had no reason to doubt her sincerity.

Ringing the doorbell, I thought of my phone in the truck, under the seat where I'd dropped it when Emerson had glanced away from me to make sure we were going the right way. Hopefully, when Ian tried to call and didn't get me, his law enforcement brain would kick in and he'd know exactly what had happened. At least the phone in my parked vehicle would alert him to my last whereabouts. From here, depending on Hartley, it was a crapshoot.

Because I didn't want to scare Emerson any more than she already was, I was working really hard to not come unglued. I was taking shallow breaths, keeping my nerves on a tight leash, and forcing myself not to throw up, even with how knotted up my stomach was. I was terrified, plain and simple, and trying desperately not to let her see it on my face.

When the door opened a crack, I saw a scared, sniffling little girl for a second before she saw her mother.

"Mommy!" she squealed, and Emerson had to put her hand on my back to keep herself on her feet.

"Hi, lovey," she soothed. "Just stand right there for me, okay? Freeze like a popsicle, until we find out what the man wants."

Saxon turned her head to listen, and then her little six-year-old face lifted to me. "Are you Miro?"

"Yes, I am."

She took a deep breath. "He wants you to come in, and if you do, I get to go out there with my mom."

"Okay, then, lemme in," I said, smiling openly so she'd know everything was going to be all right.

She turned again, listening, looking at her mother. "He says we can go, Mom, but we have to be superquiet and not talk to anyone until we get to the end of the street. If we're not good girls, he's gonna be mad."

"Yes," Emerson whispered. "Whatever he wants."

Saxon listened again. "He wants you to put the gun in the mailbox in front of the house."

"Yes," Emerson agreed frantically.

Saxon told the psychopath what Emerson had said, repeating it for him even though he could clearly hear both mother and child perfectly. It was a control measure, and for perhaps the hundredth time in my life, I thought about how clever he was. The man was a master of manipulation; he had a singular focus and no one could doubt his follow-through. It was such a waste that his mind was broken.

"He says okay," Saxon told me. "You can come in now."

I moved forward as she came out, slipping easily by me, and I closed the door behind her. I heard mother and daughter scurrying down the front steps, and then everything else was gone as Craig Hartley stepped out of the shadows to face me.

I was certain my heart stopped. How was it even possible that I was with him again? Every part of me screamed for flight, but all I could do was stand there and stare. He'd kill me if I moved, and on the cast, I wouldn't get far if I punched him and tried to get away.

"Miro," he whispered.

I had to keep breathing for as long as I could and try to keep from trembling even though I was suddenly freezing from the inside out.

"My God, man, how many lives do you have?"

"Hopefully enough," I replied glibly.

He moved forward until I felt the muzzle of the gun against my abdomen. "How in the world did you break your ankle? That's awfully klutzy, don't you think?"

"Came down on it funny," I answered as he slipped his hand between the open lapels of my olive-green wool overcoat and pressed it over my heart.

"You're scared."

I shrugged, but it took effort. Modulating my voice, repressing both my fight-or-flight instincts, and appearing calm was taking all of my concentration. "Of course I am. The last time we saw each other, you took out one of my ribs."

"Yes, I did," he replied, sliding his hand down my abdomen to my belt and then burrowing underneath two layers, Henley and T-shirt, to my skin. "But the scar is barely there. I did a good job with the surgical glue."

I wasn't going to explain that my best friend had gone in through the same incision he made just to make sure he hadn't butchered me inside.

"I tell you," he said warmly, running his fingers over the muscles in my abdomen. "Your body is really something. I bet all the boys want to fuck you."

There was only one boy for me, and hopefully when Hartley was done with me, I'd still be pretty enough for Ian Doyle. God, not that I would tell him that. I could only imagine the knock-down, drag-out fight we'd have about how shallow that would make him sound.

"I feel you're not focusing on your imminent peril."

I was so tired of being scared, of jumping at my own shadow, of thinking that the bogeyman was behind every door, even the refrigerator, in every room before I turned on the light or on my front stoop whenever I left the house. I had a reoccurring nightmare that I would open my eyes in the morning and find Hartley looming over me.

"Miro," he said, pressing the gun hard up under my chin. "What do I have to do to get you to tremble in my presence?"

All of it, from the start—back when I was a detective—was mind games. He had always told me that one day he'd have me, would be there when I woke up in the morning, and at some point along the way I'd internalized that threat and given it life. I'd turned him from a logical threat to a supernatural one, and that knowledge coming as a blast of realization chased out the fear and replaced it with anger.

"We're going to take a ride, you and I, and once we're all alone, I can teach you some respect. I suspect that further instruction is needed."

No.

Never again.

"You fuck," I growled before I forgot caution, shoved him back hard, turned, and limped away as fast as I could.

"Miro!" he roared, and I heard the gunfire a second before my right bicep felt like it was blown off.

Running down the hall, Hartley behind me firing wildly, I skidded on the heavily waxed floor as bullets bounced off studs inside plaster walls, cracked glass in picture frames, and destroyed a vase beside the bannister I ran by on my way to the dining room.

Plates exploded in the hutch, another vase, and water splattered everywhere as I flew into the kitchen. I stood behind the door, my heartbeat pounding in my ears, panting not from exertion but fear, and when he sprinted by me, I flushed from my hiding spot and went out the same door he'd come in.

A bullet hit the wall beside my head, and I had a fleeting thought that maybe Hartley had tired of our dance and was ready to simply shoot me dead.

"Come on, Miro," he yelled after me. "There's more parts of you I want in my collection."

I squelched down the urge to puke and almost went down—the rubber grip on the bottom of my cast had shitty traction and once again I was back on the wax. But I managed to scramble up the staircase, the cast making all kinds of noise as it collided with each step.

Why did I go to the second floor—why not out the front door? Outside was always better than in. But Hartley was between me and my truck—and my gun—and because going to the basement was never a good idea, I bumped up the staircase ahead of him and hopped and hobbled down the dark hallway.

It was a huge house, three stories, and as I limped through it, I opened every door I passed, finally careening through one and darting inside what looked like the master suite. I ran inside the roomy walk-in closet, closed the door to a crack behind me, and searched for anything I could use to defend myself with. I listened at the same time over my own pounding heart and then simply… stopped.

Even if I happened upon a gun safe, what was I going to do, stand there and try and figure out the combination? And how long did I have before he found me? I had to be smarter than the serial killer.

I wasn't some virgin in a slasher flick; I was a deputy United States marshal. I needed to start acting like one. If I was protecting a witness, I would have been on the offensive from the get-go. What had taken me a moment to realize was that in this instance, I was the witness.

If I lived, I was never going anywhere without Ian again. With him by my side, I never worried about the outcome. I simply knew I'd live. And it wasn't that I couldn't save myself, but the autopilot of certainty was a very compelling argument for having a partner.

I started taking clothes down, suits, shirts, and stacking them in my arms, layering them thicker and thicker until my bicep with the bullet in it was screaming as I stood there, legs braced apart, close to the door, waiting.

"Miro!" he roared from out in the hall. "I won't be able to stay here much longer. Do you really want me to go? You want me to keep haunting your life? Won't you eventually go mad?"

It was a definite possibility. The not knowing was the worst. I would rather be dead than have Hartley able to scare me for the rest of my life. It was like those awful stories where people were missing and their families didn't know what happened. They couldn't grieve, and hope was so hard to hold on to year after year. In all my years in law enforcement, I'd never met anyone who ever said limbo was the preferable option. Bad news, the worst news, was still closure.

"I can hold out longer than you," I yelled through the door, finally becoming the cat in our game, sick to death of being the mouse.

I heard him running toward the sound of my voice, and seconds later I saw a line of light under the closet door. The bathroom was beside me, and I knew he was in there, checking, realizing where I wasn't and where I was before I heard only silence.

Later I would think, *What a stupid plan! Who came up with that?* and realize that there had only been me there, so the idiocy was mine alone.

From the outside, the light flipped on, the door was thrown open and he strode into the closet at the same second he fired at me from point-blank range, to the left, aiming for my heart.

The bullet should have ripped through my chest, but ridiculously, I had all those clothes in my arms, propped against my chest. A stack of layers—so many that it had to look like I was moving in the middle of the night or stealing them in a snatch-and-grab from a department store with the wheelman waiting right out front.

So instead of me going down from a gunshot wound that should have killed me instantly, the bullet hit the layers and altered course, sliding along the top of my shoulder, barely grazing me. At the same second, my adrenaline kicked in and I charged, driving over him in a play that any defensive end would have been proud of—and not because it was particularly agile, but because it got the job done.

Hartley went down hard, slammed to the floor, his head hitting with a thump. I hurled the clothes sideways, found him disoriented and winded, and before he could lift the gun, I fisted my hand in his sweater, lifted him toward me, and punched him in the face.

I hit him many times, stopping only to grab the gun and toss it out of his reach. I stood up and kicked him in the ribs to get him to fold into a fetal position and in the head to knock him out.

I waited, checking for movement, then walked out of the closet, retrieved the Heckler Koch HK45C with the suppressor he'd been using, and walked back to him and made sure he was breathing.

I had the momentary thought that, really, shooting him in the head would be the best end to my day. No one would miss him, I'd be saving the taxpayers a crap-ton of money, and no one would even question why I'd shot an unarmed man. He was Craig Hartley; of course I had to kill him.

The issue was that the more I thought about it, the less appealing it became. Hartley had done enough to me. I didn't need his death cluttering up my psyche for the rest of my life.

Slamming the door shut, I grabbed the chair from the vanity table, wedged it under the closet's doorknob, and staggered over to the bed. I would have gone downstairs and out to my truck to get my phone, but I didn't want to leave Hartley alone. It was fortunate the people who owned the house had a landline—which amazed me in the age of the cell phone—and I used that to call Ian. He picked up on the first ring.

"Hello?"

"Hey, guess where I am?"

"You're out in Park Ridge for some reason. Kohn tracked your cell phone because you didn't pick up the fifty times I called. Where the fuck are you?"

"With Craig Hartley in a really nice house that I hope is for sale because I don't want to think about the—"

"What?" he gasped.

"What?" I heard Kohn echo in the background before I heard him loudly exclaim, "Where the hell are you, Jones?" Ian had put me on speaker.

"I caught Hartley."

"Oh, no," Ian groaned. "No-no-no."

"I'm fine," I soothed him. "I'm gonna need to go to the hospital. Can you come here and pick up my truck?"

"*Your truck?*" Kohn was incredulous. "Who cares about your fuckin' truck? Are you gonna die?"

"Jesus, Kohn," I grumbled. He wasn't helping in the least.

"Miro!" Ian shouted.

"No, come on, I promise it's not like that. I'm not gonna die. I have a bullet in my arm is all, I'll be fine."

"You're gonna make Ian pass out, you fuckhead," Kohn insisted.

I wanted to use an endearment, tell him I loved him, tell him not to worry, but Kohn was there too, and then I heard Dorsey ask what was going on. "Ian, come see me."

"I—"

"Have Kohn drive you."

"What? Fuck no!"

"Ian," I gentled him, suddenly a little light-headed, realizing blood was dripping down the fingers of my left hand. I was maybe bleeding a bit more than I thought. "Let Kohn drive so you get here in one piece. You're gonna have to drive my truck, so it makes no sense to bring another car, right?"

"I—yeah—yeah, okay."

"You need to hurry," I said as I lay on the bed. "I want you here before the ambulance, before they move me."

"Have you even called an ambulance yet?" Kohn asked.

"Actually, no, and I need you to call the bureau—unless Kage wants you guys to come collect Hartley. Go ask him and let me know. I'll wait."

"You will not wait. We'll take care of the FBI, you hang up and call the ambulance, you stupid fuck!" Kohn flared angrily. "We're on our way."

The line went dead and I knew Kohn had hung up on me. Ian wouldn't have. I called for help and stayed there, lying down and guarding the closed door as I spoke to the 911 operator. There were no windows in the closet; this wasn't a horror movie where I'd barricade the door, leave it, and come back to find it open and the murderer escaped. The reality was, if he opened the door, I'd shoot him in the head. With all the lights on, I wouldn't miss.

CHAPTER 19

AS I predicted, the FBI, as well as the ambulance, were there before Ian and Kohn. Sadly, the older couple who owned the house had been killed and left in the basement, but that had happened a full twenty-four hours before Hartley went out and kidnapped Emerson and Saxon Rice. I was told by the FBI agents on site that Emerson's husband was going to make a full recovery. The bullet that Hartley put in him had missed everything vital. I was so glad Hartley hadn't ruined another family.

Sitting up in bed in the emergency room at Advocate Lutheran, I was thrilled to see Ian walk by me down the hall.

"Hey!" I called after him.

Kohn was a few feet behind him, so he heard me first and whistled for Ian. As soon as Ian appeared in the doorway, he exhaled sharply. What was interesting was that even though Kohn came into the room, Ian didn't move.

"Come here," I coaxed softly, seductively. "I wanna see you."

He moved fast, one moment at the door, the next beside the bed, slipping his hand into mine, the other cupping my cheek.

"Guess what, I was wrong," I teased, waggling my eyebrows at him. "Both bullets only grazed me."

"Both bullets?"

"Yeah, isn't that lucky?"

"Oh yeah, that's great, that's so much better."

"What? Nothing to dig out? That's not good? Come on. All you do is put some Neosporin on both of 'em and a Band-Aid and call it a day."

"I think I wanna strangle you to death," Kohn assured me.

"How the hell did Hartley get his hands on you again?" Ian erupted.

"Wait—"

"Are you kidding?" he roared louder, stalking a few feet away before rounding on me. "We're gonna have to get you a panic button. Jesus Christ, M!"

"Stop yelling," Kage said as he breezed into the room.

For a second I was speechless, because in all the years I'd worked for the man—including when he came out to collect Ian and me from the middle of the countryside—I'd never seen him in anything but a suit and tie. But it was Saturday, now about eight at night, and he was in black jeans and biker boots, a crew neck white T-shirt with a charcoal button-up, and a pale gray cable-knit sweater with button neck over that. I had noticed how big he was before, but in something that clung to his broad shoulders and massive chest, the effect was a little disconcerting. He could break me in half, and I was not a small guy.

Crossing his arms made the size of his biceps readily apparent. "Tell me what happened, from the beginning."

So I explained as Ian fumed beside me and the hospital staff came in and took care of me, doing exactly what I suspected would happen: cleaning my abrasions, applying salve, and bandaging me up. When the nurse was explaining wound care, Ian interrupted her and promised that he knew what to do.

"Are you sure?"

"Green Beret, ma'am. I swear I can handle it."

She was sure I'd be in good hands.

As soon as I was done explaining to Kage, the FBI showed up. Since I was ready to be discharged by then but still waiting on a doctor, the special agent in charge went to speak to the on-call resident, and I was released four hours after I arrived.

I rode with Ian and Kohn back downtown to our building on Dearborn and rode the elevator up to the office in silence. Once we were off, we all headed toward the meeting room.

"Why're you pissed at me?" I prodded Ian.

"I'm not."

"It certainly seems like it, and I don't think it's fair."

"Why not?"

"Because I didn't do anything wrong? What would you have done?"

He had no answer.

Once inside, I sat down, and when Ryan and Dorsey joined us, they brought bottles of water with them.

As we all took seats—except for Kage—the door opened again and we were joined by six FBI agents. The person in charge was Special Agent Oliver, and Rohl and Thompson were among those he'd brought to speak to me.

"Where is Hartley now?" Kage asked Oliver.

"He's at County Hospital with ten agents, as well as a contingent of uniformed Chicago PD officers. He's not going anywhere."

"Why's he in the hospital?" Kage wanted to know.

"Marshal Jones broke his collarbone."

Kage grunted before turning to me. "Shall we begin?"

It was interesting: Whenever the agents started to ask too many questions, Kage shut them down. When they tried getting loud, especially Oliver, Kage lifted his hand for me to stop. It didn't take too many times for them to realize he wasn't playing around.

Ian, sitting beside me, had trouble not fidgeting, and every once in a while he'd take my hand under the table and gently squeeze.

We were there for hours, well after midnight, before the entire story had been told and recorded by the marshals service and the FBI. When we were finally ready to break, Kage asked if Hartley was going back to Elgin.

Oliver glanced up at him. "No, he's not, and you made certain of that, didn't you?" He barked with so much disgust in his tone that he surprised me, and from the quiet that settled over the room, I was guessing everyone else as well.

It was quite the outburst, angry and accusing, full of venom, almost hatred, and from the way his face screwed up into a snarl, Oliver had to be furious. But even hearing all that, seeing it, wasn't what threw me. It was my boss.

Never had I seen Kage grin, and it was even more startling to witness because of the way he did it… arrogantly, evilly, like he'd won. I was seeing no trace of the man I knew, the unflappable one, the chief deputy who personified grace under pressure. This man was enjoying

Special Agent Oliver's discomfort, the wicked curl of his lip told me so, and I couldn't get over the change in him.

"How in the hell did you get him transferred there? He doesn't even meet the requirements!"

"Oh, he most certainly does," Kage assured him snidely. "He's successfully escaped once, he killed again while at large, there is the threat of his followers contacting him, and last but not least, he assaulted a deputy United States marshal. He's a prime candidate for ADX Florence."

I turned to Ian and found him staring at Kage with the same expression I must have been wearing—one of utter mind-blown daze.

Holy. Fuck.

It was overkill, and I was humbled. While I knew it wasn't just me who Kage had done it for, I was the one he looked at every day, so at the moment, it was feeling damn personal.

The only way Dr. Craig Hartley was getting out of that supermax prison was in a body bag. I'd been there once, invited to tour the facility, and the utter isolation once you were inside the soundproof cells, how easy it would be to lose all track of time, the immovable concrete furnishings, timers on the lights and the sink and shower, an automated existence that stripped away all your humanity... I couldn't get out of there fast enough. It had been hard to breathe. I couldn't think of a worse fate for the egomaniac Hartley was. There would be no one to worship him; in fact, there would be no one at all. It was exactly what he deserved. To not be studied or asked for help, instead put in a box and forgotten.

I was mute, so struck by the level of endgame that Kage, without putting a needle in Hartley's arm, had achieved. He'd killed my bogeyman. Hartley could never again haunt my dreams. It was completely, and utterly, done.

"I wasn't saying he should be remanded back to Elgin," Oliver shouted, done in by my boss's smirk and seeming boredom, "but another prison where we would still have access to him for purposes of—"

"I wanted him stuffed in a hole twenty-three hours a day, and guess what? Now he is."

"You're being completely shortsighted! Hartley has never been the kind of prisoner who needs that!" Oliver choked, clearly incensed even as he took a quick breath.

"Oh no? I have a marshal who would disagree with you. I have people who lost their parents who would also. I have nineteen women who lost their lives, and lastly, I have a little girl who was kidnapped, and her parents had to live through that."

"Yes, but—"

"I've had someone I love kidnapped. It's a nightmare I wouldn't wish on anyone."

I was struck by Kage's voice when he said that last part, how it rose slightly, got louder, and I wanted to ask what had happened even as I knew it was not my place to ever even broach the topic. It was clear that remembering the incident still hurt, and for a moment, I wished we were closer so I could offer him some word of comfort.

"You're putting emotion into a situation that—"

"No," Kage said flatly. "I asked my boss for ADX Florence for Craig Hartley and it's done. His paperwork was signed four hours ago, and tomorrow he'll be transferred. If you want to see him from now on, you'll have to put in a request six months prior."

"Amazing how quickly things can work when we want something, isn't it, Chief Deputy?" Oliver said, his tone sharp and accusatory, the perspiration on his forehead and upper lip pronounced.

Kage could not have appeared any more unimpressed if he tried.

"What about the people Hartley's saved by helping us with our investigations over the years since his incarceration? It seems to me you've conveniently forgotten all that."

"The risk doesn't outweigh the reward," Kage answered mildly, nothing Oliver was saying doing anything to change his mind. "And my boss—and yours, I might add—agree with me."

I was the one they had sent to talk to Hartley whenever they wanted his insight, so I actually understood what Oliver was saying. The doctor had saved lives by steering law enforcement in the right direction at times, and the fact that a lot of the people perpetrating the crimes were from his legion of fans who contacted him, who he could name, didn't hurt either. So I got where Oliver was coming from, that one marshal's life wasn't worth what could be gained by continual access to Hartley. But I didn't get to decide. My boss did, and apparently, to him, the scale tipped in my favor.

Oliver moved quickly then, apparently pushed to the breaking point, and I could tell when he drilled two fingers into Kage's collarbone that he was far more upset than I was even giving him credit for since he took his life in his hands by putting his on my boss.

"You've always been a self-righteous asshole, even when you were a police detective!"

It was interesting to watch Kage simply stand there and wait until Oliver realized what he'd done and let his hand drop. I knew Kage wouldn't report Oliver; it wasn't his way. But Oliver would know for the rest of his life that he'd lost his shit in front of witnesses.

"Will that be all?" Kage asked like he could give a fuck.

Oliver muttered something under his breath and the FBI agents filed out of the room. None of us said a word, and when they were gone, Kage closed the door behind them and turned his steely slate blue stare on me.

"You won't have to worry about Hartley again. Now that we have him, we're not going to let him go. His following, such as it is, will no longer have any access to him. Everything will settle down now, Jones."

"Yes sir," I answered, still shaken by what he'd done, and at the finite end I was suddenly facing. The surge of overwhelming emotion made it hard to speak.

I was safe.

Ian was safe.

We were all safe because of Sam Kage.

I exhaled all of it, the prickling disquiet of life balanced on the edge of a razor, the burden of uncertainty and dread.

I inhaled relief and calm and most of all, gratitude for my life, because it belonged to me again. It took great concentration not to throw myself into Ian's arms.

"Jones."

"Sir?"

"Take your laptop home with you and file the reports from there. Since you missed having today off, take Monday, and you and Kohn, too, Doyle. All three of you take Monday. I won't call unless I need you."

"Thank you, sir," I said, standing up. "For all of it, for everything."

"Yessir, thank you," Ian said roughly, rising beside me.

All five of us were on our feet as he walked out the door without saying another word.

Dorsey nodded before turning to me. "Damn, Jones, boss man dropped Hartley in hell for you. ADX, that's some serious shit."

"Yeah," I agreed after a moment, glancing around the room, "but he would've done it for any of us."

Kage was built strong and solid, a little scary, and a lot protective, which was why we'd all take a bullet for him, no questions asked.

"It's what he does."

No one could argue that fact with me.

ONCE WE were home, I wanted to talk to Ian, but he made me go upstairs and take a shower while he made us something to eat. Since he was finally talking to me, even though all he was doing was issuing orders, I didn't stand there and debate but instead simply did as I was told.

It was difficult—no water on my cast, no water on either of the new wounds where the bullets grazed me—but I managed to wash all the important parts and even get my hair back to looking like I had a messy top cut and not like I'd just rolled out of bed in the morning. I hadn't been using any product lately. I hadn't cared about anything, but now I felt like me again because it was all finally over. I had kicked Hartley's ass and the experience fixed what was broken. I'd been off balance, and I'd been knocked back into alignment. I felt like dancing. Or at least having dessert before dinner.

Everything had survived the chaos of the day, even the cupcakes, so I was surprised when I came back downstairs in flannel pajama bottoms and a T-shirt to see them shoved on top of the toaster while he fried the steaks.

"Why are the cupcakes ostracized?"

He glanced over at me, scowled, and then returned to his dinner prep.

"Hello?" I said, walking over to the counter and getting the container. The four cupcakes were all beautifully frosted, and I couldn't wait to eat one.

"Aruna, as usual, is thrilled to have Chickie spend the night," he muttered.

I shrugged, peeling the wrapper away from the sides of the confection. "She loves him, they all do. It's no big deal."

"Yeah, so I was thinking that I really need to decide what's best for him."

"Uh-huh," I said distractedly, the cupcake being the important thing. I deserved it after the day I'd had.

"I mean, it's gotta be fair to him, not just what I want."

"Sure," I said as licked some of the frosting off.

"I don't wanna be selfish."

"Yeah, no, you… wait, what?" I asked, lost as to why we were talking about the dog.

"For Chickie."

"Yeah, no, I got that we're talking about Chickie. I just don't know *why* we're talking about Chickie."

"Because I have to think about what's best for him. Weren't you listening?" he asked, turning his head for only a moment to glare at me before going back to cooking.

"I wasn't really, no, but Ian, come on. You're best for him," I said, putting the cupcake down on the counter, realizing he was actually making a decision about his pet.

"How can you say that?" he asked, not pivoting to address me, instead keeping a visual on the steaks. I liked mine rare, so at least one of them wouldn't be in the pan much longer. And while it was nice that he was being attentive to my food, I would rather have had his entire focus on me. "They take him camping, hiking; he has a huge backyard to run around in; he watches over the baby, he loves Liam and Aruna and—"

"Ian." Why he was rambling I had no idea.

"—I know they'll make him part of their family and—"

"Ian."

"—he deserves to have the best person love him and maybe that's not me and I should—"

"Please stop."

He went silent.

It hit me then that my boy was having a panic attack and I hadn't realized it. Of course, I had a really good excuse and all, but still. He needed all my attention now. "Ian, honey, is it at all possible that you're talking about something other than the dog?"

"Oh, come on, Miro, gimme a break," he snapped.

God, could he be any more obvious?

In the current scenario, I was the dog and Ian was deciding on the best home for me. It was ridiculously transparent, and what was funny was the timing. I'd gotten my life back, Ian too, and so now was the best time for him to rethink what was in my best interests. If I was stronger, I would have slammed him down onto the couch. As it was, I had to settle for being logical and nonchalant, which included eating the cupcake.

"I think it's you," I pronounced, picking the dessert back up.

"What?"

"I think you're the very best thing for Chickie."

"How?" he almost yelled, and I heard it then, the fear in his catch of breath, saw how tight and bunched his shoulders were, and how hard he was clutching the spatula.

"Because," I began, taking a bite and getting frosting on my nose, "Chickie enjoys doing all those things with Aruna and her family because he knows he'll get to come home to you."

"No, I—"

"Think about it," I insisted, licking off more icing. "You run with him every single night that you're home. You take him with you everywhere, he sleeps at the foot of the bed, and he would protect you with his life. He can be a sweet ole dog to Aruna and her family because he knows he doesn't live there. He lives here."

"But is that fair to him?"

"You ever notice how happy he is when you pick him up?"

"Sure, he's a dog. Dogs get happy when they see you."

"Yeah, but he doesn't make a total ass of himself for anyone but you," I concluded. "He likes a lot of people a whole lot—me, Aruna, Liam—but you're the only one he's stupid in love with."

He snorted out a laugh before turning to look at me. "You think my dog is—what are you doing?"

I couldn't answer; I had a mouthful of cupcake. I was really glad I'd sprung for the jumbo size.

"Why're you eating that right now?"

I swallowed enough to speak. "I was eating this before."

"You were?" Which told me everything I needed to know: he'd been completely lost in his thoughts and hadn't noticed me even when he was looking right at me.

Smiling so he could see how full my mouth was, I went back to chewing, glad that me acting like a dork was jogging him out of his crappy mood. I wanted the hot, sexy Ian from earlier in the day, not the introspective brooding guy worried that he wasn't good enough for me.

"Your lips are blue, do you know that?"

I laughed. And when I did, some of the crumbs sprayed out.

"You're disgusting."

"Stop it," I tried to get out, because he was making me laugh, but it was muffled, and his expression—total revulsion—cracked me up more.

"Put that—gimme that," he grumbled, reaching for what was left of the cupcake, only to see me pivot so I had my back to him. "What the hell, M?"

I cackled and he reached over my shoulder for the cupcake, but I danced away, cast thumping on the floor as I moved awkwardly, slipping by him to lean on the other side of the counter by the refrigerator.

"You're gonna ruin your appetite and you're getting too skinny."

I straightened up and lifted my shirt, showing off the hard abdomen I knew he was a fan of so he could see that "skinny" was not the appropriate word. He needed to grasp that I was strong and healthy, and though I didn't have the defined six-pack he did—there was no washboard there—I was by no means underweight.

"What're you—"

"Can you see me?" I asked, releasing my shirt, arching an eyebrow, and waiting.

"Of course, that's a stupid question."

"I don't think so."

"I don't understand."

"I think you're stuck in a time loop."

"What?" He made annoyed-Ian face that was part scowl, part squint, with a little bit of judgment that I was a dumbass thrown in for good measure.

"You need to stop remembering me in a hospital bed or focusing on the cast and bandages when you look at me, and just focus on me being the guy who sleeps with you."

He nodded.

"Can you do it?"

Second nod.

"Are you sure?" I asked softly as I reached down and grabbed my already semierect cock. Just being anywhere near Ian turned me on a little, so the fact that I was hardening was not a surprise.

In response, I saw the muscles in his neck cord as his gaze zeroed in on my hand.

"Ian?"

"Yeah," he rasped, head snapping up. "You, not your injuries, I got it."

It was excellent news.

"You need to eat your dinner," he said automatically, even though I watched his pupils dilate and saw him swallow hard, like maybe his throat was dry.

"I will," I promised, licking some frosting off my lip.

"Is it good?"

"Yeah, come here."

He closed the distance between us fast and leaned in and kissed me hard, tasting my mouth, sucking on my lips and then my tongue as I opened for him. I went boneless under the onslaught, and when he tipped my head back, I had to grab for the counter beside me so my knees wouldn't buckle.

When he tore his mouth free, I yelled in protest. "How dare you stop!"

"Shut up," he groused, moving the pan with the two steaks in it off the fire before plating each one.

"I don't want to eat," I growled.

He put both plates in the oven, didn't even try to add the tossed green salad or the asparagus tips I'd bought earlier in the day at the farmers' market. Instead he turned off the burner, wiped his hands, turned, and lunged at me.

"Oh thank God," I moaned in delight, shivering with anticipation as he gently pulled my shirt off—I was wounded after all—and then took my face in his hands and ravished my mouth.

"Take me, have me, use me, whatever you want," I said, trying to keep my lips on his even as I issued my desperate plea.

"God, I want you so bad," he whispered, shoving a hand down the front of my pajamas and squeezing my already erect length.

Many of Ian's exes had said he was inattentive in bed and a lousy lay, but I'd never believed it, even before we hit the sheets the first time. I'd been proven right, of course. Ian was everything I craved in a lover, demonstrative and possessive but also gentle and submissive. It was difficult to imagine how no one but me had ever been treated to the man who spent so much time making love to my mouth that I was whimpering and whining and begging him to do something else, anything else, as soon as possible.

"Where do you want me?"

"Let's go upstairs and get in bed."

"Oh no," I husked, pulling free of his hands and yanking off my pajama bottoms. I left them on the kitchen floor before limping out to the living room. I pushed the coffee table back to make room, snatched the chunky cable-knit throw from the couch, and spread it out on the floor.

"What're you—"

"Grab the lube, Doyle, and get over here," I ordered, sinking slowly to the floor. "Or I'm starting without you."

I heard him on the stairs, pounding up them, rattling around in our nightstand and then running back down, appearing over me, not even the least bit winded.

"You're still wearing a lot of clothes."

He was naked in moments, stripping quickly before he lay on top of me, pressing his mouth to mine, insistent. His movements were practiced, fluid, as he reached between us, captured our cocks in his long-fingered hand, and stroked us together from balls to head.

There was no hesitation in him. He was not looking to me to tell him what to do. At this moment he was the aggressor I normally was, and I found I was more than ready to let him have me. I could barely wait.

Twisting away from him, I rolled to my stomach and lifted myself to my hands and knees.

"Oh," he murmured, his accompanying chuckle low and dirty. "I've got you now, huh? You want me bad."

"Hurry," I growled, my skin screaming out for his touch, trembling with the thought of him finally unleashing himself on me.

"No," he whispered, pulling me sideways into his arms. His bare chest was warm on my back, his left arm wrapped under my chin, around my neck as his other hand stroked my cock.

I tried to buck forward, the motion involuntary, his skin on mine made me ravenous for more.

"Grab the lube," he whispered against the curve of my ear before nibbling on the lobe. "Reach back and slick my cock for me."

It was hard to do with how tight he was holding me, but I managed, and the feel of his long, silky length sliding though my slippery fist coupled with the issued order was even more arousing than I thought it would be.

"Stop," he rumbled softly as he pressed a finger inside me.

"Ian," I husked, pushing back against him, wanting more.

"Feel okay?"

"Oh, yes."

He added another finger, pushing in, dragging out, circling slowly, maddeningly, scissoring and caressing, opening me up, relaxing the muscles with limitless patience.

"Fuck me already," I demanded brokenly, my voice full of gravel.

"Don't rush me. I'm loving this."

"Why? Just get—"

"Your body is so beautiful and responsive and…. God, look at you."

I shivered as he rubbed my prostate. "Ian," I drawled out his name. "Don't you want to be buried inside of me?"

His sharp exhale made me smile as the answer was obvious.

"I'm ready. Have me."

As he took hold of his cock, his hand bumped me before he pushed gently between my cheeks and didn't stop until he was pressed against my entrance. "I'm gonna go slow."

Arching my back, lifting my ass, I nearly swallowed my tongue when he kissed the side of my neck before pushing inside the tight ring of muscle.

I had forgotten what it was like, it had been so long, the twinge of pain, the pressure and stretch before the feeling of fullness. There was no way to hold back the guttural moan of heat.

"M?" he asked sharply, his worry evident.

"I want you—could you listen?"

"Yes," he answered as he drove into me, hard, fast, balls against my ass, as deep as he could go in that one powerful thrust.

I had nothing to grab and I needed it, had to have it, to be braced so he could hammer into me. It was utterly necessary.

"Fuck, you feel so good."

I thought I'd want to lie on our sides together, have him slowly undulate against me and pump in and out in a languid rhythm. But what I wanted was for him to hold me down and put marks on me and fuck me until I screamed his name.

"Ian, please."

"Tell me," he said raggedly, his voice thick with passion.

"On my knees."

He shifted positions with me, following as I rolled to my stomach and lifted. He moved inside me, his cock brushing over the spot that made me jolt under him and tighten around his length. I let my head slip down between my shoulders, trembling, feeling my balls tighten as he pounded into me, one hand tight on my hip, the other on the back of my neck.

I wanted to grab my cock, but I had to lock my arms and curl my fingers into the blanket. If I held tight, I wouldn't give when he pistoned inside, and that was what I wanted, to feel his cock fill me and then pull out again and again. I wanted to be used hard.

"I have wanted you like this for so goddamn long," he groaned, pummeling me, giving me the fucking I craved, shoving his cock in to the hilt until I screamed his name and came thick and hot, nothing left of me in that moment except my desire for him.

He came, and I felt him ejaculate before he collapsed across my back, hand on my chin to turn my head enough so he could kiss me.

"It's stupid—" He kissed me. "—to say right now—" Another. "—but M, I—" He sucked on my tongue, my lips. "I love you. You're all I want. All I'll ever want."

I smiled against his lips.

"I'm so fuckin' lucky and I want you to know I know. I'll never take this for granted, never take us for granted. I swear to God."

"I love you too," I promised. "But you know that already."

"Yeah, I do," he sighed, twitching as my muscles contracted around him, the suction too tight for him to ease free.

"You should pull out," I said, even though I wasn't really ready for that yet.

"In a second," he informed me, his voice soft, like a caress, before he kissed me again. "I like where I am."

And God, so did I.

AFTER THE blanket got wadded up and thrown in the washer, we took a quick shower together and finally ate dinner, only about six hours late. The steaks were good, as were the accompanying asparagus tips and salad. Since he'd cooked, I did the dishes as he cleared the table and dried. As he moved around me to put things away, I noted the whistling.

"You're going to be impossible to live with."

The waggle of eyebrows told me he was, just in case I had missed the smirk or the swaggering walk across the kitchen. He leaned in and kissed me, all heat and dominance, pressing me back into the counter, flipping the dish towel over his shoulder so he could take my face in his hands. He slowed then, his kisses becoming long and deep, and I lost track of anything but his wicked tongue, his teeth on my lips, and his soft, urgent noises. When his knee spread my thighs and his hand slipped up under my T-shirt to my nipple, rubbing, pinching, I almost came right there. Apparently in all the months we'd been having sex, he'd been watching and listening and now knew exactly the things that turned my key, big time. When he leaned back, just enough to speak, we were both panting.

"I enjoyed what we did," he murmured, "and I want to do it again, whenever I want, whenever I need, whenever you do."

"Uh-huh," I agreed, more kissing and stroking taking precedence over words at the moment. My hunger for him had not been sated; he'd be under me as soon as I got him to bed.

"And if we both want something at the same time, then we should be able to talk about it or—"

I chuckled. "I don't see us fighting to top."

"Yeah, but what if we do?"

He was worried, not wanting his new craving to interfere with our dynamic.

"Could you see that happening?"

He thought a moment. "I... no."

"How come?"

"Well, because mostly I like it how it's been... I need it how it's been."

"So, you see," I confirmed. "We're okay, baby, I swear."

"Yeah?"

"Yeah."

"Nothing's changed?"

"No."

He cleared his throat. "Then can we leave the rest of this cleaning for tomorrow and just go to bed?"

I had the urge to laugh, a big sound bubbling up out of my throat, not because anything was funny, but because of how happy I was. "Yeah, we can do that."

His sigh was long as he turned for the stairs. "You know, sometimes I'm so happy I worry that I'm gonna wake up."

"I know the feeling," I agreed as I followed behind him.

"But then," he said, rounding to face me. "I see you and I recognize this is my real life."

"Good, because you're stuck with me now."

"From the beginning, yeah, I was." He exhaled sharply. "Thank you for loving me."

Fucking Ian, only he could stop my heart. "It's my pleasure."

He cleared his throat. "Would it also be your pleasure to marry me?"

"Yes, of course it would," I said without thinking. I wanted it so bad. "Crap, what I meant was—"

"No," he sighed, the smile lighting his whole face. "I finally got an honest answer that was all you and none of your worry about what I thought."

"But—"

"I just want to talk about it, all right? I want you to know that the place I was at before, where I could never see me wearing a ring, isn't where I am now."

"How come?" I asked softly, trying to keep the thunderous excitement out of my voice. I didn't want to spook him.

"Because now I realize that being a marshal or being a solider isn't my whole life—those two things aren't all that I am." His voice was thick with emotion, low and husky. "You're in there too; you're actually the most important part because I carry you with me wherever I go."

Jesus. His words annihilated me and made me putty in his hands. "Gimme kiss," was all I could manage to say.

His cocky grin was there as he leaned in and kissed me tenderly, sweetly, ending with the whispered, "I love you," in my ear.

"Okay," I said, shivering with happiness. "So we'll talk about getting married."

"We'll talk about *when*, not *if* anymore."

"*When*," I repeated, unable to keep in the smile of pure joy. "Okay."

His chuckle was warm. "All right, come on, gimpy," he said as we reached the bottom of the stairs. "This time, can I carry you up?"

"No, but you can help me and hold my hand and let me have you when we get up there."

That smile of his made those gorgeous warm eyes of his crinkle in half. "Give me your hand."

His was warm in mine when I squeezed tight.

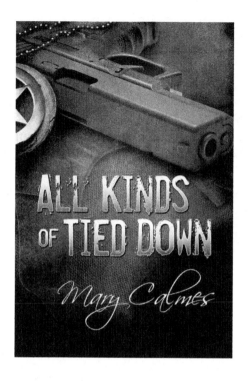

Deputy US Marshal Miro Jones has a reputation for being calm and collected under fire. These traits serve him well with his hotshot partner, Ian Doyle, the kind of guy who can start a fight in an empty room. In the past three years of their life-and-death job, they've gone from strangers to professional coworkers to devoted teammates and best friends. Miro's cultivated blind faith in the man who has his back… faith and something more.

As a marshal and a soldier, Ian's expected to lead. But the power and control that brings Ian success and fulfillment in the field isn't working anywhere else. Ian's always resisted all kinds of tied down, but having no home—and no one to come home to—is slowly eating him up inside. Over time, Ian has grudgingly accepted that going anywhere without his partner simply doesn't work. Now Miro just has to convince him that getting tangled up in heartstrings isn't being tied down at all.

www.dreamspinnerpress.com

MARY CALMES lives in Lexington, Kentucky, with her husband and two children and loves all the seasons except summer. She graduated from the University of the Pacific in Stockton, California, with a bachelor's degree in English literature. Due to the fact that it is English lit and not English grammar, do not ask her to point out a clause for you, as it will *so* not happen. She loves writing, becoming immersed in the process, and falling into the work. She can even tell you what her characters smell like. She loves buying books and going to conventions to meet her fans.

A Matter of Time Series from MARY CALMES

www.dreamspinnerpress.com

Also by MARY CALMES

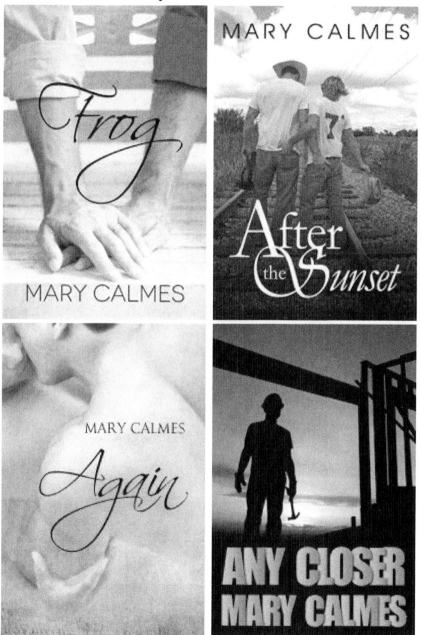

Change of Heart Series from MARY CALMES

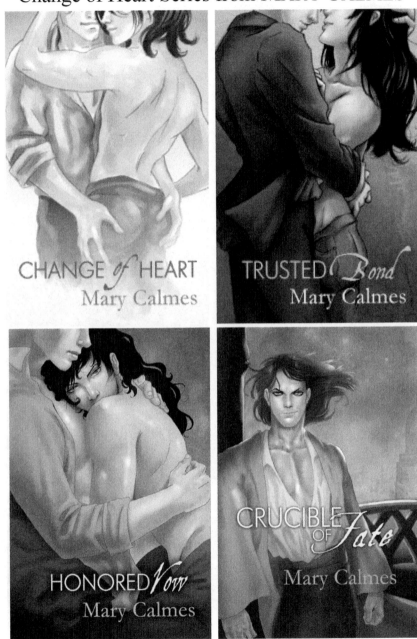

www.dreamspinnerpress.com

A Change of Heart Novel

Jin Church is back where he started, alone, wandering, and uncertain of his path. It's not by choice but by circumstance, as he remembers he's a werepanther... but not much else. He knows one thing for sure—he needs to find the beautiful blond man who haunts his dreams.

Logan Church is trapped in a living hell. His mate is missing, his tribe is falling apart, and he's estranged from the son he loves with all his heart. His world is unraveling without his mate by his side, and he has no one to blame but himself.

If Jin can regain his memory and Logan can overcome the threats to his leadership, then perhaps they can resume their lives. The question is: Is that what they want? Back to the same house, the same tribe, the same troubles? They can choose from various roads leading to their future... or they can forge their own path.

www.dreamspinnerpress.com

CPSIA information can be obtained at www.ICGtesting.com
Printed in the USA
BVOW11s2109011015

420344BV00010B/139/P